RAZING THE DEAD

Razing the Dead

Sheila Connolly

WHEELER PUBLISHING
A part of Gale, Cengage Learning

GALE
CENGAGE Learning®

Farmington Hills, Mich • San Francisco • New York • Waterville, Maine
Meriden, Conn • Mason, Ohio • Chicago

Copyright © 2014 by Sheila Connolly.
A Museum Mystery.
Wheeler Publishing, a part of Gale, Cengage Learning.

Wheeler Publishing Large Print Cozy Mystery.
The text of this Large Print edition is unabridged.
Other aspects of the book may vary from the original edition.
Set in 16 pt. Plantin.

LIBRARY OF CONGRESS CATALOGING-IN-PUBLICATION DATA

Connolly, Sheila.
    Razing the dead / by Sheila Connolly. — Large print edition.
        pages ; cm. — (Wheeler Publishing large print cozy mystery) (A museum
    mystery)
    ISBN 978-1-4104-7380-6 (softcover) — ISBN 1-4104-7380-5 (softcover)
    1. Pratt, Nell (Fictitious character)—Fiction. 2.
Murder—Investigation—Fiction. 3. Large type books. I. Title.
PS3601.T83R39 2015
813'.6—dc23   2014037026

Published in 2015 by arrangement with The Berkley Publishing Group,
a member of Penguin Group (USA) LLC, a Penguin Random House
Company

Printed in the United States of America
1 2 3 4 5 6 7 18 17 16 15 14

ACKNOWLEDGMENTS

Most writers use people and places they know when they write a book — it's so much easier than starting from scratch. This was particularly true for me with this book.

Anyone who has spent time in the Philadelphia area in the past few decades or who is familiar with the skyline will most likely recognize the man who inspired the character of Mitchell Wakeman in this book. Likewise, anyone who knows the township of East Goshen in Chester County should be able to name the individual who inspired Ezra Garrett. As it happens, I knew and respected both of them (they're both gone now) and I hope they'd be pleased with the characters I created for them.

My family lived in Chester County for decades, close to the Paoli Pike, so it was easy to write many familiar places into the book. But despite that long association, until recently I had never explored the site of the Battle of Paoli, also called the Paoli Massacre, even though I drove past the historic marker for it hundreds of times. Nor had I ever studied the story behind that event, but to put it in simplest terms, that small battle had a significant impact on the early course of the American Revolution. Today there is little more to see than a level grassy field, but the war memorial there is one of the oldest in this country.

Like many battles, it was chaotic — made more so because it was a sneak attack fought by night — but that gave me the opportunity to ask, "what if . . . ?" As a result, I created a plot element that I believe is consistent with what we know. My apologies if I have offended any purists who dislike authors who tinker with history — I have been one of you.

Many details of the story reflect real places. The Chester County Historical Society is a delightful institution with excellent collections, but I have given the place a director who is neither based upon nor resembles any actual employee there. Ezra Garrett's farm did indeed belong to a single family for at least two centuries, until it was sold to QVC in the 1980s. The portion that lies along the Paoli Pike looks much as it always has.

In crafting this story, what I wanted to convey was how much our history is still with us. The past is not dead but lives on in unexpected ways.

Thanks as always to my tireless agent, Jessica Faust of BookEnds, and my eagle-eyed editor, Shannon Jamieson Vazquez of Berkley Prime Crime, for sustaining this series and giving me an excuse to visit Philadelphia regularly. Thanks, too, to the wonderfully supportive mystery community, including organizations such as Sisters in Crime and the Guppies as well as the great crowd of writers I count as friends. And of course, thank you to all the readers who follow Nell Pratt as she grapples with managing a Philadelphia museum, trying to sort out her love life, and solving those murders that keep springing up around her.

Three can keep a secret, if two of them are dead.

— Benjamin Franklin

CHAPTER 1

I was standing at the sink making a stab at clearing up the breakfast dishes when Special Agent James Morrison of the Philadelphia FBI came up behind me, wrapped his arms around my waist, and kissed my neck. So much for dish washing.

"When do you have to leave, Nell?" he asked.

"Ten minutes ago, and I still have to get dressed."

"Anything important on your calendar this morning?"

I turned to face him, which put us in contact from the neck down. "I don't want to be late." I was lucky that I held a job that let me call my own hours — I was president of the Pennsylvania Antiquarian Society, so in theory I could come and go as I chose. But I preferred to set a good example for the rest of my staff, which meant that under normal circumstances I arrived early and left late. But circumstances over the past month had been anything but normal.

Actually, I would be happy to be late — again — because time with James felt . . . precious. It was barely a month since he had nearly bled to death under my hands, and the scar that curved along the inside of his arm was still raised and red. The Philadelphia FBI office had been generous in allowing him a month's leave to recover — in tacit recognition that it was their fault he'd gotten injured in the first place — but we were nearing the end of that grace period, and I had noticed James becoming increasingly restless as his health improved.

But for now? It looked like I *was* going to be late again.

I was surprised a while later when he rolled to face me, and said, "I think we should look for a bigger place."

Wait — *we*? Admittedly, I had been spending most of my time at his apartment near the University of Pennsylvania in Philadelphia, returning to my own small house in the suburbs only now and then to swap out clothes. Until now we'd been careful not to talk about anything long-term. We'd been living in the present, waiting until he recovered. I'd originally moved in to take care of him — I've always acknowledged to myself and anyone else who would listen that I'm a lousy caregiver, but I'd felt I owed it to him. Besides, there was no one else to do it. While he might have deep Philadelphia roots, on a day-to-day basis he was as much of a loner as I was.

But a serious discussion had been looming on the horizon, like a coming storm. After all, we weren't young, and we should be old enough to know our own minds. On the other hand, I'd been married once for about fifteen minutes and it hadn't worked out, and I'd lived alone since, and James had never been married, a fact that continued to mystify me. I mean, he was smart, good-looking, held a responsible job, and could be tender and funny and sexy when he took off the strong-silent-FBI-agent mask.

There was no question that the last month, here with James, had been . . . like nothing in my life. James hadn't been a demanding patient. If anything, he'd been too stoic at first, never admitting when he was in pain, never asking for anything, not even a Tylenol. Thank goodness that phase hadn't lasted more than a week or two. After that a new and unexpected James started to emerge, one with a sense of humor and an

13

element of playfulness that his serious FBI persona hadn't previously let him show.

But *we*? As in *together,* with our names on a lease? Or even a mortgage? I fought a moment of panic and realized he was looking at me oddly because I hadn't answered him. I scrounged up a smile, and said, "Are you asking me to move in with you? Like, officially?"

"For an intelligent woman, you can be kind of dense. Yes, Nell, I think we should look for a place for both of us, together."

"Oh. Well, then, yes, you're right." *Damn it, Nell, you were going to try to get over your fear of commitment, weren't you?* I took a deep breath and looked him in the eye. "Yes, James, I would be delighted to live with you. But right now I need to leave for work, and I can't blame my late entrances on your medical crises forever. Because you're about ninety-seven percent back, right?"

"I am, and I don't want you to use that as an excuse to move out again. My lease is up the end of August, and I'm sure someone would grab this place in a minute. So we've got a little time to work out the details."

"Good." I leaned over and planted a kiss on him, then backed away so he couldn't pursue it. "Then I'm going to work. Shoot, look at the time!"

"I can drop you off," James volunteered.

"Then you'd better put some clothes on."

Ten minutes later we were out the door. Normally I could have walked to the Pennsylvania Antiquarian Society from James's apartment, especially in the nice summer weather. I'd found I enjoyed the walk — unless it was raining, in which case I could drive — and all the walking was doing wonders for my waistline. Well, that and all the worrying I'd done over the past month. If you're not a stress eater, worrying is a rather good way to lose weight.

"You have plans for today, apart from your meeting with your boss?" I asked, as he pulled up in front of the bluestone portico of the venerable Society building. It was only an hour later than my normal arrival time. Well, maybe an hour and a half.

"Get a haircut. See if any of my suits still fit. Talk to Cooper and see when I can start back at work. I feel ready, and my doctor's okayed it. You want me to call a Realtor?"

"Oh. Uh, yes, I guess." *Nothing like showing unbridled enthusiasm, Nell.* "See you later." After a serious kiss, I climbed out of the car and went up the steps. I nodded at Front Desk Bob, a retired policeman who staffed our reception area, and headed

15

toward the back hall. While I waited for the balky elevator to make its stately descent, I greeted the massive marble statue of Edwin Forrest in his role as Coriolanus that guarded the back hall. "Don't worry, Edwin — I'm going to see to it that you get moved to a better place, where more people will see you." Luckily, there was no one around to hear me talking to a sculpture, but I had a lot of strong feelings about Edwin.

Upstairs on the third floor, I stopped by my assistant Eric's desk. "Good morning, Eric. Anything I need to know about?"

"Mornin', Nell. Actually, there is. Mitchell Wakeman called and asked for an appointment with you, so I penciled him in for eleven. Is that okay?"

That left me all of half an hour to get my head around this meeting. I didn't know Wakeman personally, but I knew that he was a major player in Philadelphia development and construction — he'd had a finger in every major building project that had happened in the city for the last couple of decades. I'd have to Google him to remind myself of the details. "Did he say what he wanted?"

"No, he just said there was something he wanted to discuss with you. The man himself, not his assistant. I can cancel if you want."

Based on his comment, Eric must have recognized the name, and Eric was a lot newer to Philadelphia than I was. Maybe Wakeman wanted to give the Society a whole lot of money — or upgrade our creaky century-plus-old building. Hey, I could dream. But his visit could be an opportunity, and if it was, I was going to grab it. "No, that's fine. I'll be happy to talk to him. Do you know if Latoya's in?" Latoya was the Society's vice president for collections, who managed all the stuff that was inside the building, and there was a lot of it.

"I believe so."

"Then ask her if she can come see me ASAP."

"Will do."

"Thanks, Eric."

I barely had time to sit down behind my desk when Shelby stuck her head in the door. "Everything okay?" she asked. " 'Cause you've been keeping kind of irregular hours. For you, that is."

I gestured her in, and she pulled the door shut behind her. Shelby had been one of my first hires at the Society. In fact, she had replaced me as development director when

I was unexpectedly bumped into the corner office. But more than that, we were friends. "Everything is peachy-swell. Hunky-dory. Pick your own term."

"Things are going well with Mr. Agent Man?"

"Swimmingly." I hesitated, then said in a lower voice, "He wants us to find a place together."

"About time!" Shelby said, grinning. "So, he's back in fighting form?"

"He is, and he's talking with his boss today about going back to work. I have to say we're tripping all over each other at his place, and mine's not any better, plus it's kind of out of the way for him. We need more space. And more closets."

"Well, congratulations. I'm happy for you. He's one great guy." She cocked her head. "But you don't look exactly thrilled."

"Is it that obvious? Look, I know he's a terrific guy and we get along pretty well, but . . . what happens if it doesn't work out?"

"Then you find another place to stay. You gonna sell your house?"

"Thus far our discussion about this move has been about three sentences long, so I don't know." I lived in what had once been a carriage house behind one of the gracious

18

Main Line mansions in suburban Bryn Mawr. The exterior of the house was still gracious, but inside, it had been chopped up into offices by a succession of professionals. At the moment it was owned by a group of psychologists. I wondered how easy my place would be to sell — it was kind of small and had no land attached, and it was in somebody else's backyard. Something I'd have to think about. If James and I took the next step. *If?*

Shelby stood up. "Well, I'd better get to work. But let me say this: If you let him go, you're an idiot. Get over your fear of whatever and move forward."

"Thank you, Doctor. That's what I plan to do." Maybe.

We were interrupted by Latoya. "You wanted to see me, Nell? Oh, hi, Shelby."

"Hi, Latoya," Shelby said. "I was on my way out. You want to have lunch, Nell?"

"Let me get back to you on that, Shelby. I've got an appointment at eleven, and I'm not sure how long that will run."

When Shelby left, I turned my attention to Latoya. We'd had a rocky relationship ever since she joined the Society a few years earlier, back when I was still director of development. As vice president for collections, she usually had conveyed the sense that fundraising was somewhat inferior to collections management. She'd had some difficulty adjusting to my unexpected promotion to president — which had made me her boss. I hadn't wanted to force the issue, but now that I was settled in the position, it was time for me to take a firmer hand. It was hard to do, but I knew it was best both for me and the Society. I just hoped Latoya would adjust to our new working relationship.

"Is this about the registrar position?" she asked bluntly.

"It is. What progress have you made?"

"Actually, we've had a lot of applications since we posted the position. Which I will say surprised me, but given the economy, I guess I ought to have expected it. Unfortunately, many of the applicants simply aren't qualified for a senior position here."

"Have you considered moving Alice into the position?" Alice was an intern, very young but very talented.

"She hasn't said anything to me, and I'm not sure she wants it. To be honest, I really don't think she's ready. She has the ability, but not the depth of experience. I hope she'll stay on, though. Do you disagree?"

"Actually, no. I think you're right. Her job description may change a bit, depending on the skills the new registrar brings to the table. Well, keep looking and keep me informed. The collections here are still superb, and we're in sore need of someone who can work with the new software and finish sorting them out. We really need to dig out from under all the stuff we've got piled up." Not only was the documentation of the Society's collections mired in the past, but we'd been handed a mountain of uncataloged material by the FBI recently, and we were bursting at the seams.

"I'll do that." Latoya stood up, then hesitated. "Nell, we really do need to do something to improve our image in the public eye. Almost all of our publicity lately has been about theft and murder, and I can't imagine that our members are happy about that. Not to mention our donors and the board."

As if that was my fault? "I recognize that, Latoya. If you have any ideas, I'd love to hear them. Maybe we should have an all-hands staff meeting devoted to this, to find out what people have been saying about us and figure out how to fix it." Now that I didn't have to worry about James from day to day, I could devote more energy to my own responsibilities.

"Good idea. Let me put my ideas on

paper, and we can talk."

"Sooner rather than later, please."

"Right." Latoya left, but as soon as she had cleared the door, Eric stuck his head in.

"Mr. Wakeman is downstairs. Want me to bring him up?"

"Please." The man was early, and I hadn't had time to check out what we had in our records about him or think through what he might want. When Eric left to retrieve Wakeman, I figured I had about three minutes, so I did a quick online search about my guest. My fuzzy memory was more or less correct: he was a big-time developer in Philadelphia and the surrounding counties. Which didn't give me a clue about why he wanted to see me.

Two and a half minutes later, Eric ushered in a tall, greying man in his fifties, whose expensive clothes seemed to have a mind of their own and were flying in several different directions — necktie loose, shirt coming untucked. But I was pretty sure he wasn't here for a fashion consult.

I stood up and extended my hand. "I'm Nell Pratt. What can I do for you, Mr. Wakeman?"

He shook it firmly. "I'm working on a new

project, and I want you to help."

Music to my ears.

CHAPTER 2

Mitchell Wakeman sat heavily in one of my antique guest chairs, legs sprawling. "Nice to meet you, Ms. Pratt. I've been seeing your name in the papers a lot lately."

I was never sure how to respond to statements like that. It really would be nice to get some press for something related to Philadelphia history instead of my involvement with its crime rate. I hedged a bit. "And how did that lead you here to the Society?"

Wakeman nodded once, as if noting my tacit acknowledgment of the events he was talking about. "I'll come to the point. Please keep the details of what I tell you on the q.t. — we're still in the preliminary planning stages and I don't want to spread it around yet. You know, drive property values and construction costs up in the neighborhood."

"I understand, and I hope I am always

discreet about any confidences. What are you asking for?"

"Now that the economy is turning around a bit, I think the time is right for a project I've been nursing along for a while — a multipurpose development in Chester County."

"Multipurpose? Meaning a combination of residential and commercial?"

"Yes, but even more. It's a unified development that brings together everything you need, kind of like a little community of its own. You know — housing, restaurants and cafés, shops, dry cleaner, maybe even some medical offices."

"Like a retirement village for senior citizens?"

"For all ages. Condos first, then maybe houses in a later phase."

"Sounds interesting. Will this be in commuter range?"

"Good question. Like I said, it's in Chester County, so it's in commuting range. Plus SEPTA's been talking about extending one of its lines out farther that way. I'd like to encourage that. I've initiated very preliminary discussions with management there about a sort of public-private venture, but nothing is set in stone yet."

"I live near the Main Line. So, this would

be out beyond that?"

"Yeah, that's where the land is." He leaned forward and lowered his voice a notch. "I've got a nice parcel of land in Goshen, a working dairy farm until recently. I knew the owner for years — his family owned the place for centuries. When he hit ninety, Ezra decided to sell before his kids started squabbling over what to do with it. I was happy to take it at a fair price. The deal was already done when he passed last year, but he had a life interest in it."

"This all sounds wonderful, Mr. Wakeman, but where does the Society fit in this?"

"You know about Duffy's Cut?"

"Yes, of course." Duffy's Cut had been in the news a lot over the past couple of years — it involved the tragic death of over thirty Irish immigrants working on the "cut" or railroad cutting in Malvern, a town in Chester County, in the early nineteenth century, and the cover-up by the railroad company, which had buried the bodies fast and never reported the deaths. They'd been found only recently. "Various historians and members of the media have done some research on it here. How does that apply?"

"Frankly, I don't want another Duffy's Cut to happen on my project. It's not just the legalities about digging up old bones —

I can respect that. What I want is to be ready if something like that comes up, so I'm not caught with my pants down. Goodwill is important in making a project like this work, and it's hard enough without worrying about any messes in the press. You see what I'm saying?"

"I think so," I said cautiously. "You want the Society to look into the history of the property you are considering to make sure there aren't any unpleasant surprises hidden there? Or, if there are, to make sure you're prepared to handle them?"

"Exactly." He sat back and smiled at me. "Can you do that?"

I thought for a moment. He was right to come to the Society. We had the best collections of documents about Philadelphia history anywhere, although there was a good small historical society in West Chester. But I still wasn't sure what he was asking. "Do you want to hire a researcher to look into this?"

"You mean one of your hourly intern types who'll take a year or two? No, I want the best. I want someone working on this pretty much full-time until I'm sure you've turned over every rock and nothing crawls out."

Full-time? I wasn't sure I could help him

27

there. Our staff was pretty limited. There was Rich, an intern whose main job was to slog through the Terwilliger Collection, mainly documents from generations of local Terwilligers — Pennsylvania movers and shakers who went back to the early eighteenth century. The family had included several Society presidents, and its latest member, Martha Terwilliger, was on the Society board. The short answer was, Rich was fully occupied and Marty wouldn't be happy if I tried to divert him from "her" project. That only left new intern Alice, who was untried. She'd been hired in part to keep her benefactor uncle happy, although so far she'd done a great job for us. But no way was she ready to tackle a major research project like the one Wakeman was proposing. Still, I didn't want to tell him that we couldn't handle it or send him off to one of the local universities to find a historian, who would probably want to write a book about it anyway. And academic historians were slow, because they insisted on being careful and accurate, with footnotes on every page. I didn't condone the quick-and-dirty approach, but I thought we could deliver what he wanted. "Mr. Wakeman, I'll be blunt. We don't have enough staff at the moment to provide what you need. But we can recruit and hire someone qualified to take on this project on a full-time basis, if you're willing to pay for it. And we do have all the resources here on site."

"Of course I'll pay for it," Wakeman said impatiently. "But I want somebody good, and I want whoever it is to keep his or her mouth shut until I'm ready to go public with this."

"That's not a problem. I take it you want this to happen immediately?"

He grinned. "Yeah, like, last week. How much you gonna charge for this?"

I named a figure that equaled six months' salary for one of our interns — plus fifty percent. I figured the extra would cover speed and silence, of course, and I knew he had the money.

Wakeman didn't blink. "When can you start?" he asked.

"As soon as I can identify him — or her."

"Let me know. I'll want to meet him — or her. And if this goes right, there might be something extra in it for the Society."

"I'm sure that would be welcome."

Wakeman stood up. "Great. Here's my card. Give me a call when you have somebody for me to talk to." He turned and strode out, and I frantically gestured to Eric to see him out of the building, since Wakeman couldn't use the elevator without a key. Pitiful security, I knew, but it was all we had.

After they were gone, I sat at my desk for a few moments, stunned. I recognized this as a true opportunity: Wakeman Property Trust was a major player in the greater Philadelphia area and was rolling in money. If we did a good job, there would definitely be rewards, tangible and intangible. And we were clearly the best organization to dig into the history of that particular plot of land. The problem would be finding someone who could do it.

Well, Marty Terwilliger was a good person to start with. She knew everybody in Philadelphia and was related to half of them (including James). Funny — I hadn't seen much of her in the past few weeks. Of course, I hadn't been around much myself in the past few weeks because of James. But it was definitely time to climb back in the saddle. I picked up the phone and dialed Marty's cell.

She answered on the fifth ring. "Nell? What's up?"

"Nothing bad, I promise. I've got a research project I'd like to discuss with you. Can you do lunch today?"

I heard what sounded to me like a hand

clamping over the phone and a rumble of voices. Then Marty came back. "One? At that place around the corner?"

"Great. See you there."

I checked my watch: twelve fifteen. The meeting with Wakeman hadn't taken long, because he'd come right to the point. I hated bits of time that weren't long enough to start anything but were too long to waste. I decided to spend it doing some more online research into Mitchell Wakeman. From my days as Society fundraiser, I was sure he had never been a member of the Society or given us any substantial amount, so I wondered what had made him think of us. It was gratifying to know that we had a solid reputation — apart from a few recent problems — but Wakeman could have hired just about anyone in the business. How hush-hush was this project of his? Had he come to us because he thought none of his construction colleagues would see what he was up to? The next time I looked up, it was twelve forty-five, there was a stack of printouts on my printer, and Shelby was leaning on my doorframe smiling.

"Earth to Nell?"

"Have you been standing there long?"

"Maybe. What had you so absorbed?"

"I'll explain over lunch if you want to

come along. I'm meeting Marty around the corner in twelve minutes, so we should get going. Say, have you seen much of Marty recently?"

Shelby wrinkled her brow. "Come to think of it, I haven't. Maybe Rich is too tied up with general stuff to work on the Terwilliger materials?"

"That never stopped her before. I've been so distracted that I hadn't even noticed she wasn't around. But she said yes to lunch quickly enough when I called today. Maybe there's something else going on in her life."

"Heaven forbid Martha Terwilliger should have a life!" Shelby said in mock horror. "Let's go find out."

Marty, unfazed by the August heat, was waiting outside the restaurant when Shelby and I arrived. We gathered her up and ducked into the air-conditioned restaurant as quickly as possible and found a quiet table in the back. Once we were settled with tall glasses of iced tea in front of all three of us, Marty looked me over critically.

"You're looking good. How's Jimmy?"

"Are those two statements related?" I parried.

"I'd say yes," Marty said. "Has he asked you yet?"

"Asked me what?" I said, stalling.

"Yeah, what?" Shelby said, smiling and looking back and forth between us.

"About moving in together," Marty replied.

I struggled to answer. How come she knew before I did? "Yes, he mentioned something like that this morning."

"You gonna do it?" she asked. Marty didn't bother with-beating around the bush. But I supposed she had a right to be interested, since she was the one who'd introduced me to James and the one who'd glued me back together when he'd been injured, and forced me to step up to take care of him. "Your house is cute, but it's not adequate for two people. Kind of like a burrow built for one."

"Marty!" I protested. "It's a perfectly nice Victorian carriage house, but I know it's small. And how the heck do you know anything about it? Have you even seen James?"

"We had lunch a couple of times while you were at work."

"So, was this your idea or his?" I was working up a head of steam. Was Marty trying to manipulate my life now?

"His. He asked me how I thought you'd react. I told him you'd back off, and then you'd waffle for a while, and that he should just wait it out because you two belong together."

Great. My own life was not my own, apparently. "Shelby, were you in on all this, too?"

"No, ma'am!" she said quickly. "But I do agree with Marty. Why don't you skip the waffling part and go straight to yes?"

"Hey, give me like fifteen minutes to think about this, okay? Besides, a few other things have intervened. Which is what I wanted to talk to you about." I looked around the room: midweek, after one, the restaurant was sparsely filled, and there was no one seated at a table near us. "I had a very interesting discussion with a certain prominent local developer this morning."

"Mitchell Wakeman, right?" Marty said.

"How did you know?" I asked. The woman was uncanny.

"Before you ask, no, he's not a relative, and no, I didn't send him to you." She grinned at me. "He figured out where to come all by himself."

One question answered, to my happy relief. "I'm glad to hear that. How, then?"

"Because you say *prominent, local,* and *developer* in one sentence, and he's the obvious choice. What did he want?"

"Time-out," Shelby interrupted. "Who is

this guy? I mean, I know the name, and I know his reputation, but he's never been involved with the Society."

"You haven't been around Philadelphia very long, have you?" I said. "He and his various companies more or less shaped the current skyline of the city. He's had a finger in every pie in half the state. He's been on boards and panels and who knows what around here. Does that about cover it, Marty?"

"In a nutshell. He's one of the good guys. Politically connected, but he uses it for good, not evil. He's made tons of money, but legally, and not by trampling or squeezing anybody for it. Never been a member or given us any money." By *us* I knew Marty meant the Society, to which she was fanatically devoted, just as her father and grandfather had been. "What did he want?"

"You mean I actually know something you don't?" I smiled at Marty. Our salads arrived, which kind of quashed conversation for a few minutes. Plus I suddenly felt a little funny talking about this in public after Wakeman had specifically asked me to keep things quiet. I decided to change the subject, at least temporarily.

"So, now that James will be going back to work, I should be in the office more. I feel

like I've been out of the loop for a while."
All too true: the first couple of weeks of
looking out for my injured warrior had been
kind of rough. Sure, I'd had plenty of ac-
cumulated sick leave and vacation time, but
I was also the relatively new president of a
venerable institution, so I was torn between
nursing and doing my job. It would be a
relief to get back to normal, if I could
remember what that was. "What have you
been up to, Marty?" I said innocently.

Shelby picked up my drift. "You know, I
haven't seen much of you, either. Something
new going on?"

Marty seemed to be at a loss for words,
which was unusual.

"Marty, are you blushing?" I asked with a
grin.

"No!" she protested quickly. "Well,
maybe." She smiled, kind of. "I'm seeing
someone."

"Ooh, tell us!" Shelby said before I could
say much the same thing. Marty had been
married a time or two, but as far as I knew
she hadn't been involved with anyone for a
couple of years now.

"What's his name? Do we know him?" I
asked.

"I'm not going to play twenty questions
with you. He's a professor at Penn, special-

izing in urban history and economics. Widowed, grown kids. And before you ask, not related in any way, shape, or form to the Pennsylvania Terwilligers."

"So how did you meet him?" I pressed.

"I went to a lecture he gave. He was interesting, so I hung around to ask him a question after. Things kind of went from there. And that's all I want to say right now."

"Stay away for a couple of weeks, and the earth shifts on its axis," I sighed dramatically. "But I'm happy for you, Marty. I hope it works out."

"Just like you and Jimmy, huh?" Marty shot back.

And we finished the lunch with non-business-related girl talk. After, standing outside the restaurant, I said, "Marty, do you have time to come back and talk to me about this mysterious special project of Wakeman's? Shelby, you're welcome to join us. Based on what he said, I think this is about local history, which isn't exactly up your alley, but you've come up with some good stuff in the past. If you aren't too busy."

"Hey, lady, anything that puts me in the good graces of a local power broker works for me," Shelby said happily. "Let's do it!"

CHAPTER 3

Settled once again in my office, I began, "Before we get into it, anybody have any new thoughts on the registrar position? Latoya told me she's been getting applications but that many of the people simply aren't qualified."

"Alice is working out well," Marty volunteered. "She's smart. Or maybe I mean *intuitive.* I can't see her chained to a computer all the time, but she's great with descriptions and making connections."

"I agree with both your points. Latoya and I discussed her earlier, though, and I'm not sure she's ready for it, nor would it send the right message to bump her up to the position right now. Which leaves us nowhere. Latoya hasn't found any candidates that she likes. Maybe it's just that it's summer and things are slow."

"Or nobody wants a job that's both boring and unlucky," Marty said. "I'll ask around again. Have you talked to Jimmy about it?"

"Why would I?"

"In case you haven't noticed, the FBI uses analysts. Maybe somebody over there wants a change of pace. Or maybe he'd remember a good candidate they didn't hire. Can't hurt to ask."

"I suppose." I made a mental note to mention it to James later. "Now, back to the Wakeman project. Here's the deal: Mr. Wakeman approached me directly because he's planning some sort of mega-development out in Chester County, and he doesn't want to run into any problems like Duffy's Cut."

"What's Duffy's Cut?" Shelby asked.

"How much time have you got?"

"Hey, this is business, isn't it? Take all the time you want, boss."

"Okay, you've both been to my house in Bryn Mawr. The train that serves the town is now the SEPTA R3, but it's always been known as the Main Line. It's what's left of the main line of the Pennsylvania Railroad, which served all the upscale communities west of the city. The 'old money' families."

"They took trains? I thought they all had chauffeurs," Shelby said with a smile.

"Well, some of the gentlemen had to get

to their clubs, so the train was simple," interjected Marty.

"Anyway, the Main Line used to end in Paoli, and then it was extended to the next town over, Malvern," I continued. "Now, the Malvern stretch was originally built for a different railroad in the nineteenth century. When the bosses needed laborers back then, they'd take immigrants straight off the ships in Philadelphia — mostly Irish and mostly those with no local connections. In 1832, dozens of them died on the Malvern railway job in a cholera epidemic, and nobody ever notified the relatives back in Ireland, and the railway all but destroyed the evidence. The bodies were buried in a ditch under the tracks and more or less forgotten. When the bodies were finally discovered in 2009, archeologists saw what they thought looked like evidence of blunt-force trauma, so the site was declared a crime scene rather than a dig. There are some nasty rumors that some of the workers may have been killed off to stop the spread of the disease."

"That's awful!" Shelby exclaimed.

"Exactly. When the mass burials were uncovered, it became a big issue, of course, with various factions blaming others retroactively, and then the current railroad wouldn't let the historians finish the dig, which only made things worse. I read all about it at the time — it's kind of in my backyard, it's local history, and it's a compelling story. Anyway, Wakeman's property is only a couple of miles away, and he doesn't want to run into any surprises like that or set off another firestorm among local historians. Malvern and the local towns are already pretty sensitized to the issue, so he wants to be sure that everything is clean and aboveboard. That's why he came to us — he wants somebody to do a thorough history of the site he's optioned, to make sure there aren't any bodies there, literally or figuratively. Worst case, if there are, he wants to be ready to manage the situation."

"Wouldn't hurt our reputation much, either," Marty said. "Did he tell you exactly where the site was?"

"He said it was a dairy farm. He bought it before the old owner died, but he's only taken possession of it recently. He also said it's near a rail line, but there's some talk of extending that, and I think that would figure into his development plans."

"What's he want to build?" Shelby asked.

"He called it a mixed-use development that combines housing, commercial space, recreational stuff — a whole package. I was impressed, if it's true. I mean, I've seen enough ugly suburban sprawl, so if he can do it efficiently, with a solid plan and with the local communities on board, I'd have to applaud. If it all checks out, I'd like to help him. The only problem is, we don't have anyone available to do the work right now at the Society. We're already short-staffed. Either of you have any ideas about where we can find somebody qualified for a short-term appointment?"

Everybody was silent for a couple of minutes, apparently thinking hard. Then Marty said, "Did he mention money?"

"He said he'd pay the salary of a researcher, if we needed to hire one. We didn't get into anything about supporting the institution, if that's what you're asking, but he kind of hinted. So, Marty, you know everybody and everything that matters about eastern Pennsylvania. What's your take on this project? Is it something we should be part of?"

Marty contemplated the ceiling. "I've known Mitch Wakeman and his wife for years, but sort of socially, and we're not close. He lives way out in the burbs, with said wife and a bunch of his kids. I've never heard anything negative about him, and as far as I know he is a good planner, and doesn't jump into a project unless he's pretty sure he has the funding lined up, so he's left no half-built messes behind. As for the project itself . . . I think I know the parcel he's talking about. Plenty of room, but he is going to have to look at access roads, water supply, wastewater, all that stuff. I don't think any of them is a deal-breaker, if he's got enough money to put into it. The train upgrade might be harder because there are a bunch of different agencies involved, but I'm not sure it's essential to the project."

Marty leaned back in her chair. "He's going to need local approvals from the township out there. I don't know what Wakeman's relationship with that bunch is like, although I think it's a good bet that he knows them already. And I'm sure he's thought about all of this. The Society's role is a very small part. Still, it's nice of him to think of us."

"Great, so you're in favor of going ahead? Do we need board approval?"

"I'll talk to them, but I don't think anyone will have a problem — well, unless one or two of them have butted heads with Wakeman in the past, which has been known to happen, because he can be kind of, well, abrupt. Let's hope not, anyway. It won't cost the Society anything if we can find a warm body with a brain to take it on, and it'll make us look good. Assuming, of course, that we don't find something like another Duffy's Cut that puts the kibosh on the project or drags it out for years."

"And what would do that?"

"Let's not borrow trouble," Shelby said. "First you need to find a researcher. What's his timeline? Or maybe I mean, when did you tell Wakeman you'd get back to him?"

"Uh, I don't think I said. But ASAP, at least with a yea or a nay."

"Maybe Ethan knows a grad student . . ." Marty said, her expression softening.

Shelby and I exchanged a look. "Ethan being the man of the moment?" I asked. "Does the man have a last name?"

"Uh, yeah. Miller," Marty said, then shut up again.

"A grad student might be a good choice, if he knows anything about local history," Shelby commented.

"I'll ask," Marty muttered. "So, what're you going to tell Jimmy about the whole moving-in-together thing?"

Nice deflection, Marty, I thought. "I, uh, don't know. We'll have to talk about it." My cell phone rang in my bag. I fished it out: James. Marty and Shelby wouldn't mind my answering. I punched the button to connect. "Hey there. Were your ears burning?"

"What? Oh, I get it. Say hi to Marty."

"And Shelby," I added. "So, what's up?"

"You free for dinner tonight?"

"Out? Are we celebrating?"

"Close enough. I'll meet you at the Society at six, okay?"

"Fine. See you then." We both hung up. I looked up to see Marty and Shelby watching me with closely matched smiles.

"Ah, true love," Shelby cooed.

"You two are the very soul of romance," Marty added.

I refused to take the bait. "Come off it, guys. This is my place of business. He and I will get mushy over dinner tonight, and no, you can't tag along."

"Wouldn't anyway — I have plans," Marty said, looking smug.

"So, we're about done here. Marty, you're going to ask Ethan if he knows of any eager researchers who want to take on a short-term project like this. Shelby, maybe you can do a little digging about Wakeman and see if there's anything we need to know — and check out his record on charitable donations while you're at it. Oh, and I'll ask James if there are any leftover FBI analysts who might fit the registrar position. Anything else?"

Shelby stood up and saluted. "No, ma'am. That about covers it. I'll let you know if I find anything interesting."

After she'd left, I turned back to Marty. "This thing with Ethan serious?"

"Maybe. Look, I'll lay off you and James if you don't ask any questions about Ethan. If there's anything you need to know, I'll tell you."

"Deal."

Having sent Shelby and Marty off with their marching orders, I whiled away the rest of the afternoon with paperwork and correspondence and all the other stuff that keeps an institution going. At five, Eric popped his head in.

"You need anything else, Nell?" he asked.

"No, I'm good. Look, Eric, thanks for covering for me over the past few weeks. I know I haven't been around much, but I hope things will get back to normal now."

"I was happy to help out. And I'm glad Agent Morrison is back on his feet. It must have been hard on you."

"It was, but we're past that now. Thanks for asking. I'll see you in the morning."

Eric left, and the rest of the administrative staff on the third floor trickled out until I was the last one. I'd mentioned getting back to normal, but what *was* normal? I'd been in charge of the place for over a year now, and every time I thought things had settled down, another crisis erupted. Sometimes I wondered how we managed to keep the doors open and staff employed, but we had. Sometimes I wondered how I had managed to survive all of it — and a few times it had been a close thing — and come out of it with renewed enthusiasm for what I was doing. The Society and the history that it held were worth fighting for . . . although I really would prefer it if people stopped fighting and just enjoyed the bounty of the place.

I was lost in thought when James called to say that he was downstairs waiting for me. I gathered up my bag, turned out the lights, and went down to meet him.

I almost didn't recognize him. The haircut made a big difference — he'd gotten kind of shaggy over the past month, but a major scalp laceration did not lend itself to regular trims. And I'd forgotten how good he looked in a suit. Had anything else changed? Maybe a little. His face seemed thinner, and there were a few more lines at the corners of his eyes, but they just added dignity. I felt almost tongue-tied. "Hey," I said brilliantly.

"Hey yourself," he said, smiling.

"Damn, you look good."

"Thanks. I can't button the jacket — I need some serious gym time. But it's summer, so nobody should notice. You ready to go?"

"Are we walking?" I asked, and James graciously escorted me down the stone steps of the Society.

"I thought we'd go to Vetri — that's close."

"Nice! If I'd known, I would have dressed for it."

"You look lovely."

I bit off a remark along the lines of "What, this old thing?" I was trying to learn to accept compliments, and James's were always sincere. "Thank you. So this really is a celebration?"

"I hope so. I've been cleared to go back to work. You're back on the job full-time. And we made it through, you and I."

"That we did," I said, taking the arm James offered, establishing our status as a couple for all the world to see.

CHAPTER 4

We strolled slowly, given that the heat of the day still lingered in stone and concrete. Since the restaurant was only a couple of blocks away, we arrived quickly despite the leisurely pace, and once inside we were seated immediately.

"Wine?" James asked.

"Please," I said, and watched as he ordered a bottle of white. When the waiter had departed, I said, "You know, you look very pleased with yourself."

"Shouldn't I be? I'm fit again, I've got a job I enjoy — plus my boss now figures he owes me because he didn't listen to me when it counted — and I've got you. Not necessarily in that order. Nell, I can't thank you enough for sticking by me over the past month. I know it wasn't easy."

"No, it wasn't, but I wanted to be there. After what happened . . ." I stopped, unsure how to go on. "The aftereffects linger on," I finally said. When he started to protest, I held up a hand. "No, I'm not having flashbacks or waking up in a sweat at night. It's just the stress of being understaffed at work, and we're having trouble filling this registrar position, which keeps getting bigger and more complicated. We're still not done with the conversion to the new software system, and then there's the flood of new items, thanks in part to all the FBI stuff you dropped on us, and we'd barely made a dent in that when things hit the fan. So, as I said, it's not over until we're fully staffed and things are running smoothly again." I took a sip of my wine. "Marty said I should ask whether you knew anyone who might be interested in the job. You don't, do you?"

James thought for a moment. "Actually, I might know somebody who would be a good fit for that position, but he may surprise you. Let me talk to him and see if he's interested."

"Does he have a résumé?"

"I don't know if he's written one lately. It's kind of an odd situation . . . No, let me check with him, and then we can talk about it."

We lapsed back into silence for a moment. "Is there something else that's bothering you?" James asked.

"You told Marty about what you asked me this morning," I said bluntly. It still rankled, although I wasn't sure why.

"What? Oh, you mean about finding a place together? Is that a problem?"

"I guess I'm not happy that she knew before I did. You might have asked me first."

He cocked his head at me, looking genuinely confused. "I'm sorry, I didn't mean to overstep, but you know Marty . . . Wait, are you saying you don't want to?"

"No, not exactly. But I want to think about it, okay? I mean, spending this past month with you has been . . . interesting, and parts of it have been intense, but I haven't had time to look at the big picture."

He looked down at his wine glass and swirled the contents rather than look at me. "Is that one of those 'it's not you, it's me' lines?"

"No! I'm happy that you've asked, but I need to figure out what I want, and what works for us together."

He looked at me then, and his eyes were less warm than they had been. "I told you, my lease is up at the end of the month. When do you think you'll have an answer?"

Suddenly my eyes were filled with tears. "Oh, James, you only asked me this morning. It's a big step for me. Just give me a little time, please?"

The waiter appeared to refill our glasses and take our orders, providing a welcome break. Why was I being such an idiot? I loved James. He was smart, sexy, gainfully employed, and he said he loved me. What else could I possibly want?

The problem *was* me. I had trouble trusting people, and I didn't let them get too close. I knew it was an issue, but I'd never figured out how to get around it. Yet, if there was ever a time to work it out, this was it. I knew it was an insult to James, that my hesitation signaled I didn't really trust him, not all the way, when he'd been up-front about how he felt without pushing too hard. Heck, he had every right to push — he wanted to get on with his life. Why didn't I?

Once our food arrived, it gave us something else to focus on. The wine was smooth, the food was delightful, but the company was . . . subdued. It certainly didn't feel much like a celebration anymore, and that was my fault, which I regretted. After passing on dessert but agreeing to espresso, James settled the bill, and said, "Are you coming home with me?"

"If you want me to," I said.

"Always," he said, and he smiled to show he meant it.

■ ■ ■ ■

I woke up in the morning before James and I lay still in bed, thinking. James and I had been thrown together intimately, in more ways than one, for the past month, but I still knew in the back of my mind that I had a place that was all mine, one I could escape to if I needed. Was I ready to give up my escape hatch? To the world it looked like I had all my ducks a row — great guy, good job, nice life. What more did I want? I rolled over to find James watching me. I smiled at him. "How many bedrooms?"

He smiled back with what looked like relief. "Three? That way we each get office space."

I liked the idea of a hidey-hole with a door, all my own. "Sounds good."

We moved on to talk particulars. James's third-floor row house walk-up was probably better suited to a graduate student than to a senior special agent for the FBI, but it had worked for him, at least until now. He had few possessions and didn't seem to care much about "things." In contrast, I was a collector — pretty items that caught my eye, heirlooms I treasured that had belonged to my grandparents, and a lot of stuff that just seemed to accumulate. As my stuff migrated, his place had become increasingly crowded. It hadn't been too bad when James had been laid up, but now that he was more himself, we kept bumping into each other. Not that that was always a problem, but still. We discussed parking spaces and the like, then James asked, "Nell, you're sure about this?"

"Yes, I am." Maybe. I wasn't sure I was sure, but I was going to work very hard to convince myself. "Now, let's celebrate for real."

I made it to work on time, but only by skipping breakfast. I picked up a large coffee on the way.

"What's on the calendar today, Eric?" I greeted him as I arrived at my office.

"Mr. Wakeman called again, asked if you had some time free this afternoon to look at something. You don't have anything scheduled, but I didn't want to book it without checking with you first. Should I call him back?"

"Sure. Anything else?"

"Ms. Terwilliger called, said she might have someone for that thing you told her about. I assume you know what she means?"

"I do. Did she say if she'd be coming in today?"

"She didn't mention it. You want me to call her, too?"

"I'll do it, after I've talked with Mr. Wakeman, since the calls are kind of related." Eric looked game but confused. I decided to take him into my confidence. "Hey, come on into my office and I'll explain."

Eric followed me in and shut the door. "Is this something secret?"

"Not exactly, but let's keep it low profile. You know who Mr. Wakeman is?"

"Kind of — I Googled him after that last meeting. Big local builder, right? I see his name on construction sites a lot."

"Exactly. He's done a lot for the city. Anyway, he's hatching a new development in the suburbs and he doesn't want to run into any archeological or historical surprises at the site, so he's asked us to look into it for him. It's a very responsible thing for him to do, and I'm pleased that he came to us. But since we're a bit shorthanded at the moment, we'll have to recruit somebody short-term to do it. That's where Marty's call comes in — I asked her if she knew anyone who might fit the bill."

"Got it. Is this project hush-hush?"

"It's still in the planning stages, so the less said the better for now. Not that I don't trust you, Eric, but you never know who's going to overhear something in the city and run with it. If everything goes well, the site will get a clean bill of health and we'll come out smelling like a rose. Maybe with a nice contribution to go with it."

"Let's hope so. Thanks, Nell, for filling me in. I'll call Mr. Wakeman for you now."

I barely had time to take a sip of my coffee before Eric told me that Mitchell Wakeman was on the line. I picked up. "Good morning, Mr. Wakeman. What can I do for you?"

"I wondered if you'd like a tour of the site, so you know what we're talking about?"

"I would like that. When did you have in mind?"

"This afternoon? I could pick you up about three — it's maybe an hour away, out toward West Chester."

"That sounds good, if you're willing to drop me off in Bryn Mawr on your way back."

"No problem. I'll come by at three, then. Thanks." He hung up. He knew I wasn't going to be doing the research myself — I couldn't claim to be a local historian — but I figured that the big cheese at the Wakeman Trust preferred to talk to his counterpart at the Society, and that would be me. Actually, I was kind of intrigued by the idea

56

of seeing a major development project like this from the ground up, literally. Assuming it was done responsibly and tastefully, without upsetting the neighbors or the ecology.

And I'd get a ride home out of it. Though "home" was a loaded term right now . . . I shook myself and picked up the phone to call Marty, and she answered quickly. "Hey, Nell. I think I've got a researcher for you. You want to meet her?"

"That was fast. Give me a quick rundown, will you?"

"Penn grad student, needs some cash because her grant funding dried up all of a sudden. Doing a masters on urban planning, majored in American history in college. Smart, and a hard worker."

"Sounds just about perfect. Marty, how do you do this? Come up with people at the drop of a hat?"

"Ethan's her advisor. It's a good fit, isn't it?"

"It is. Look, Wakeman offered to take me on a tour of the site at three this afternoon. If this person's free, she could come over here and talk to me at two, and if I like her, I can introduce her to Wakeman and we could go out together and see what's what."

"Good idea. I'll call her and let you

know." She hung up. Why did I talk to so many people who hung up abruptly? Was that better or worse than the ones who rambled on and wouldn't get off the phone? Anyway, I was glad that the pieces seemed to be falling into place nicely.

Eric rapped on my doorframe. "Nell, there's a guy downstairs, says Agent Morrison sent him over to talk to you. You want to see him?"

I wasn't sure I knew what James's idea of a registrar candidate would be like, but I was willing to talk with the man. My goodness, this morning was moving at an incredible pace. Maybe the stars had realigned while I wasn't looking. "All right. Can you go down and bring him up?"

"Will do." Eric disappeared.

I straightened what little there was on my desk and tried to get my head into interview mode. Maybe I should send this person straight to Latoya, but James had pointed him toward me, so I might as well talk to him first. At least I knew what the registrar's job required in the way of qualifications, having interviewed quite a few people for it in recent months. Whoever we hired needed to have solid computer skills and some serious database-management experience. A background in history, particularly for the

Philadelphia area, would be extremely helpful. Someone who really cared about local history would be even better.

Eric returned quickly, and I looked up from the job description I'd retrieved from my file to greet the newcomer — and then adjusted my gaze down: the man was in a wheelchair.

CHAPTER 5

The man didn't smile. "I'm Benjamin Hartley. James Morrison said you have a position open. Don't get up." He looked to be fortyish, with close-cropped hair, and not exactly happy. He rolled his wheelchair closer to the desk and extended his hand. I shook it; his grip was as strong as I would have guessed. "Not what you expected, huh, Ms. Pratt?"

"I'm Nell," I answered with a smile. "Frankly, Mr. Hartley, I wasn't expecting anybody, not this fast. I only mentioned it to James last night. How do you know each other?"

"Went to college together. Then he went with the FBI and I went to into the military. We stayed in touch."

All right then. A military guy? I wondered why he was here for this position, and how he could possibly fit. "What did James tell you about the job?"

"That it's mainly computers and historical stuff."

"Do you have a résumé?"

"Nope. Just got out of rehab — physical, not alcohol or drugs — and I haven't had time for that kind of stuff. But I need a job."

Nobody would accuse this guy of sucking up to a potential employer, or of pulling his punches. But if James vouched for him, I had to assume he had a good reason. Even out of loyalty to an old friend, he wouldn't send over someone totally unqualified. "You haven't interviewed for a job for a while, have you?"

"No. Why?"

"Because you're giving me a lousy first impression. Why are you here?"

"Because I need to work, and I've got the qualifications."

I took a moment and counted to ten. "Okay, let's back up. You're no longer in the military?"

"Right. I'd had enough of that. And if you're wondering, I'm in this chair because of a stupid car accident, after I got out. At least I've got decent insurance."

"You're cleared physically to work full-time now?"

"Yes." He didn't elaborate.

I suppressed a sigh. To be honest, the

61

registrar position didn't require a lot of interaction with other people, just technical skills. "Why the attitude, if you want a job here? Are you pissed off because you think this is a charity offer? I assure you it's not. We need someone in this position — but it has to be someone who can do the job."

Ben looked at me for a moment, and finally he smiled, which changed his face altogether. "Sorry, you're right — I'm being rude. It's just that I'm kinda new to this whole disability thing, and I don't want anybody's pity. I want to work, and I can do the job. Can we start this over?"

"Happy to. Welcome, Mr. Hartley. Tell me, why do you think you're suited to the position of registrar at the Pennsylvania Antiquarian Society?"

"It's Ben, please. I've got an undergrad degree in history, and ten years in data management for the US Army. I'd just gotten out, hadn't even started looking for something new, when this happened." He waved at his legs. "But the rest of me still works fine."

"Thank you for telling me. I never know these days which questions are politically incorrect and which ones you could sue me for. Are you from Philadelphia?"

I was willing to discount his hostile entrance — he was having a hard time dealing with being in a wheelchair, both physically and psychologically. Once he started talking, Ben relaxed and became a much more pleasant person. He was intelligent and well-informed about computer issues — or at least, better than I was. And he knew something about history and the local scene. Mobility wasn't really an issue for the position, except for retrieving files off a high shelf now and then, but someone could help out with that. Could he maneuver through the stacks? Easy enough to find out. We already had handicapped access to enter the building from the side street. I decided I liked him.

"You considering other people?" he asked after several minutes.

"To be honest, we had a fair number of applicants for the position because of the general economy, but most of them don't have the credentials. You're the best qualified by any standard. Let me bring in my VP for collections, Latoya Anderson. The position reports to her."

I picked up the phone and punched in Latoya's number. "Latoya, could you come to my office for a moment? I'd like you to meet a candidate for the registrar position."

She appeared thirty seconds later — not

hard, since her office was just down the hall. "You might have given me some warning, Nell."

"I would have, but I was as surprised as you. Latoya, meet Ben Hartley. He's applying for the registrar position. Before you ask, no, I haven't seen his résumé."

Latoya appeared bewildered for a moment, looking at Ben and then back at me as if to see if I was joking. Then she pulled herself together and sat down in the chair in front of my desk. "Tell me about yourself, Ben. What interests you in working at a place like this?"

Now that he was warmed up, Ben handled himself well, and I watched the two of them interact, feeling encouraged. Latoya and I had had our disagreements, but she was a professional, and she had the best interests of the Society at heart. I didn't think she'd be petty enough to reject Ben just because I'd been the one to bring him in, and he was responding to all her questions appropriately. After a few minutes, Latoya stood up. "Thank you for coming in, Ben. Nell and I need to discuss your application, but I promise we'll get in touch with you shortly. I'll be down the hall, Nell." She left quickly.

"How'd I do?" Ben asked me.

"Not bad. Could you work with her?"

"She always have a stick up her butt?"

I stifled a snort of laughter. "Yes, she does. But she is good at her job, and she knows the collections."

"Fair enough. Yes, I believe we could work together."

"What do you think of the work? Feel you'd be up to the job?"

He nodded once. "I believe I could handle it, if you'll give me the chance."

"Let me confer with Latoya. But I will call you either way, I promise. Thanks for coming in. Oh, by the way, the job would start, like, yesterday. We are so behind, you would not believe it. Is that a problem?"

"Nope. Except I'd need some time off on a regular basis for rehab sessions."

"We could work that out. I'll see you out." I escorted him out of the office and to the elevator, then called to alert the front desk that he was on his way down so they could take him to the handicapped lift. Then I headed for Latoya's office.

She was at her desk. "What do you think?" I asked.

"He's qualified." She said it with a noticeable lack of enthusiasm, but then, I'd seldom seen Latoya excited about anything. "Where'd he come from?"

"James Morrison recommended him — he's a personal friend of James's. But that doesn't mean we're obliged to hire him, if you object."

"Why would I object? He's the best of the lot so far, or at least he talks a good line, and I have no reason to doubt him. And there's a kind of symmetry — bringing in a guy the FBI recommended to handle a load of stuff that the FBI dumped on us. You want to call him, or shall I?"

"I will. And he's available to start immediately. Do you have time to acquaint him with the software and the collections?"

"I'll make time."

"Latoya, are you sure you don't have any issues with hiring Ben? I'd rather hear them now than have you looking for him to fail."

She gave me a cold look, but I didn't flinch. Finally she said, "All right, I'll admit I feel as though he's being shoved down my throat. The collections staffing is my responsibility."

"Latoya, I recognize that, and I'm not challenging you here. You've done a good job with attempting to recruit suitable candidates. If Ben can't do the job, he should be treated like any other employee. Agreed?"

Latoya straightened up and looked me in

the eye. "Fair enough. I didn't mean to imply —"

I cut her off before she could finish that statement and erase any positive progress we'd made. "Thank you for agreeing to give him a chance."

My, weren't we all sweetness and light? But I wasn't going to complain. And just like that, we'd filled the position. I needed to let James know. Back at my office, I hit the speed dial for him.

"Agent Morrison," he responded crisply. "Oh, sorry. Hi, Nell — I was trying to get back into the routine. What's up? Did Ben call you?"

"Was he supposed to call first? He showed up, interviewed, and it looks like he's hired. Even Latoya seemed to like him. So, thank you. But if he's faking it, it'll be on your head."

"I'm not worried. He's a good guy who's had a hard time lately, but I'm sure he can handle it. You're welcome. I may be home late tonight — lots to catch up on here."

"Oh, about that — Mitchell Wakeman invited me to go tour his development site in Chester County, and I asked if he could drop me off in Bryn Mawr after. Is that all right?"

"So you'll stay out there?" He kept his

tone neutral.

"Yes, for tonight." I started to make excuses, like I needed to find some clean clothes, but then I stopped myself. It was still my house, and I wanted a little alone time with it.

"Okay. We can talk tomorrow. Gotta go." He ended the call.

Which left me feeling vaguely unsatisfied. But, hey, I'd said yes to him starting a real estate hunt, hadn't I? I got up and ambled down the hall to Shelby's office.

She was surrounded by stacks of paperwork but looked up when I arrived. "Hey there. Before you ask, I don't have time for lunch if you want me to finish this anytime soon." She waved at the piles in front of her. "You need something?"

I flopped into a chair. "No, not really. Things just seem to be moving awfully fast. In a good way. James sent us a possible registrar candidate, and he's already been interviewed and I think we're offering him the job. Marty says she has a good possibility for the Wakeman research slot, and I'm going to meet her this afternoon. And the man himself invited me to go out and look at the development site this afternoon. Oh, and I told James we could go ahead and look for a bigger apartment."

Shelby sat back in her chair and laughed. "Lady, you weren't kidding when you said things were moving fast! But it *is* all good, isn't it?"

"I think so. I hope so." I hauled myself up out of the chair. "I'll let you get back to work. I'm going to go find a sandwich and wait for Marty's pick of the day to arrive."

I left the building to get a sandwich and was surprised that the streets of the city seemed positively calm compared to the whirlwind that had been my morning. At least things were falling into place, although it might have been easier if they'd been spread out a little more. But I couldn't complain. I rewarded myself with a bag of potato chips to go with my tuna on rye and ate lunch in the break room at the Society.

Lissa Penrose, Marty's latest find, arrived seven minutes before her scheduled appointment at two. At least I'd had time to finish my sandwich. She turned out to be a tall, self-assured woman who looked to be in her later twenties, with straight, shoulder-length brown hair and glasses that hovered between hip and nerdy. Given what I guessed her age to be, I wondered if she had worked for a while or traveled or done something else before returning to school — she seemed a bit past the usual age, although these days a lot of younger people were returning to school rather than trying to find satisfying work.

I stood up and offered my hand. "Welcome, Lissa. I'm glad you could make it on such short notice."

She shook briefly but firmly. "Thank you for seeing me so quickly."

"Please, sit down. How much did Marty tell you?"

She sat. "Just the outline — that there's a developer who wants to vet a large suburban property before he proceeds with a major development project there, and he wants the Society to review any potential historical problems. I assume he has other people working on other aspects, such as any possible contamination of the site and the water supply."

A smart young woman. "Good heavens, you're already way ahead of me! I hadn't even considered the contamination question. Are you thinking there might be some overlap with the Society's part, if there was an old factory or something on the site?"

"Exactly. We should be prepared to coordinate. If I get the gig, of course."

"Good thinking. So give me the snapshot version of your credentials." Good thing I was in interview mode today.

"Born and raised in the Philadelphia suburbs — north of the city. Went to Juniata as an undergrad. Then my mother got sick, so I spent a couple of years taking care of her. She died last year, and since she left a little money, I applied for a graduate program at Penn and got in. But the money didn't stretch as far as I'd hoped, even with a grant, so something like this would be perfect."

"It is short-term, you know. Three months max."

She nodded. "I know. But Marty gave me an estimate of what it pays, and that would go a long way for me."

"How do you know Marty?"

"I don't, really. I know Ethan — he's my advisor — and I've run into Marty several times in his office. She's like a walking encyclopedia of who's who in Philadelphia, isn't she? Ask her what a particular neighborhood in the city was like in 1840 and she can tell you who lived there and who built the houses on that block. It's amazing."

Either Ethan kept people waiting, or Marty was at his office a lot. "It is a gift, and we're very lucky that she's involved with the Society. You know Philadelphia yourself, obviously. Your undergrad degree was in history?"

"History and urban planning — I hoped to work for the city, in their community redevelopment department, but then life kind of got in the way."

"Have you used the Society's collections before?"

"I have, although not extensively. But this would be a very focused project, wouldn't it?"

"It would." I made a quick decision: she was a good fit. "I don't know if Marty told you, but the developer — by the way, it's Mitchell Wakeman — wants me to see the building site this afternoon. Would you like to tag along?" Why not see how she got on with the person she ultimately had to please?

"Sure, I'd love to. I know something about Chester County, but I can be more efficient about researching it if I'm familiar with the specific part he's looking at. Tell me, what if we do go ahead with the historic assessment and we find something, like that George Washington slept there — could that derail the project?"

I considered her intelligent question before answering. "That's complicated, I think. In undertaking any project like this, I'm sure you know there are a lot of people you have to keep happy — local governments, the federal government, environmentalists, historians, neighbors. How much clout each group has varies a lot, and I don't know if just one of them can put the kibosh on it. They might be able to delay it with lawsuits and the like. Does that worry you?"

"Not really — you're paying a flat fee for the project, not on an hourly basis, right? So even if I've mined all your resources before the three months is up, would I still be paid the full amount?"

"As long as you get the job done and Mitchell Wakeman is satisfied, I don't see why not. But it's his call."

"I know. Right now, I'll take what I can get, and this sure beats waitressing."

"I hope so."

CHAPTER 6

Front Desk Bob announced Mitchell Wakeman's arrival just before three, and the unusual level of respect in his voice suggested that even he knew who he was dealing with. I gathered up my things and, with Lissa trailing behind me, I went down to greet him.

"Mr. Wakeman, good to see you again. Do you have time for a quick tour of the Society?"

He seemed restless, as if the stately grandeur of the Society's lobby made him uncomfortable. From all I'd heard and read, he was pretty much a no-nonsense and hands-on construction guy, so maybe he really didn't feel at home surrounded by all this shiny marble. "Maybe another time. Who's this?" he asked, nodding at Lissa.

"This is Lissa Penrose. We're considering her to fill the researcher position you described to me. With your approval, of course."

Lissa stepped forward and offered her hand. "It's a pleasure to meet you, Mr. Wakeman. From what Nell has told me, it sounds like you're proposing an ambitious project."

I thought she hit just the right note with the man — respectful without being fawning. Points to her.

"Nothing I can't handle." He turned back to me. "I'll trust your judgment about who to hire — I'm told you know your stuff. You ready to go?"

"Yes. Do you mind if Lissa comes with us? She should see the site, so she knows the context."

"Sure, fine. Let's go — I'm double-parked."

We went out the door. His nondescript sedan was parked directly in front of the steps. No fancy cars or chauffeurs for Mitchell Wakeman, apparently. Silly me, to have expected the trappings of wealth from a multimillionaire developer. I got in front, and Lissa slid into a seat in the back, and then we set off for Chester County.

Wakeman drove efficiently and not overly aggressively, and with the low mid-afternoon traffic we made good time. We engaged in impersonal small talk on the way. I tried to probe discreetly about the man's interest in local history, and he proved reasonably well informed, although not particularly reverent about the past that was still much in evidence around us.

When we reached the suburbs, he said to me, "You live out this way?"

"Yes, I've lived in Bryn Mawr for a while now. I guess I like to keep my work and my life separate. I like to have a place to escape to. I like the contrast. Does that make sense to you?"

"Yeah, sure, I get that."

"You live even farther out, don't you?"

He glanced briefly at me, as if surprised that I knew. "I do, for a lot of the same reasons. Nice country, west of the city. Open space."

"And you're proposing to put a major development in the middle of it? Sorry, I don't mean to be rude — I'm just trying to understand how you see this."

"I understand. I guess the bottom line is, I want to do it right. People are moving out that way, and they're going to need housing. I want to show that it's possible to create a community that has all the things people want, but without dropping it like a flying saucer in the middle of a place and wondering why the people who've lived there for years are pissed about it. I respect the history of the area, and the geography and the ecology."

"That sounds admirable. Are there any other examples of that kind of development?"

He tossed off a couple of names that meant nothing to me. "Thing is, it takes big money to put together the whole package, not just a bunch of houses and a couple of stores in the middle of nowhere. I've got the money, so I can make it happen. Does that sound crude to you?"

Was he smiling? "No, just practical. And I see your point. Trying to do it piecemeal means you run the risk of the whole project losing steam, and then you're left with a half-finished mess."

"Exactly. Almost there." I turned away from him to look out the window and check out where we were and realized we'd reached Paoli, on Route 30, a road I knew well, since it ran close to my house. Past the train station he turned off to the left. "Hey, you in the back — you've been quiet. Do you know where we are?" he asked as we drove along.

Lissa spoke up promptly. "We just left what was once the Philadelphia and Lancaster Turnpike, which was the first incorporated major toll road in the country," she said, just loudly enough to make herself heard. "We're on the Paoli Pike, that leads to West Chester, which became the county seat in 1786. But we're not going that far, are we?" I noted that she pronounced Paoli correctly: pay-o-lee. People who didn't know the region and had only read the name often got it wrong.

Wakeman looked pleased by her response. "Nope, we're stopping just this side of it."

I watched the houses roll by, the space between them increasing the farther we went. I loved this time of year: everything was lush and green, which somehow made it quiet, apart from the cicadas. But inside the car you couldn't hear them. Wakeman drove through a couple more town centers, usually no more than a few public buildings, such as local government offices and post offices, and a scattering of stores. Sometimes it was hard to believe that we were no more than thirty miles from Center City. We passed a sign for a stable, and there were sleek horses grazing in a field by the road. A mile or so farther on, Wakeman turned onto a smaller road on the right, which climbed a hill, then he turned in to an unpaved gravel driveway on the left. A hundred feet farther he stopped the car and turned off the engine. "This is it."

We all climbed out of the car and stood looking out over the rolling hills to the south. I knew the town of West Chester was only a couple of miles down the road, as was a shopping center, but here all was serene and unspoiled.

"Let me show you what we're planning," Wakeman said, after giving us ample time to take it all in.

I looked down at my shoes. I hadn't been planning on a hike when I'd dressed in the morning. "Uh, I don't think I've got the right footwear."

"No problem. I always carry boots in the trunk — a lot of construction sites are muddy. Let's see if we can find something to fit you."

If Mitchell Wakeman had appeared un-comfortable in the venerable rooms of the Society, here he was clearly in his element — expansive, enthusiastic, talkative. He quickly found boots for both Lissa and me, even if our feet slopped around inside the too-large boots, and appeared ready to walk the entire site with us, outlining each detail.

"Before we set out," I said as tactfully as I could manage, "could you tell us about the general layout? How much land are you talking about? Where's the center going to be?"

Wakeman pulled a rolled plan from the trunk and laid it out on the hood of the car. "We're here, at the top of the hill." He pointed to the center of the map.

That much I could have figured out for myself. I looked around me: nice old stone farmhouse at the top; a ramshackle wooden dairy barn just down the hill from the house, with an adjoining tall silo; various dilapidated sheds, whose use I couldn't identify, scattered around. "How much land do you have altogether?"

"About a thousand acres, irregular shape," Wakeman replied promptly. "We plan to build on no more than a third or it in the first phase. We want a mix of housing and open space, plus a buffer zone along the perimeter roads. I've got options on some of the abutting properties if we want to expand in the future."

"A thousand acres?" I said, incredulous. "How on earth did you find a single parcel that big in this day and age?"

"Told you — the Garrett family's been here since seventeen-whatever. Ezra was a great old guy. One of eleven kids. Ran a dairy operation here all his life. I got to know him through a couple of civic organizations we both belonged to. And he was smart. Some people might have figured he'd be sentimental about keeping the old place in the family, but he knew damn well the land was worth more as housing than as a dairy farm. I'd guessed it would come to that, so that's why I approached him. I did tell the kids that I'd keep the old farmhouse as a community center — they liked that."

"The underlying property must have been part of a Penn land grant, although I doubt that the Garretts were the first owners, but I can check," Lissa said suddenly. "Either way, it's amazing that they've kept the land together this long."

"That's the kind of information I'm looking for — Melissa, is it?"

"Lissa," the girl corrected him quietly.

"Lissa, got it. You dig into all that stuff. Great selling point when the houses are built — own a piece of history, going all the way back to William Penn." Wakeman turned away and surveyed his domain. "So, basic facilities up here, kinda behind the hill so you won't see it from the road — market, post office, café, a couple of doctors' offices, bank, that kind of thing. Houses set back, scattered around. We keep the trees when we can, plant some new ones to fill in. No ticky-tacky rows of matching buildings, even for the condos. The lots might be small, but the houses'll be staggered so you aren't looking into your neighbor's bedroom, you know? My planning people tell me most of the residents, at least in the beginning, won't have children, so no strain on the local schools. Golf course on the far side." He waved vaguely to the east, or maybe it was the north — I couldn't tell. "Hey, it's easier to show you. Follow me."

He struck off up the hill, his long legs leaving us behind. Lissa and I exchanged a look and followed.

Thirty minutes later we had covered what felt like the entire thousand acres, although that might have been a small exaggeration. We'd made a big loop around the perimeter, with Wakeman making grand sweeping gestures all the way. I had to admit the man had a vision for the place, and he seemed committed to doing it right, making the new buildings fit into the landscape. His enthusiasm was obvious, and I admired that; he'd been doing this a long time, and it was heartening to see someone who still enjoyed his work after so many years.

"Let's finish up down by the road — I want you to see how it will look to anyone passing by." He pointed down the hill toward the Paoli Pike, the way we had come in.

It was well after five o'clock, and still hot. I was sticky and sweaty, and my feet hurt. I wanted to go home and take a nice, cool shower. But I also wanted to remain in Mitchell Wakeman's good graces, for the benefit of the Society — besides, he was my ride home, and maybe he could drop Lissa at a train station along the way. I dredged up a smile and said, "Sounds great." Lissa shot me a dirty look, but heck, she was younger than I was, so she couldn't complain.

We dutifully trooped down to the bottom of the hill and looked back up at the skyline. If I squinted, I thought I could see a hint of Wakeman's vision for the place.

He was still talking, energy undiminished. "And like I said, we'll keep a lot of this part as a buffer, maybe halfway up to the ridge there. Keep that nice little pond over there." He pointed. "Scenic. Reeds. Geese sometimes. Besides, it's too wet to build on, so might as well keep it." He stopped suddenly. "What the hell? Nobody's supposed to be dumping there." He took off abruptly toward the pond, loping downhill on his long legs. But when he reached it he stopped and stood staring down at the water. He seemed frozen.

I picked my way through the marshy grass, stumbling a bit in my too-big boots, until I came up beside him and looked down to see what had seized his attention.

I should have guessed that things had gone a bit too well today and I would have to pay the cosmic bill.

Before us bobbed the body of a dead man, facedown in the pond.

For once, it seemed, the industrial titan Mitchell Wakeman was at a loss. "What the . . . ? Who is it?"

"How on earth should I know?" I snapped.

Lissa had finally made her way down to stand beside us. She looked at the pond, and said, "Oh." Then she turned quickly, walked to the edge of the road, and threw up.

I'd been through this before. I pulled out my cell phone and hit 9-1-1.

The good news is, out in the suburbs, where there are lots of small towns, the police station is never far away. The bad news is, because these are small, peaceful towns, there are seldom police officers on staff who have much experience investigating deaths. In five minutes, a squad car arrived and two youngish uniformed cops climbed out. I'll give them credit for doing things correctly, all by the book: they approached us and looked down at the body and nodded sagely; they asked us who we were and what we were doing there; and then they escorted us back to Wakeman's car and told us to sit there and stay put. Then they walked away so that they were out of earshot, conferred briefly, and made another call.

Five minutes after that, another car arrived, and two more officers climbed out. One was older and clearly had more authority. He spoke briefly with the first officers, then came up to Wakeman, who was leaning against the car with a thousand-mile stare on his face, and introduced himself. His deference suggested that he recognized Wakeman's name if not his face. Then he turned to Lissa and me, and we explained again how we had come to be in an idyllic cow pasture on a fine summer's day, staring at a corpse. Who nobody had yet identified. The cops had wisely left the body right where it was, presumably to avoid mucking up any potential evidence.

"What happens now?" I asked. I had a passing familiarity with Philadelphia procedures, but I wasn't about to assume they were the same here.

"We wait for the coroner," the officer said

promptly. "That's who decides if it's an unnatural death and figures out who it is. He'll be here any minute — the county office is right down the road."

For a brief moment I nursed the hope that whoever it was had fallen into the pond (which looked about a foot deep) and drowned. Or chosen a rather unlikely method of suicide, in plain sight of a well-traveled road. I couldn't convince myself that either was likely.

"Will you be handling the investigation?" I asked, more to make conversation than because I cared. I knew I had nothing to do with this death. I couldn't swear to Wakeman's innocence, but why would he have brought me all the way out here to witness his discovery of the body?

"Depends on what the coroner has to say, and who it is." The senior officer looked over at Wakeman, standing a dozen feet away sucking on a cigarette, and asked, "That's *the* Mitchell Wakeman, right?"

"Sure is," I said.

"What's he doing here?"

"You'll have to ask him." I didn't know what details of the project had gone public, and I wasn't going to talk out of turn.

The coroner arrived. The senior officer conferred with him, and then the pair of them went back to the pond, and the coroner took pictures of the body, the pond, the field, a pretty flower . . . well, probably not that last one, but it seemed that way. I was getting punchy. After the coroner had taken the appropriate photos, he enlisted the assistance of a junior officer and together they extricated the body from the pond, which, as I had guessed, turned out to be shallow but muddy. They laid the body on the grass at the edge of the pond and stared down at it. The coroner shook his head and said something, then knelt and fished a wallet out of the dead man's hip pocket and flipped it open to look at the driver's license. He looked up at the senior officer and nodded, then stood up again.

This was beginning to feel like watching a television show with the sound turned off. Whatever conversation there was was drowned out intermittently by the sound of passing cars, some of which slowed to see what all the activity was about, only to be shooed on by one of the younger officers. I watched the senior officer walk over to Wakeman and exchange a few words, then the two of them went over to where the body lay, and looked down. Wakeman shook his head; apparently he didn't recognize the man.

Then Wakeman came back to where Lissa and I were still standing. "Sorry to have dragged you into all this," he said.

"Don't be. You didn't have anything to do with it. Did they tell you who the guy was?"

"Local, according to the cop — he's the zoning officer for the township. Which I guess makes it likely that he's tied into the project, because that seems like the only reason he'd be here. Like I said, sorry."

"I'm sorry, too. It's clear this project means a lot to you, and this isn't going to make it any easier. Can we go?"

"Not yet. I think the local cops have decided they're in over their heads, since I'm kind of a public figure, and they've called in some bigger guns, and I talked to some people, too. They should be here shortly, and they may want to talk with us. So we sit tight for now."

I nodded, then turned to Lissa. "You okay?"

She shrugged. "I guess. I've never seen a dead body before, not outside of a hospital. It wasn't quite what I expected."

"I know what you mean." All too well.

We sat for a while, saying nothing. It seemed to incongruous, to be sitting in the midst of the bucolic splendor of a Chester County summer while a body lay on the grass below, discreetly covered with a piece of plastic. We talked sporadically about insignificant things. At some point, Lissa said, "You know, you wouldn't know it to look at it now, but a lot of history took place around here. As I said earlier, that road down there has been a major road since the late seventeen hundreds. Washington and his hapless troops were all over the place around here, and we're not all that far from Valley Forge." She stopped for a moment, then looked past me and nodded toward an approaching car. "Looks like the cavalry has arrived."

A plain car pulled up behind the police cars and parked. The door opened — and James stepped out.

I didn't know whether to laugh or cry.

CHAPTER 7

We regarded each other across twenty feet of driveway. I felt I had the advantage: I figured the local cops had indeed recognized this death was beyond their scope and had asked the FBI to step in — which they had every right to do — so seeing an FBI agent here was not altogether surprising. What the odds were that James would pick up that case, and that he'd find me here in the middle of yet another murder investigation, I couldn't begin to guess. For a brief, wistful moment, I wondered if this was where I was supposed to sob gracefully and fling myself into his manly arms and let him comfort me, but I stifled it. We were both here as professionals and should act accordingly.

He made the first move. Wakeman and the senior cop were deep in conversation a few yards down the hill, so James approached me first.

"I don't believe it," he said in a low voice. "What are you doing here?"

"Getting a grand tour of the proposed development site from the developer himself." I nodded down the hill at Wakeman. "What are you doing here?"

"The local police put in a call for help, but I'm pretty sure it was your developer pal who asked. Whoever caught the call thought a nice suburban death would be a soft entry back into the game for me, so I got sent. It never occurred to me that you'd be involved." He leaned back, because Lissa had come up behind us.

I made the introduction. "Lissa, this is Special Agent James Morrison, from the FBI. He's been called in to help out the local police with the investigation. James, this is the person Marty recommended to handle Wakeman's research into this site. Although she may not be interested after today." Dealing with dead bodies — recent ones, at least — had not been part of the job description.

"Good to meet you, Agent Morrison. I take it you know Nell?" Lissa asked, her composure returned.

"Uh, yes, we're . . . we've . . ." James fumbled for an answer.

I rescued him by saying, "I'll fill you in later, Lissa. James, don't you need to check in with the local authorities?"

"I do. I assume they told you to stick around?"

"Yes, since we discovered the body. And Wakeman was our ride, anyway."

"We'll sort it out." James turned away and started down the hill to where the main players were gathered, waiting.

"I can't wait to hear the story," Lissa said drily as she watched him go.

I was torn between admiration for her observational skills and an urge to swat her, and say, "Hands off, he's mine." Very mature of me. I settled for "We might as well sit down to wait — this may take a while."

We sat in Wakeman's car, leaving the doors open, our feet pointing downhill, and watched the machinery of a police investigation grind along. "You said something about being involved in murder investigations? Do you know what happens now?" Lissa asked, indicating the police.

"Well, I've only seen things from the civilian side, but I'll tell you what I know. The coroner's here and he's identified the body and apparently declared the death a crime, since they called for reinforcements. That means there will be an autopsy to determine the exact cause of death and when it happened. Then they'll start interviewing people. Apparently, the victim is a local guy, so they'll start with his wife, if he had one, his colleagues and friends around here, and then anyone who might have wanted him dead."

"Sounds logical enough. Why did they call in the FBI?"

"Manpower, for one — most police departments don't have a lot of staff these days. Access to information, for another — the FBI can look at phone records, financial information, all that stuff, a lot more quickly. They've got better forensic facilities, too. And I'd guess that the fact that Mitchell Wakeman is involved means there'll be more public attention to this, even if he had nothing to do with it, so I'm going to guess the locals are covering their butts."

"You think the project will go forward?"

It seemed a little early to ask, but Lissa was probably worried about this job opportunity drying up. "I'd guess yes. Unless someone can prove that Wakeman committed the crime himself or had direct knowledge of it, both of which seem unlikely. He's probably looked into most of the history carefully already. He just wants our official seal of approval — not that I'm suggesting you sugarcoat whatever you find. He seems very heavily invested in this project, and I don't mean just financially."

"I agree — he seemed really enthusiastic when he was showing it off. I like his vision for this place," Lissa said.

I watched Mitchell Wakeman talking to the group of police and James; he was remarkably patient. "I'd like to think he's honest and he really does care, but I can't say that I know him well. Look, if you'd like to back out now, I'd understand."

Lissa smiled, more to herself than to me. "No, I'm good with it. It's a shame about that poor man, but after all, it isn't the first time people have died here, and we had nothing to do with his death."

We fell silent again. The shadows were lengthening and swallows were swooping above the meadow, snagging slow-flying insects. I watched James at work. He seemed to have things well in hand. He was talking to the officers, but he appeared neither too deferential nor too assertive. He knew he was on their turf and he didn't want to create any more friction than necessary, but somehow he managed to make it clear that he was in charge without ruffling any feathers. It didn't seem like his reentry into work was proving too taxing, I was glad to see.

I just wished I didn't have quite such an up-close-and-personal view of it.

I watched as the coroner's van loaded up the covered body and sped off toward West Chester, then James and the local police chief conferred with Wakeman. After a lot of nodding, the group split up, with James and Wakeman coming toward us. Lissa and I stood up.

"Ladies," Wakeman said, "I know you probably have questions, but I need some time to think about how this is going to proceed. I didn't expect anything like this. Agent Morrison says he'll see to getting you two home, so I'll leave now. I'll be in touch."

"I understand," I said — and I did. "I hope everything works out for the best."

We stepped away from his car, and Wakeman pulled out. Thirty seconds later I saw his car on the Paoli Pike below, headed toward West Chester.

"What now?" I asked James.

"Have either of you eaten?" he said.

"Uh, it's been a while. I'd ask you both back to my place, but I don't think I have any food."

"I hear the Iron Hill Brewery in West Chester is nice," James said. "We can eat, and then I'll take both of you home."

"Deal," I said.

It took us no more than five minutes to reach the restaurant, and we even found a parking space on the street. Inside, the place was comfortably filled, but we got a table quickly and ordered a locally brewed ale and exotic pizzas all around. When the waitress left to fill our orders, I asked, "How much can you tell us? Or can't we talk about this?"

"You were on the scene before I was, obviously." James looked around carefully, but there were few people in earshot, and they all seemed deep in conversation with their tablemates. "How did Wakeman react when you all found the body?"

"You mean, did he set us up to witness his reaction? I doubt it. As far as I could tell he was honestly surprised — he started out annoyed that somebody was dumping stuff on his site, until he got closer and realized what it was we were looking at. He seemed pretty legitimate to me."

"Did he recognize the victim?"

"I don't think so. I think the coroner told him who it was. Why? Is there some reason he should have known the guy?"

"What was the man's name?" Lissa asked.

"George Bowen, a township employee in charge of land use and zoning, among other things."

Lissa and I exchanged a look. "Do you know if he was involved in Wakeman's project?" I asked.

"On some level, probably, though it seems highly unlikely that the head of a major corporation would be talking directly to a small-town local official — Wakeman's probably got about eight layers of people to do that. On the other hand, we can't dismiss it altogether."

"Are the police handling the local interviews?" I asked.

"They were going to talk to Bowen's wife — some of them know her, and they live close by. They'll talk to his township colleagues in the morning. They're better equipped to handle that than I am, but I may sit in."

"What was the cause of death?" I prompted.

"According to the coroner, a blow to the head, possibly in combination with being strangled, and his best guess before an autopsy was sometime late last night — certainly after dark. And before you ask, we don't yet know if it happened where he was found or somewhere else. We'll be sending a couple of our forensic people over."

"So if this man was hit on the head *and* strangled, he was murdered?" Lissa asked. "How awful." We all grew quiet. I surprised myself by reaching out and taking James's hand; he in turn looked startled, then smiled and clasped it in his. We kind of lost a few moments looking at each other. "I'm glad you're here," I said quietly.

Lissa was watching us with some amusement. "So, Agent Morrison, Marty tells me you're her cousin?" she said, shifting conversational gears. As well she should, for all our sakes.

"Yes, but don't ask me to explain how," James said. We all laughed, then kept the conversation on lighter topics and away from murder.

Our pizzas appeared and we dug in happily. I hadn't realized how hungry I was, but everything tasted good. It was full dark when we finally emerged from the restaurant, and we hadn't worked out who was going where. I had said I wanted some alone time at my house — but that was before we'd stumbled into another murder. But now there was Lissa to consider. So I saw three choices: James took me home and deposited me on my doorstep, then took Lissa back to the city; the three of us crashed at my place, which would definitely be a strain on my hospitality; or we stuck Lissa on a late train and had some personal time together, which seemed kind of unfair to Lissa, who had seen the same body that I had and had every right to be upset. Why did all this have to be so complicated?

In the end, James made the decision. "Let me take you home, Nell, and then I'll take Lissa back with me. Where do you live, Lissa?"

"Near Penn," she said. "But I could take a train."

James brushed off her offer. "That's near me, so it's no bother. Nell, does that work for you?"

What could I do but agree? I'd asked for space, and I was going to get it. "That's fine."

Late in the evening, it took no more than half an hour to reach my house. I got out of the car and was surprised when James did, too. "I'll walk you to your door," he said.

The door was ten feet away. But it was dark. I hadn't been home in ages, so I'd left no lights on. James took my arm and guided me to it, and waited while I found my keys. Then he looked at me and said softly, "You all right?"

I nodded. "Yes. It wasn't . . . awful, and I didn't know the man. Maybe I'm getting jaded, after what we've been through. But thanks for asking."

James leaned in and kissed me, the kiss gentle, warm. Then he broke it off, sooner than I might have liked. "I'll talk to you in the morning."

"Hey, are you all right yourself? First case and all? Maybe, since I'm in the middle of it, you should step back?"

"That doesn't worry me — and it has nothing to do with us, right? You're just a bystander this time. Good night, Nell." He turned and went back to his car, and like a school-girl I watched as he drove off until I could no longer see him.

Then I let myself in to my dark, empty house. It was very quiet, and once I turned on the lights I could see it was also rather dusty. When had I last spent any time there? Weeks, at least. I stalked to the tiny kitchen and opened the refrigerator: pathetic. I filled a glass with peach iced tea and wandered around while I drank it.

I could have gone with James and Lissa, back to the city, back to James's apartment. Why hadn't I? Did I value my independence more than my relationship with a great guy? Where would that leave me in forty years? Sure, there were no guarantees in life, and an FBI agent was always in danger, more or less — as I knew only too well. But being scared of possible negative outcomes in the distant future was a stupid reason to avoid living life in the now.

Well, I'd said yes to finding a place together, hadn't I? Okay, maybe it was a qualified, halfhearted sort of yes, but it was still a yes. He understood — I thought. Now all we had to do was find a place that made us both happy — and I had no idea what that would be.

I took that much-needed shower and went to bed. Alone.

CHAPTER 8

The next morning I woke surprisingly early, given the events of the prior day, and lay in bed reviewing what was going on. I should have checked with Latoya to confirm whether Ben Hartley, our new registrar, would be starting today. I had no way of gauging whether his military computer skills would translate to cataloging antique items and documents, but data was data, wasn't it? And James had recommended him — shoot, yesterday we'd been too distracted to talk about Ben. I reminded myself to find out a bit more about Ben's backstory and how he and James had kept in touch.

I couldn't do much about Lissa's position until I knew if there would actually be a need for it now, and under the circumstances I wasn't about to badger Mitchell Wakeman about that. But I meant what I had said to Lissa the day before: this planned development was a big project, and unless all evidence pointed directly to Wakeman or a member of his project crew, it probably wouldn't derail the project. Of course, that assumed the murder was solved and the killer identified sooner rather than later. Lissa had seemed surprisingly calm throughout the whole experience — after she'd thrown up. And she was observant. Of course, being able to read people wasn't quite the same as being able to read documents, but her apparent competence was reassuring.

Okay, moving on. James had said he was going to start the process of finding a new place for us to live — of course, that had been before he'd been assigned to the Wakeman case. Did I want to get involved in house or apartment hunting? Well, maybe first we should pin down what we were looking for. I liked living in the suburbs: I liked the privacy of a freestanding house; I liked the open space; I liked being someplace that was away from work. I liked having choices for commuting. James lived in the city, in an apartment. Would he want to stay in the city? Style-wise, my little carriage house was late Victorian, and while I hadn't gone overboard with decorating it in a true Victorian spirit, I liked that it was older and had a history of its own. James's apartment was definitely modern, stark, rectilinear. Where would we find a middle ground?

Enough. I jumped out of bed and started my day.

I arrived at the Society early, at least compared to recent days, but Eric had beaten me to the office anyway. "Mornin', Nell. Coffee?"

Eric and I had long since worked out a coffee agreement: whoever arrived first made the first pot. "Sure. Did I miss anything yesterday afternoon?"

"While you were out finding bodies?"

"Shoot, did it make the papers already? How did they find out so fast? It was only the one body."

"Since Mr. Wakeman was involved, it did — you know he's news. Speaking of whom, he's already called this morning."

"Did he want me to call him back?"

"No, he left a message, and I quote: 'Project is a go. Lissa can start ASAP.' Make sense to you?"

"It does. That's good news, I think. A man of few words, isn't he? But decisive. So we will have a new, short-term intern. Can you figure out what paperwork we'll need? Funding will come from Wakeman or some subsidiary of his, and it's a term appointment — three months."

"Will do. Right after I get you that coffee. Oh, and Latoya said that other new hire would be starting day after tomorrow."

Bless Eric. I'd hired him because Shelby knew him, and he was a nice kid and needed a job, but he had far surpassed my expectations. By now I couldn't imagine running my office without him.

Coffee in hand, I settled myself in my office and contemplated where to begin. I should call Lissa, but I wasn't sure if I had her phone number. Should I call Ethan at Penn to get it? I didn't have his phone number, either, although that should be public information. Marty would know it, though . . .

As if by magic, Marty materialized at my door. "Someday I'll figure out how you do that, Marty," I said. "I was just thinking about you."

Marty dropped into a chair. "Good things, I hope. How'd Lissa work out?"

"What, you haven't heard?"

"Heard what?"

"We went out to see the site yesterday and found a body. Eric said it was in the paper."

"You've got to be kidding! No, I haven't had a chance to look at the paper this morning. This was a body on Wakeman's patch?"

I nodded. "It was. The three of us were

walking the grounds and we found him in a pond."

"Anybody know who he is?"

"Apparently an official with the township there. You don't have any friends or family in Goshen, do you?"

"Maybe. Old neighborhood, there — mostly Quaker, way back when. What was the guy's name?"

"George Bowen, I think. James will know."

"Why?"

"Because the local police called in the Mounties, and he got the case."

Marty laughed heartily. "You're kidding! I would've loved to see that little meeting! They really think they need the FBI out there?"

"I think that was Wakeman's involvement. You know he wants only the best."

Marty gave one of her ladylike snorts. "What's your take on Wakeman, now that you've spent some time with him?"

"Overall I'm impressed. He seemed like a straight-arrow guy, I guess. Not at all pretentious. He was really excited about this development project of his, and happy to show it off. At least, until we found the body."

"Did Wakeman know the dead guy?"

"He said not."

Marty shot me a look, and I wondered if I had sounded more skeptical than I intended. But she didn't pursue it. "So, you took Lissa along on this little jaunt?"

"Yes. I thought it made sense — she could get a feeling for the physical lay of the land. And I wanted to see how she got along with Wakeman, although they probably won't run into each other again."

"What did you think of her?"

Something in Marty's tone made me look more carefully at her. "She's smart, and she's very calm — didn't panic about the body, and she asked intelligent questions. She was older than I expected, but she explained that she'd taken some personal time off before going back to school. Wakeman okayed her. How did you come to recommend her?"

"I met her at Ethan's office, and he said good things about her. And she needs the money."

Marty sounded a bit abrupt, even for her. In the time I'd known her, Marty hadn't been involved with anyone, or at least not seriously. And she'd kind of hidden her involvement with Ethan, although since I'd been a little preoccupied, I could have missed the signs. Was she worried that Ethan had some interest in Lissa? I felt I was treading on shaky ground with my next question — although Marty had never hesitated to involve herself in my private life, I rationalized. "Do Ethan and Lissa have a history?"

Marty shrugged. "Maybe. I haven't asked."

"Okay," I said cautiously. "But you have no problem if the Society hires her for this project for a couple of months?"

"Nope. If Ethan vouches for her, she'll do a good job." Marty's tone made it clear that she wasn't going to comment further.

"Fine. Do you know where I can reach her? I want to tell her the project is moving forward."

"Sure." Marty pulled a scrap of paper out of her pocket and scribbled a number on it, then handed it to me. "That's Ethan's office — his assistant should know where to find Lissa."

"Thanks. Was there something else?"

"When's your registrar showing up?"

"Day after tomorrow. I left it to Latoya to deal with the formalities, since he'll be working for her." I did a double take. "Wait, how did you know we'd made an offer?"

"James told me that he was thinking of recommending Ben and asked if I thought Ben could handle the job."

"Hang on. You know Ben, too? Why was there any question about whether he could handle the job?"

"I don't know him personally. James wanted to know what the job requirements were. Ben's had a rough time since the accident, and he hasn't worked lately, which looks bad on his résumé. But he's smart and hardworking, and he'll want to prove himself."

"Will he fit in here?"

Marty smiled. "With this crew of misfits? I wouldn't worry. Just don't expect him to be real sociable."

I sighed. But at least the registrar position didn't require a whole lot of social interaction, just computer skills and a good eye. And as for those, anyone I hired would have to demonstrate them directly, whatever his or her baggage and background. "Ask Latoya about his start date. And don't co-opt him to do all the Terwilliger stuff first."

"Would I do that?" Marty said, batting her eyes with exaggerated innocence. She stood up. "I'm going back to the processing room, by way of Latoya's office. See you later."

She had no sooner walked out the door when Shelby appeared. Good thing I hadn't planned to get anything like work done this morning. "Hi, Shelby — what's up?"

Shelby took the chair that Marty had vacated. "You've got a new corpse, I hear."

"Did my name come up in the paper?" I asked, almost afraid to find out.

"Nope, but Mr. Wakeman's did, and I knew where you were going yesterday afternoon, so I put two and two together. How many does this make?"

"Too many. And to top it off, James caught the case when the FBI was called in to help."

"My, my — just like old home week. What is the great Wakeman like?"

"Surprisingly normal, for a multimillionaire mogul. He seems to like what he does, and he had a great time showing us his plans for the place."

"So this body in the pond won't slow the project down?"

"Apparently not, according to him, because we have the go-ahead to start the historic research on the site. Best case, the murder investigation will be wrapped up quickly and we'll do the research here and give him a gold star and everything will go as planned." That had to happen sometime, didn't it?

"Let's hope so. They're sure it's not an accident?"

"So the coroner says."

"What a shame," Shelby said, then pivoted the conversation away from murder to ordinary Society business.

After she left I tried to remember what I'd originally planned for the day. I heard the phone ring, then Eric call out, "Agent Morrison for you."

I picked up. "Hello. Is this official business?"

"Just wanted to see if you had time for lunch. I can bring sandwiches."

"A working lunch? Sure. Here?"

"One?"

"Okay. Uh, there isn't a problem with anything, is there? Have you solved yesterday's murder?"

I could hear him chuckle. "I may be good, but I'm not that good. I just wanted to touch base with you. See you at one." He hung up, leaving me slightly confused. But that was a state I was used to.

"Eric?" I called out. "I'm having a quick lunch with Agent Morrison at one, here in the building. You have something to keep me busy until then?"

He appeared in my doorway with a sheaf of papers. "Sure do."

CHAPTER 9

At one, I went downstairs to let James in. I was beginning to wonder if I might as well go ahead and give him a key, since he was at the Society so often. He arrived on time carrying a bulky bag. I had to admit he was looking good, considering what he'd been through over the past month. Concussions were sneaky, and sometimes left nasty aftereffects, but he hadn't complained. It was back to business as usual.

But the old, serious James was back, and I realized how much I would miss the warm, funny James now that he was back to work.

We decided to eat in the first-floor conference room, which was usually empty. After we had doled out food, I asked, "Are you okay?"

"Why wouldn't I be?" he responded.

"First day back and a lot of running around yesterday. You got thrown into the deep end pretty fast."

"I'm fine, Nell. Really. I wanted to talk about yesterday, and what we've learned."

"By the way, Wakeman called early this morning and left a message, and said that the project was still on. Is that true?"

James took a large bite of his sandwich. "Close enough. It's not as though the township called a meeting last night and hashed it all out, but I gather the relevant parties put together a conference call and decided that the project was important to the community and, barring any legal issues, it would go forward as planned."

"You think Wakeman leaned on them?"

"I don't know, but I don't know if it would have been necessary in any case. You want the details on the dead man?"

"Please." I picked up my sandwich and started eating, chewing while I listened.

He opened a file but rattled off the key points without looking at it. "George Bowen, age fifty-seven. Engineer by training. Lived in the township and worked for them for about ten years. Wife who works in West Chester. Two kids, both married and living out of state. Volunteered for a lot of civic activities. Interested in local history. All-around nice guy, from what everybody says."

"Do you believe 'everybody'?" I made air

113

quotes as I said the last word.

"No reason not to."

"So nobody had a reason to want him dead."

"Not that we've found, but it's been only a day."

"Have your forensic guys done their bit yet?"

"At first light this morning. Mr. Bowen did not die at the pond but somewhere else yet to be determined."

"How do you know this?"

"There's no evidence of a struggle or an attack in the area around the pond, which would have held impressions since the ground around there is soft and damp. There are, however, some interesting footprints leading up to the pond, but they couldn't follow them through the grass to the point of origin."

"So you're saying someone carried George Bowen to the pond?"

"You do ask all the right questions. Yes, he was carried. He weighed about one eighty, so it would have taken a strong man to carry him without dragging, and there are no signs that he was dragged — that we would have seen."

"Obviously the field isn't exactly well lit. Could a strong man have slung the body over his shoulder and carried him across the field from somewhere else? In the dark?"

"Like a fireman's carry? Maybe."

My questions just kept bubbling up. "Why the pond? I mean, it's kind of close to the road. Anyone driving by would have noticed someone dumping a body there."

"It would have to have been in the middle of the night, when it was darkest, and there was the least traffic. That squares with what the coroner said about time of death. Still, getting him there had to be quick. You're right — nobody could stroll around with a body and expect not to be noticed for long. As for your first question, so far all we know is that the pond is not where he died. You saw for yourself that it's not deep enough to hide a body, so maybe the body was dumped there simply to distract our attention."

"So you've narrowed the search to a strong man. Does that help?"

"Not a lot," James said cheerfully. He must have been used to it. "His wife came home about six but he wasn't there. She wasn't surprised, because the township holds a lot of after-hours meetings, and sometimes they run over into dinner. She ate and watched television for a while. She was mildly worried when he wasn't back by the time she went to bed, but not enough to act on it. I gather it's happened before."

"Did they have problems?"

"Not that she'd admit, but she was obviously upset, and people under those circumstances usually fall back to the 'don't speak ill of the dead' mode. No doubt the police will be talking with her again."

"So he could have been having an affair, and maybe the other woman's spouse or boyfriend or whatever found them together and went ballistic?"

"It's a possibility, but there's no evidence. Yet. But it's early days."

"And that's all you've got?"

James gave me a smile tinged with exasperation. "Nell, this happened yesterday, and we've just started. But, yes, there's nothing obvious jumping out. The guy lived within his means, had a small balance remaining on his mortgage. His kids are happily married and solvent. No unexplained money coming in or going out of his bank account, no overextended credit cards. If he wasn't dead, he'd be a model citizen."

"But he is dead. So what happens now?"

"We continue to investigate. If we don't turn up anything on George, we look at people who might have something at stake in this property, or in the development going forward. People in the township, or in any other townships that might have been competing for the project. People on Wakeman's management team. We'll keep widening the circle and digging deeper."

"Sounds like archeology, doesn't it? That reminds me, what about the research on the history of the site?"

"What about it?"

"Should we — Lissa or the Society — be looking for anything that might provide a motive?"

"Ah, Nell — things aren't always all about the Society, or history, or you."

I was stung, oddly enough. "Hey, I was there, remember? At the same time that this guy coincidentally ended up dead in the pond when Mitchell Wakeman was showing off his dream project to a pair of wonky historical researchers. Are you saying to ignore any historical information that might be relevant? Without even knowing what it is?"

"I'm sorry, I didn't mean to hit a nerve. No, I won't rule out a connection, but I'm not going to make any assumptions about it, either. Is that fair?"

"I guess," I grumbled. This was stupid. I was not a crime investigator; I managed a building full of history investigators. Past and present did not often collide, and when they did, they seldom resulted in corpses. But it was unsettling nonetheless.

"I missed you last night," James said softly.

"Me, too. You got rid of Lissa?"

"Are you jealous that I went home with a younger woman?" He smiled.

"No, not really. If anything" — I leaned in close — "I'm guessing Marty thinks Lissa's got her eye on Ethan. But don't you dare tell her I said that."

James raised one hand, and said solemnly, "I am an agent of the federal government. I know how to keep secrets."

"This is Marty we're talking about."

"There is that. But you don't have to worry, Nell. We're good, you and I."

"We are." At least, I hoped so. Oh, how I hoped so.

"But you've got to remember, Nell, that what I've told you today has to remain between us. I shared it with you only because you're already involved, so you have a right to know at least some of the details."

"What if Lissa asks questions? She was there, too."

"Just tell her you don't know anything beyond what's in the papers and that it's an ongoing investigation, which is true."

"Speaking of which, how did the papers

get onto it so fast?"

"I can't say for sure," James said, "but it's possible that Wakeman and his people put the story out there to make sure they look transparent."

That was an angle I hadn't considered. "What about Marty?"

James looked pained. "Why would she stick her nose into this?"

"Because she's Marty. Are you going to swear there wasn't a Terwilliger living in West Chester in seventeen-whatever?"

"No. If she asks for details, just point her to me, okay?"

"I'll be happy to." Enough about the crime, since there wasn't much information to go on — yet. "So, what's the story on Ben? Or can't you talk about that without breaking all sorts of confidences?"

He sat back and thought for a moment before answering. "Look, I know there are a lot of things you as an employer can't ask or consider in hiring someone, at least in theory. I know you well enough to know that your main goal is to find someone who can do the job for the Society."

"Why are you dancing around the question? Is there something that I should know that I'm not supposed to ask about?"

He sighed. "Not exactly. Okay, you already

know that I met Ben in college. We weren't exactly best friends, but we hung out together, along with some other guys. After college he joined the army and stayed on for quite a while, as a number cruncher, an analyst, not a combatant. Then he left, and he was trying to figure out where he fit in the private sector, and then the accident happened — by the way, it wasn't his fault. He got T-boned by a drunk and ended up in the hospital for a while and then in rehab. He's understandably bitter about it. I'll tell you in confidence that he's had trouble adjusting to civilian life in a wheelchair — he used to be an active guy. What he needs most right now is to have a job, one that lets him feel useful and productive again. He's smart and he's got the skills, and I think he can do what you need here. But there may be some speed bumps along the way, because this is far from a military organization."

I had to smile at that. "You think? Thank you for telling me, and you know I'll keep it to myself. I might have to share this with Latoya, but I will only if I think it's necessary."

"Don't handle him with kid gloves, Nell," James said. "Let him do the job. Just give him a little time to settle in, okay?"

"Of course." I gathered up my lunch trash and stuffed it back into the original bag. "Was there anything else?"

"Where will you be tonight?"

"Where do you want me to be?"

"With me."

So simple. Shouldn't it be? "Okay. Dinner?"

James smiled. "I brought lunch. You can figure out dinner."

"Deal."

And we went our separate ways, slowed only by a rather steamy kiss before we emerged from the old conference room.

CHAPTER 10

When I got back to my office, I found Lissa there waiting for me, chatting with Eric. "Hi, Lissa," I greeted her cheerfully. "How come you're here? Did you hear?"

"Ethan asked me to check some references for him. Hear what?" she asked.

"Wakeman wants to go ahead with the project — he apparently isn't the type to let a little problem like a dead body stand in the way of progress. Was that why you're here?"

"I'll admit I wanted to know if you'd heard anything. Does that mean I can get started?"

"Come on in and we can talk about where we go from here. Eric, did you manage to figure out what paperwork we need? Mr. Wakeman and his crew may have plenty of money, but that doesn't mean they pay their bills on time, and I'd rather get this on his desk before he gets distracted." *By more than a body,* I added to myself. But busy men were busy men, and I should send paperwork to him before he forgot who we were and what he'd asked us to do — and what he'd promised to do for us.

"On your desk, Nell."

"Thank you. Lissa, come on in."

She followed me into my office and took the chair I pointed to. "I should start by asking, are you okay?" I asked.

"What do you mean?" she replied, looking confused.

I sat down behind my desk. "Well, after finding the body yesterday. Sometimes you think you're fine at the time, but it catches up with you later. I won't hold it against you if you want to back out, after what you saw."

She looked down at her hands briefly, then back at me. "It's not a problem, really. I mean, I know I threw up, but after that I found the whole procedural part kind of interesting. I hope you don't think that makes me weird or something."

I thought I'd reserve judgment on that for now. People cope with traumatic events in different ways, and if Lissa's way was to observe details in order to distance herself, that was fine with me.

"Besides," she went on, "I really do need

the money."

"I understand. Mr. Wakeman seems to approve of you, so I'll get the paperwork in the pipeline as soon as possible. So tell me, how do you plan to approach this? I don't intend to interfere with however you want to do it, but I'm curious. You should know up front that I got into this field via fundraising, so I wasn't trained as a historian or a researcher. I don't always know all the details."

Lissa nodded once. "Okay. As I understand it — before having done any real research — Mr. Wakeman bought a thousand acres of Chester County farmland that has been continuously owned and managed by the same family since the seventeen hundreds. I'm sure he's got a small army of real estate lawyers who have done title searches to make sure the title is clear. I would review all of those, because who knows? Sometimes modern lawyers don't understand the language of seventeenth-century deeds. Just double-checking, plus I can give Wakeman a nice folder of reproductions of all the original documents, even if all he does with them is use them for PR and impressing the homebuyers."

"Do I detect some cynicism?"

She shrugged. "Maybe. But this is the

modern world, and nobody's going to buy that land just to keep the pretty views. I'd rather see Wakeman follow his vision than watch another cookie-cutter development go up."

"I agree, for what it's worth. So, say you've made sure the title is clear — what next?"

"I think I mentioned that it's worth checking for any old factories or trades that occupied any part of the farm. For example, early paint factories left a lot of nasty chemicals in the soil, and remediation is expensive. And there are other polluters. Again, he's probably covered all that, but sometimes nobody recognizes the hazards from a factory that's not even there anymore."

"Okay," I said cautiously. I was way out of my depth here, but it all sounded interesting. "You're familiar with the Duffy's Cut story?"

"The Irish cholera victims? Of course. Really sad. But that should have nothing to do with the Garrett property — the railroad is a couple of miles away."

"But what about other historical events? I guess my question in this context would be: what kind of archeological discovery could delay the project? Say, the equivalent of an ecologist finding that some rare and unique tree frog has made its sole habitat in the middle of the property?"

"My guess is that's Mr. Wakeman's primary concern, or at least why he invited the Society to the party. He can hire plenty of biologists and pollution experts, so my task is to look at the history of the place. As I said, I'd start with the deeds. And then I'd start looking at contemporary accounts in local collections. Here at the Society, of course, but a lot of things still hide out in other institutions. And even if they've been transcribed, there are often things that are missing or misinterpreted, so it's best to see the real documents. I'm sure the people at the Chester County Historical Society will help."

I nodded in approval. "I would think so. I've heard they've got good people there. It all sounds great, Lissa — exactly what Mr. Wakeman needs. Let's hope there are no more unpleasant surprises. Will three months be long enough?"

"I think so, unless I have to travel. But most of the materials should be right here. Thanks for giving me the chance, Nell."

"You're qualified, and better yet, you're here on the spot. And you've already started."

"Thank you." She cleared her throat. "If you don't mind my saying so, I read some of the online reports about other . . . complications you've been involved in."

"And yet you came back?" I said in mock horror. "I'm sorry that my abysmal luck seems to be slopping over to this project."

"Not your fault, is it? How could you have known there would be a body there?"

"Thank you for the vote of support. I really was hoping that this would be a clean-and-simple project, but I should know better by now."

"That's okay. The history will still be there waiting, no matter what happened to that poor man. And no doubt Mr. Wakeman has enough pull to see that it's all cleared up as quickly as possible. All quite legally, I'm sure."

I couldn't argue with that. "You want me to show you around the office, introduce you to the rest of the people you're likely to run into here?"

"Sure, that would be great."

Outside my office, Eric stopped me. "Latoya confirms Mr. Hartley will be starting tomorrow morning. You want to see him then?"

"Sure. I'll see if Latoya has shown him around. He'll have to figure out the software for himself, because I'm clueless about it, but he can ask her. You can go ahead and set up a time, unless I've got something else scheduled that I don't know about."

"Will do, Nell."

I guided Lissa in the direction of the processing room, where the collections and items that needed to be cataloged were kept, awaiting attention. It was a large, open space with shelving around the perimeter and large tables in the center of the floor. Normally it was a comfortable space, but since the FBI had deposited what could be years' worth of items seized under a wide range of circumstances and had asked us to figure out exactly what they had, the space had become a lot more crowded. I pushed open the doors, led Lissa in, and gave her a minute to scope it out.

Interns Rich and Alice were already in the cataloging area. Ben would sort of be their boss, officially responsible for cataloging and entering all collections into our electronic database.

"Rich, Alice, meet Lissa Penrose," I said when I had their attention. "She'll be working on a short-term project looking into the history of the land for Mitchell Wakeman's Chester County development project." It wasn't like the project was exactly secret

128

anymore, since George's Bowen's murder had been splashed all over the news media.

"Hey, Lissa," Rich said, raising a hand in greeting. "Whoa — that the place where they found the body yesterday?"

Just as I'd guessed. "That's it. And before you ask, yes, Lissa and I were there, along with Mr. Wakeman." I moved on quickly. "Rich, if you come across any references to the Garrett farm or Goshen among the Terwilliger stuff, please pass it on to Lissa. Oh, and I don't know if Latoya has told you yet, but we've filled the registrar position. Ben Hartley should be starting here tomorrow — I'll check with Latoya and let you know if that changes. I hope you'll help him out, because I don't think he's worked in a cultural institution before, although he knows computers and information management. But most of his experience is military." I debated about explaining more, like his accident, but decided to let Ben work things out for himself.

"Will I have some place to set up, or do you want me to work in the reading room?" Lissa asked.

I hadn't thought of that. "Normally I'd say you could snag a space in here, but as you can see it's kind of chaotic. Let me think about it. Anyway, this is where the photographic and scanning facilities are. You have a laptop you can use?"

"Of course. I'll figure something out."

"Are you familiar with our stacks? As an official researcher you'll have full access to them. I'll have to see that you get a key — ask Eric about that. You want a quick tour?" I was asking as much for myself as for her — I always welcomed the chance to prowl the stacks and marvel at the wealth of original materials we had at the Society, and I seldom had enough time to indulge myself.

"Sure," Lissa said promptly. "Rich, Alice, good to meet you. I'll probably see you tomorrow."

We spent a happy hour prowling the stacks. I have to admit I used the stacks tour as kind of a litmus test for new hires. If they wrinkled their noses at the scent of mildew and crumbling leather, I didn't think they'd last long here. I might not be a trained historian, but I loved old books and documents because of the window they gave us into the past. That's why I was willing to fight hard to preserve them and make them available to other people, so that they could share my love of them. An uphill battle, but one worth fighting, I thought. Lissa passed my test with flying colors.

By the time I had escorted Lissa to the

front door and seen her off, after getting a key for her and starting her paperwork, it was almost the end of the day. I had promised James I'd be at his place to fix dinner. Somehow I couldn't bring myself to say "home for dinner," because his apartment wasn't home. This was the first day of the new "normal," with both of us working. And if things worked out, that normal would be changing pretty soon — as soon as we found a new place for the two of us. Something we still hadn't talked about in any detail. I found my cell phone in my bag and called him on his, since this wasn't official business.

"Hi," I said when he picked up. "What time will you be . . . back?"

"Sixish, I think — nothing urgent has come up. Why?"

"Just wanted to know what kind of cooking time I have. Maybe I'll stop at the market on the way." The Reading Terminal Market, that is — one of my favorite places in Philadelphia, and one that never failed to cheer me up, not to mention that it gave me great ideas for meals.

"Works for me. See you soon." He hung up. Not exactly warm and fuzzy, but he was in his office.

I left shortly after five, to Eric's surprise.

"Both Ben and Lissa will be here tomorrow?" he asked.

"Looks like it. Fully staffed once again, and then some. See you in the morning, Eric."

I walked slowly over to the market. The streets were hot and steamy, although a breeze from the Delaware River blowing up Market Street helped a bit. I plunged into the market, struggling with myself about buying a Bassett's ice cream cone and resisted — which let me give myself permission to buy something luscious for dessert. I picked out meat and fish and a lot of fresh local vegetables, until I figured I couldn't carry any more home. Then I hopped on a Market-Frankford train, which brought me to James's neighborhood. I beat him home, so I started chopping and sautéing and so forth, aided by a glass of wine.

He walked in at six-fifteen. "Hi, honey, I'm home."

And I melted into his arms. Playing house did have its moments.

CHAPTER 11

"This is great," James said, as he all but inhaled the dinner I had prepared. He must have been fully recuperated: his appetite was back. "You haven't said much."

I poked what was left of my dinner around the plate. "Just thinking. I'm still getting back into the swing of things at work, and it must be even harder for you. Look, there are some things we should talk about."

"That always sounds ominous," James said cheerfully, as he topped off my wine glass. "Such as?"

Brave man, to jump straight into the fray. I decided to start with a less-personal item. "This case you're on, for one thing. This is all kind of weird. Look, if I didn't happen to be standing in the middle of the crime scene when you arrived, would you have been able to share any information with me? Talk about it at all? I'm not sure what the guidelines are."

His expression turned serious. "That's a good question, Nell. Normally agents are discouraged from talking about any open case. I'm not saying that agents don't go home and share with whomever they're with, but we aren't supposed to go blabbing at a bar, for instance, no matter how important it makes us feel to show off. But you're special."

"Thank you, I think. Are you talking from the FBI perspective?"

"Yes, for the moment." He smiled. "You have amply demonstrated that you are both trustworthy and discreet, so if there was an FBI seal of approval, you'd have it. And personally, I value your opinion. Particularly in matters — all right, crimes — that involve the cultural community."

"Which this one does, if one step removed. Look, I was there, and I've already got a public profile for finding myself in the middle of murder investigations, so de facto I am part of the cultural community and thus the cultural community is already involved. I should have stayed at work and sent Lissa to deal with it."

"No, you were doing your job, cultivating someone who could turn out to be a major supporter."

He was right, of course. I took another sip

of wine. "You know, in the heat of the moment I didn't think about it, but how did you end up there so fast? I mean, aren't there procedures to be followed? Local police get first crack, and then they decide whether to ask anyone else for help?"

James looked pained. "You're right, in general, but Wakeman pulled rank. He was on the phone to the higher-ups before the first squad car arrived on the scene."

"That must make for a lot of unhappy campers among the police on the case."

"You've got that right. The FBI will assist any local force that requests help, but nobody likes to have us jammed down their throats. The Chester County detectives were not pleased, so in addition to whatever investigating I'm doing, I have to smooth ruffled feathers and make nice."

"Welcome to my world. So Wakeman knows important people — no surprise there. Had you two ever met before?"

James shook his head. "No, not before yesterday. He's never been directly involved in any crime that I know of."

"Is that an evasive answer? Directly involved? That you know of?"

"I didn't mean it personally — I was just being careful. I have no reason to believe that he has ever been involved in anything that he shouldn't have. Of course, the construction industry isn't exactly as pure as the driven snow."

"Okay, you can stop waffling. What's your personal opinion of the man?"

James sat back in his chair and thought a moment. "Abrupt. Used to getting his own way. Doesn't play games. What about you?"

"I'd agree with what you said. But I'd add something: I spent a couple of hours with him on the site, before we found the body, and I think he really cares about this project. I know he's made a lot of money, but he's built some things that really made a difference, in a good way. And it's not all about ego, either — although I suppose that putting up tall buildings has a certain symbolic element. But I think he wants to do good, as opposed to doing well."

"How far would he go to eliminate anything or anyone who gets in his way?" James asked quietly.

I considered. "I don't know. Maybe I *should* know — after all, what if poor Lissa finds something that the great man doesn't like, and he tries to suppress it? That's my responsibility, in a way."

"So she's going to be working on it?"

"He gave the go-ahead this morning. Has the crime scene been cleared?"

"Yes. Everybody's forensic people have crawled all over it. Not much to show for it, unfortunately."

"Has anybody figured out where the man died yet?"

"Nope. I think there was some talk of bringing dogs in to search the rest of the property. It's a pretty big parcel, and, I might mention, liberally sprinkled with cow pats."

"Oh, you city boys. In case you didn't notice, Wakeman loaned us some muck boots, in case of mud or more likely cow pats — he'd been there before so he would know. So the FBI has dogs?"

"We know people who have dogs. The local force knows more people who have dogs. So we can get into a dogfight about dogs." James stood up. "You want coffee?"

"If you make it. Oh, and you can do the dishes, too, since I cooked."

"Later." He went to the kitchen, or rather, the kitchen corner, all of five feet away, and put the coffee on.

"I assume there's more you want to talk about?" he said, keeping his eyes on the coffeemaker.

"Yes. How are we planning to go about finding a new place?" That large elephant in the room.

"How do *you* want to go about it?" he said cautiously.

This was not going anywhere fast. "I don't know. I haven't been in the market for a long time, and I'm sure things have changed. But don't we need to figure out our parameters?"

James waited until the coffee was done, then filled two cups and brought them to the table and sat down. "Such as?"

"Like how much we can afford. I have no idea how much money you make or how much you're willing to spend. How much does this place cost you?"

He named a number that was larger than my monthly mortgage payment, for a one-bedroom walk-up in a middle-aged building. I *had* been out of the market for a while. "Ouch."

"I can afford more, if you're worried. I've stayed here because it's convenient and there hasn't been any reason to move. Until now. Were you assuming that we'd split the cost of whatever we choose? Or pay proportionately to our respective incomes?"

I realized I hadn't even considered that. "I haven't even thought that far. I'm guessing that I don't make that much less than you do, since you're a government employee and I work for an impoverished nonprofit, and

I'm sure we could adjust if we needed to. If we pooled what we're paying now" — I named an approximate figure — "what would that get us?"

"Where? City or suburbs?"

"I like the suburbs," I said, just a bit defensively. "Is that a problem for you?"

"I . . . don't know. I haven't given it much thought. But be warned: I'm not a mow-the-lawn, paint-the-house kind of guy."

"Noted. Rent or buy?" That was a big issue, since it was kind of symbolic about the level of commitment, and I sort of held my breath waiting to see how he responded.

James regarded me with an expression I couldn't read. "You really don't trust . . . us, do you?"

That hit me in the gut, but he was probably right. I took a deep breath. "I . . . I don't trust anyone easily. Look, I've known you less than a year, and under some pretty strange circumstances. And the last month has been . . . really eye-opening. James, I trust you as much as I've ever trusted anyone. And I'm pretty sure I love you, although I haven't had a lot of practice. But this is a big step for me. No one would say that we're rushing into anything, and we're not young — or stupid, I hope. But I'm still feeling my way here. Look, we can say, let's

139

find something we like, run the numbers, and make the decision based on the best financial outcome? But that's not what we're really talking about here, is it?"

"No." A long pause. "Look, Nell, if you're not ready to deal with this, I'll just renew my lease. No big deal."

I couldn't sit still any longer, so I got up and started pacing in the small space. "No, it is a big deal, because I *want* to make this decision. I just want to get it right."

He stood up and came over to me, and put his hands on my arms. "Nell, there are no guarantees. In some alternate universe, either one of us could have been killed one way or another in the past year. We weren't, and here we are. I know what I want: to live with you. But I don't want to make you miserable. It's your call."

Damn, why did I have to fall for a guy who was not only smart and good-looking, but also empathetic and patient? He made me feel small. "Where do we start?"

"Online Realtors," he said promptly, which led me to guess that he'd been looking already. "You can virtually walk through just about any place these days."

I leaned into him and laid my head on his chest. "You are unbelievable."

He tilted my head up. "No, I'm not —

just practical. Saves time."

"And no doubt you want to show me six places you've already bookmarked?"

"Yup." He grinned.

"The coffee's getting cold."

"Let it. I have a microwave. And an idea . . ."

Which led to the bedroom. I went happily. Whatever our living arrangements, some things worked very well between us. Later, in the dark, I ran my hand lightly along the scar on his arm. It would take some time to fade; the memories of how he'd gotten it would take longer. I'd come so close to losing him, before I even knew what we had. "So, city or suburbs?" I murmured into his chest.

"Both? There are some pretty nice places on the periphery of the city. Old place or new?"

"That should be obvious: old. I work with history, remember? And I like old buildings."

"Fine. Nineteenth-century houses have a nice sense of scale — high ceilings, big rooms."

"No closets, though. You don't want a yard, so we don't need much land to go with it."

"Nope. Garage?"

"Shoot, we'll have two cars. We need a big garage with a small house? That could get complicated. Oh, and don't forget — near a train line. I do some of my best work on trains." I rolled over to face him. "Do you want me to look online? But not at work, I guess — bad example for the rest of the staff, and I've taken enough time off lately as it is."

"Maybe tomorrow, after work, we can look together. That way we'll both get a feel for what we like."

"Okay. Oh, Ben's starting tomorrow. Things are moving fast. I told the guys in the processing room to expect him, but I didn't say anything about . . . the wheel-chair. Obviously they'll figure that out quickly."

"Yes. But as I told you, nobody has to coddle him. He doesn't want pity."

"I can understand that — I wouldn't, either. He should be judged on the quality of his work, period."

"Amen. Did you say something about dessert?"

"Ah, you know me too well. Yes, there's dessert, and I don't mean me."

Back in the kitchen, eating chocolate cake with an inch of mocha buttercream, washed down with lukewarm coffee, I said, "I don't know if we ever settled what we started out talking about. Your case, I mean. I'm not officially involved beyond being a peripheral witness. Of course I'm interested, but I don't feel I have the right to ask for day-by-day updates. And I don't want you to feel you have to report everything to me. So how do we work this out?"

"I'll tell you what I can. And you and Lissa should tell me whatever you find out, if you think it's relevant."

"Before we tell Wakeman?"

"How about at the same time? Unless you find a bloody weapon with the initials *MW* etched on it — then you should call me first. But he doesn't have to know you're reporting to me."

"It's not like we're going to come up with a lot of confidential information about a block of land."

"You never know. And, objectively, if you were to find something that threatened the project in any way and word got out, it could have a serious financial impact on Wakeman et al., and you and the Society could be liable. So be careful. And remind Lissa, too."

"Got it. You finished with that?" I pointed toward his dessert plate, which looked polished. "And you're still doing the dishes."

CHAPTER 12

James and I carpooled to work the next morning. Would we do that when we lived together? Our schedules were so unpredictable and erratic that it probably wouldn't work, except on rare occasions like today. Did FBI agents ever go anywhere by train? That didn't really mesh with my mental image of them emerging from unmarked dark sedans with unusually powerful engines.

When I arrived at work, Latoya was waiting for me, as was a cup of coffee, thanks to Eric. I smiled at him as I led Latoya into my office.

"What's up?" I asked.

"As you know, Ben Hartley is starting this morning. I wondered if you'd like to show him around, introduce him to people."

I took a few seconds to think about that. Did Latoya just want Ben to get off to a good start, with my apparent blessing? Or did she want to make it clear to the rest of our staff that Ben was my hire, not hers? "Why don't we just take him around together?"

"All right. I'll bring him up when he arrives."

I sat at my desk and sorted through papers and messages until I'd finished my coffee. Latoya arrived with Ben, who looked marginally less — what, hostile? Wary? — than he had the last time I'd seen him. He said quickly, "Thank you for this opportunity, Nell."

"Ben, we need someone with your skills, period. I'm glad you could join us. We're going to throw you straight into it, but first I'd like you to meet your colleagues. This way."

I led the way around the office, introducing Ben to our staff — Shelby in development; Felicity, our head librarian; even Front Desk Bob — then took him to the processing room, where Rich and Alice were already at work. I was surprised to see Lissa there, too, talking with Rich, who was explaining some document he had laid out on one of the work surfaces. "Hey, guys," I said, and waited until I had their attention. "I'd like you to meet our new registrar, Ben Hartley. He's starting today. I know you're all busy, but I'd appreciate it if you could show him how we do things here. Latoya, have you set him up with computer access?"

"Of course," Latoya said formally. "He'll be using that desk when he's working with physical objects in here, right?" She nodded toward the one in the corner that our former registrar had staked out, and I felt a pang — I had no idea if it would work with a wheelchair.

"If you need a different configuration, Ben, let us know," I said. I made the introductions. Lissa spoke up. "I'm short-term, Ben, but pleased to meet you. Uh, Nell, is it all right to talk about, you know . . . ? I haven't said much yet."

"It's already been in the news, and I mentioned it to Rich and Alice yesterday." I turned back to the others. "Lissa is working with Mitchell Wakeman on the historical background of a piece of land in Chester County, where he's planning a new development. She'll be here full-time for three months or so, unless she's out in Chester County. I know, this place just keeps getting more crowded all the time. Ben, you have any questions?"

"I need to familiarize myself with the computer and software setup. Latoya, you'll walk me through the computer procedures?" Ben asked.

"I will — as far as I understand them. I'm no computer expert myself, but I hope what you'll find in your space is current and clear."

"Great, thanks."

"Well, then, back to business. Ben, you want to have lunch today, sort of a welcome? Latoya, can you join us?"

Latoya shook her head. "I have a prior commitment, but I'll be spending time with Ben this morning. You two go ahead."

We all scattered to our respective workstations. Eric handed me a stack of papers and together we sorted through them, assigning priorities or handing them off to other staff members to deal with. It was a productive morning that passed quickly, and I was surprised when Ben appeared at my door. "We still on for lunch?"

I checked my watch: noon. "Sure. Any place around here you'd like to go?" I wondered if that was tactless. How many of my favorite restaurants would be hard for a guy in a wheelchair to access?

"I don't know the neighborhood. You can choose."

"There's a nice lunch place the next block down — nothing fancy, but good sandwiches."

"Sounds fine."

We made our way out the side entrance and to the restaurant, one where I ate (or got takeout) regularly. I'd remembered it as a place with widely spaced tables that I hoped would be easy to fit a wheelchair, and I was relieved to discover that I was right. I was going to have to rethink a lot of small things like this, if Ben stayed on. If? Well, the last registrar hadn't lasted long, and Ben faced special challenges working in our old building. Plus, who knew how well the job would suit him?

Once we were settled and had ordered the day's specials, Ben spoke quickly. "Look, if this doesn't work out, no hard feelings. I know you're taking a chance on me."

I admired his directness, even as I fumbled for an answer. "Heck, you're taking a chance on us, too. I don't know how much James has told you, but we've had some rather peculiar events happen recently."

Ben's mouth twisted in a reluctant smile. "So I've heard. But I don't know how much Morrison has told you about me, either. Look, here's the deal: I'm good with computers. I'm less good with people. That was true before this." He nodded toward his lap. "I have limited background in history, but I'm told I have a good eye and I can string together an accurate description. I'm assuming that describing something as 'old pink vase' is not going to cut it with you guys, but I can learn." Ben took a large bite of his sandwich and chewed and swallowed before continuing. "I like some aspects of history. I kind of got into military history when I was in the army — it's interesting to analyze where battles went wrong and, in hindsight, how the commanders could have done things better. The analysis that goes into that is probably transferrable to dealing with your artifacts."

"What do you mean?"

"Well, you've got a building full of things. My job, as I understand it, is to define that stuff so that you and researchers can put it together in a meaningful and coherent way. I mean, take that pink vase I mentioned earlier. It's a lot more useful if I can describe it as 'nineteenth-century Chinese export blue willow,' isn't it?"

"Bingo. And don't be afraid to ask for help — Rich in particular knows his stuff," I said.

"Look, if I can lay my cards on the table — I don't want to be a pity hire. If I'm doing something wrong, I want to hear it. I won't fall apart or blow up at anyone. Morrison probably told you I have some issues with anger, about what happened, but I don't want people walking on eggshells around me."

"I would have anger issues, too, in your place. You got a lousy deal."

"But that's my problem to deal with, not yours. Let me do the job — that's all I want. If I can't hack it, you can get rid of me. But I appreciate the chance."

The waitress arrived with our sandwiches, which provided a welcome break from our rather heavy conversation. When she had retreated, I said, "Look, is this off the record? Because if whatever government agency is responsible for employer-employee relations hears us, I don't want to have problems."

"You mean, am I going to turn you in for being legally or politically incorrect? Don't worry."

"Good. If I ask you personal questions, it's not that I'm prying, but if we're going to work together, I'd appreciate a few details. Look, the Society isn't a big place, so we all kind of know each other. Some people have been working there for years — far longer than I have. I got bumped into the president position through a strange series of events, and I'm still kind of feeling my way. Nobody makes a lot of money. Most people stay because they love history — their reward is getting to handle the real documents of our past. Carefully, of course. It's not just a nine-to-five job for most of them. Do you know what I'm saying?"

"Yeah, I get that."

"So, tell me something about yourself. Like, where are you living?"

"A few blocks from here. Ground-floor apartment."

"I thought you said you didn't know the neighborhood."

"I'm still learning how to get around in this thing." Ben slapped the arm of his wheelchair. "So I haven't done a lot of exploring."

"Do you drive?"

"Not yet. I'm told I could get a special vehicle, but I don't go far — I chose this neighborhood because it had everything I needed close by. I figured when I found a job, I could get there easily enough as long as it was in Center City."

"You live alone?" I wondered if I was pushing too far.

Ben didn't seem to mind. In fact, he grinned for the first time. "You asking if I'm a weirdo creep or if I'm available?"

"The former, I guess. As for the latter, I'm off the market."

"Yeah, I got that impression from Morrison. You know, this isn't exactly the conversation I expected to have with my new boss on my first day."

"Maybe not, but you know what? I think you'll fit in just fine."

We chatted amiably through the rest of lunch, then made our way back toward the Society. I set a slow pace because it was hot, not to accommodate Ben, who actually moved rather quickly. I followed him around to our handicap-access lift at the side of the building and rode up with him, then parted ways in front of my office, as he headed for his new work space.

I turned to find Eric frantically signaling to me. He threw a wary glance toward my office, then came around his desk, grabbed my arm, and dragged me down the hall the way I'd come.

"Eric, what's wrong?" I said quietly. I'd never seen him this upset.

"Mr. Wakeman is in your office," he whispered.

"Did we have an appointment? Did I miss something?" I asked.

Eric shook his head vehemently. "No. He just showed up and he said he had to talk to you, and I guess nobody knew how to stop him. So I parked him in your office. He's been there about fifteen minutes. I'm sorry."

"Don't worry about it, Eric," I reassured him. Stronger men than Eric had been cowed by Mitchell Wakeman, I suspected. "I've spent enough time around him already to know that he can kind of steamroll people to get his own way. I guess I'd better go see what he wants." I strode back down the hall and entered my office like I belonged there — which I did. He didn't, not right now. "Mr. Wakeman, what can I do for you today?"

Before he had a chance to answer, I noticed that Eric had left a message from James on my desk. No, two messages. And then the phone rang, and two seconds later Eric stuck his head in, looking scared. "It's Agent Morrison — he says it's important."

Wakeman was glaring at me, but damn it, this was *my* office. "Excuse me," I said, "but I have to take this." I picked up the phone and turned my back on my fuming guest. "What's going on?"

James said abruptly, "The dogs found more bodies. Two."

I had not expected to hear that. "Wow. Uh, who knows about this?"

"Just the cops and the coroner. We've called in the FBI forensic team — there's something odd about these."

"What do you mean?"

"I'll explain later, when I'll probably know more. Oh, and by the way, it looks like Bowen was killed where the bodies were found."

I didn't have time to digest that information, not with Wakeman sitting across from me. "I see. You sure no one else has been informed? Because I have a guest in my office . . ."

James sighed in pure exasperation. "Wakeman?"

"Exactly."

"Does he know?"

"I can't say, but I'll find out."

"You do that. Call me after." He hung up.

I turned slowly to Mr. Wakeman, whose expression was a truly strange mix of sheepishness and belligerence.

"Why did you want to see me?" I asked him.

"Same reason that FBI guy just called you — those bodies. We need to talk."

I sat down slowly behind my desk and gestured toward the chair in front of it. "So talk."

Chapter 13

Much as I yearned to fill the silence with polite chatter, I clamped down hard on my tongue and waited for Mitchell Wakeman to explain. I had a sneaking suspicion that not many people successfully stared Wakeman down, but he had come to me, not the other way around. In the end he kind of wilted a bit, and said, "They found more bodies on the site this morning. The dogs were out early, before it got too hot."

I nodded but kept my mouth shut. I'd just heard the same news from James, but I had no idea how Wakeman could know so fast — or why he was coming to me with this information. So far, I didn't see why he was here. I waited.

Finally, he stopped waiting for a reaction from me. He added, "They're old."

Aha. I was beginning to see a glimmering of light.

He went on, "The thing is, nobody will

say how long the bodies have been there. The science guys are gonna take a look at them. But best guess is a couple of hundred years."

Now he definitely had my attention. Centuries old? Really? That could put them in the Revolutionary War. Wow.

And had Mitchell Wakeman known or suspected they might be there? Was that why he had come to me and the Society?

"How did they happen to find them now, after all this time?" I said carefully.

"The dogs did. Looks like that Bowen guy had been poking around the place where they were buried. That's why the dogs found 'em. They were following Bowen's scent. Right to where they were buried."

This was one of the oddest conversations I'd ever had. "Excuse me, but why are you telling me this?"

He sighed. "If these bodies are as old as they say, they're *historic* old. I want you on top of this."

I suppressed a fleeting image of me lying on top of a few corpses — trying to protect them or to cover them up? "What do you mean?"

He leaned back in his chair and rubbed his face, then faced me again. "I told you, I came to you because I didn't want another

Duffy's Cut mess. People in Malvern, even the college researchers, got pissed off because the railroad wouldn't let them take the time to excavate those graves properly. You've gotta know, there could be bodies and historic sites all over the place around here, including the land I now own. All I wanted was to be ready to handle it if and when something was found, just like this."

We studied each other silently for a few moments. Then he resumed: "Finding two old bodies can cut either way. They're a piece of history — and of course my people would treat that part of the site with respect, not just slap a café on top of it. But I think we'd all be better off if we knew who those dead guys were and why they were there, and fast. And make sure we're not going to be stumbling over more. That's where you come in. I could tell you what I think the story is, or you can wait for that FBI agent guy to give you the official story. Either way, I'm betting the history angle just got a lot more important. I want you on it."

"We've hired Lissa to do the research . . ."

"Fine, keep her and let her do the book work. But I want your face out there when we talk about it for the press and the public. You're the chief here."

Maybe I was beginning to see his logic.

I'd never claimed to be an expert on old bodies, but I *was* the official face of the Society. "Let me get this straight. You think the bodies they've just found on your development site are really old, and if that's true, you're afraid you're going to have issues with the local historical community unless you handle this problem carefully. So you want me to make sure we've done all the research we possibly can, and then explain it all to the public?" And, in addition to that, the evidence suggested that the dead man — the modern one — might have found them first, but that was not my problem, so I didn't bring it up.

He nodded. "Yeah, exactly. And I don't want some little part-timer trying to deal with the press and local groups and all that crap. I want you."

I was both flattered and horrified. Did he really see me as the spokesperson for Philadelphia regional history? When had *that* happened? Or maybe he saw me as the figurehead for historical crimes around here. Less good, but his position made a strange kind of sense either way. But did I want to get involved? I could still walk away, wash my hands of him and the whole project. "If I may be blunt, Mr. Wakeman, what's in it for me?"

"What do you want?" he shot back, unfazed. I guess I was talking his language.

If we were horse-trading, that is. I wasn't about to sell him my carefully tailored opinion in exchange for, say, a new top-to-bottom security system or a modern HVAC for the stacks. Not that I wasn't tempted, if briefly. "Mr. Wakeman, let me tell you up front that I will not make false statements, nor will I spin whatever the findings are to make your problems go away. If this is in fact a historic site, there are protocols to be followed, and I have little or no control over those." Not exactly a direct response to his question, but at least I'd defined my position: I wasn't going to lie for him.

"Hell, I'm not asking you to fudge the facts. All I want is to be sure that whatever research is done on whatever they've found is rock solid and above criticism. I'm not knocking the kid you've hired, but her opinion doesn't carry any weight around here. I want you and your whole team here to vet whatever she comes up with. I'll make it worth your while."

Still vague, but I could live with that. From what I'd heard, Mitchell Wakeman kept his promises. "No matter what we find?"

"I want the truth, and I want it to be open

and aboveboard. That's all."

Maybe he *was* one of the good guys. I'd have to wait and see. "All right. What's your time frame?"

"The news of these bodies is going to hit today's news cycle, and I can't do squat about that. Can you be ready with a statement today, or tomorrow? I want to set up a press conference."

Was he crazy? Lissa hadn't even started working on the research end of things. "Mr. Wakeman, that is unrealistic. If you'd like me to stand beside you and make a nonspecific statement that we are throwing all our resources at this and will have more detailed information shortly, I can put something together. But right now we have no facts."

"The FBI will, in a couple of hours — they're handling the autopsy. Tomorrow morning, then. I'll have my people call you." He stood up and stalked out of my office and down the hall, and Eric raced to catch up to activate the elevator for him. I was left sitting at my desk, stunned. What had just happened, and what had I agreed to?

I had to talk to Lissa, fast. No, wait — I'd promised to fill James in on whatever Wakeman had to say. I hit his speed dial.

"He gone?" James answered without preamble.

"Just left. How did he find out so fast?"

"He's probably got plenty of local people on his payroll. What did he tell you?"

"He knows the bodies are old. He wants the Society to do the historic research on the property ASAP. He wants to make it clear that he's not trying to cover anything up. He wants me to be the face for the cameras, starting tomorrow with a press conference. You have anything new?"

"Not yet. Our people have the bodies — I told you there were two, right? You have anything on the history of the place yet?"

"Good heavens, no! We only started yesterday. At least Lissa knows the area pretty well. I'll ask her what she can pull together quickly so I won't look like a dithering idiot in front of the cameras. You'll let me know if you learn anything else? Like from the autopsies? That could help."

"Of course. Nell, are you okay with all this? You can still say no to Wakeman."

I gave that idea about three seconds of thought. Saying no to Wakeman could make a significant enemy for the Society; saying yes but not coming up with anything that helped him could have risks of its own. But if these were historically old bodies, the Society had some sort of responsibility to at least look at them. Besides, I didn't want to bow to Penn or anyone else around here to do this kind of research. Wakeman had come to me first. "I don't think I can or should do that. Don't worry — I can handle it." I hoped. "See you later?"

"I'll call." He hung up, all business.

On to my next problem: talking to Lissa. Heck, now that the stakes were higher, maybe she'd bail out on the whole deal, leaving me worse off than I was now. At a minimum I had to put together a short-but-coherent statement for the press, but I didn't know anything, and I'd look stupid mumbling generalities for the news. "Protect our sacred heritage," "treasure the past," blah blah blah. Not my style. Maybe I could find something to say about the interesting intersection of history and forensics — assuming the forensics folk found anything worth talking about. I hoped James would let me know in time to use it.

I hauled myself out of my chair and went to the processing room, wondering if Lissa would still be there. Luckily she was, and I gestured her over. "We need to talk," I said, keeping my voice low so that Rich and Alice wouldn't hear. Not that they wouldn't know everything in short order, but I didn't have time to explain at the moment.

"Okay," Lissa said, looking mystified as

she followed me back to my office.

When we were settled, I said, "Mitchell Wakeman was just here."

"What? Why?" Lissa asked quickly.

I explained what he had told me, and how he expected the Society to handle things. When I was done, I asked Lissa, "Is that a problem for you? You can still drop out of this if you want — I wouldn't hold it against you."

"No, I'm fine with it. In fact, it's kind of a cool challenge. I'm glad you'll be doing all the public speaking — I'm lousy at that. I'll just go do my research thing and tell you what I uncover."

"Thank you, Lissa," I said, feeling relieved. Things were happening fast, and I needed her *now* — there was nobody else to pass this off to. "Look, I expect to collect more information on the new — or rather, old — find later today or tonight, but that doesn't give us much time to whip it into shape to present publicly — Wakeman said he was going to set up a press conference tomorrow morning. Can you put something together from what you've got so far?"

"That should take about two minutes. I haven't had time to scratch the surface," she protested.

"I know, I know. But two minutes is probably the amount of face time I'll have on the news, if it comes to that, so we can keep this general until we know more." My brain was galloping ahead of my mouth at the moment. "Listen, maybe we should plan on going out to Chester County in the morning and paying a call on the historical society there. It would be good to have them on our side, and they should have useful information. You should come, since you'd be the one working with them. Can you do that?"

"Uh, yeah, I guess. Should I find my own way out there? Can you meet me somewhere?"

"You live near Penn, right?" When she nodded I said, "Catch a local train at Thirtieth Street Station. I can pick you up at the Paoli train station and we can drive from there. Okay?"

"Sounds good. Thanks for filling me in, Nell. This whole thing is crazy, isn't it?"

"That it is. Thanks for hanging in, Lissa."

Lissa's comment about transport made me realize I needed to touch base with James again. I picked up the phone.

"We're good but we're not that good," he said when he answered. "I don't have anything new since I talked to you fifteen minutes ago. What's up?"

"I talked to Lissa and she's going to do her best, but she doesn't have a whole lot to work with yet. Part of that involves whatever you guys find. *And* I think she and I need to be in Chester County in the morning, but I want to go over whatever your findings are with you before that."

Smart man: he went straight to the heart of the matter. "I'll take you home tonight."

"You are brilliant." Why hadn't I thought of that? Because I didn't want to ask for favors? "We can pick up dinner on the way."

"Great. I'll call when I can break free to pick you up."

"See you later."

James came by to collect me at the Society about six, and we fought commuter traffic all the way back to Bryn Mawr. At least James could drive and talk and think all at the same time, a very useful skill set.

"Okay, what've you got?" I asked as I buckled my seat belt.

"Wait until I get onto the Schuylkill — I need to pay attention for that. So how was the rest of your day?"

"Ben started work, and we had lunch. I like him. I introduced him around and told him he could ask Rich and Alice if he needed any help with collections jargon.

Latoya is reserving judgment, as far as I can tell, but since she hired the last one — and we know how well that turned out — I get a turn now."

We talked about minor stuff from our respective days until we were on the parking lot known as the rush hour Schuylkill Expressway, where there were few driving decisions to be made, and most of them occurred at about five miles per hour. "Okay, now talk," I said.

"I'll give you what I've got, which is more questions than answers. This morning about six, local handlers took their search dogs to go over the Garrett property to see if they could find any other locations the victim might have visited. They followed a scent that led to a wooded area on the east side of the property and stopped there. The handlers observed some recently disturbed soil and investigated further, and came upon a pair of skeletonized remains in a shallow grave."

"Okay, so based on that we now know that Bowen was there recently."

James smiled briefly at me before returning his gaze to the road. "Exactly. The handlers freaked, the dogs freaked, and they called for reinforcements — i.e., us. We arrived shortly after eight thirty. After a couple of hours, our people determined that it was not a recent crime scene, so they packed up the skeletons and transported them back to the city for further study. As you've heard, the techs said the skeletons looked old, as in centuries. They're usually pretty accurate."

"Do you think George actually dug them up?"

"Not really. He was careful, but he uncovered enough to know what he was looking at. It didn't look like a formal burial — no evidence of coffins, and no stones."

"So it couldn't have been an old family plot?"

"Probably not. The bodies weren't neatly laid out, just kind of jumbled together. Didn't look as though that piece of land had been cultivated anytime recently. But a body is a body, so we are compelled to investigate."

"Wow again. From a historical viewpoint, this is cool. From a PR viewpoint, if you're Mitchell Wakeman, this is a nightmare. My conversation with him was, shall we say, elliptical. If I read the signals correctly, if I do right by him, then the Society could see a nice contribution. Of course, he didn't come out and *say* anything like that. He's not stupid." I filled James in on the rest of

Wakeman's visit to my office, which lasted us most of the way to my house. As we drove through Bryn Mawr, debating what to pick up for dinner, James said, "So, let me get this straight. Wakeman wants you to take whatever historical straw we hand you and spin it into public relations gold?"

I turned to stare at him. "That may be the most muddled metaphor I have ever heard you utter. But the gist of it is correct."

"Did the man ask you to lie?" James said, expertly pulling into a small parking space.

"No, he did not. And I made it clear that I would not, either. He only wanted me to cast this most recent discovery in the best light, speaking for the collective local historical community. And to make sure we looked like we were concerned and acting promptly, with full disclosure of whatever we find out."

"I am honored to be in your presence — I didn't know you were an entire community."

"Oh, shut up," I said, swatting his arm. "I'm hungry."

Later, after we'd consumed our take-out dinners back at my place, I tried to think about the recently discovered skeletal remains — not easy with a full stomach and a glass of wine in me. Especially since we were sort of lying nestled on my couch. "So what does this mean, James? The bodies have been there beyond living memory, but our dead man had been poking around and found them very recently?"

"That's what the dogs would say, if they could speak."

"Let's say Bowen did find them, which seems likely. If he knew they were there, who would he tell?" I mused.

"If he told the wrong person, that could be why he's dead," James said.

That was a troubling idea. "And who would the wrong person be?"

"Ah, that's the question. I can think of several people who might have an interest in concealing the discovery, at least temporarily. Starting with your new friend Wakeman."

"Hardly *my* friend. Heck, I'm not sure what he is. A client?" I snuggled closer. "Do you think he's behind this? Because he did seem honestly upset, and I don't think he's a good actor."

"What? Oh, sorry — I'm drifting. You mean, is Wakeman behind the new death? As in, he didn't want these new bodies to be found, so he had Bowen killed to keep him quiet? I can't say, not yet. He was the one who asked that the FBI be called in, which kind of argues against it. Unless he thinks we won't find anything and he'll come out looking like a hero for trying. But I don't pretend to know how a titan of industry thinks — he may be five steps ahead of us."

"Mmm. Well, come morning I'm going to pick up Lissa at the train station and then we're going to go talk to the folks at the Chester County Historical Society, and somewhere in between I've got to throw together a convincing speech that doesn't say anything important but will sound good on television."

"I have every faith that you can do this brilliantly. Can we go to bed now?"

"I thought you'd never ask."

CHAPTER 14

James got a very early call on his cell phone, and when he was finished he came back and kissed me behind my ear as I hid in the pillow. "Two males, in their twenties, evidence of trauma. Oh, and they have indeed been dead for a couple of centuries."

"You do say the sweetest things," I murmured. I rolled over. "Your forensic guys? They're in early."

"They finished up last night, but I turned my phone off." He smiled. "Remind me what you're doing today?"

I checked the clock. "Picking Lissa up at the Paoli station at eight" — I had texted her the night before with the right train to catch — "and then we've got an appointment at the Chester County Historical Society, before the doors open at nine thirty. I need to get up to speed on Chester County history, and I don't have time to read a book or twelve. And then we're supposed to meet with Wakeman and his band of merry men so we can look intelligent and informed for his press conference, which is timed to catch the noon news. He's good at setting up that kind of thing."

"He seems pretty sure this project is going forward," James said.

"He's Mitchell Wakeman. He usually gets his way, I gather. You want the shower first? I'll go make coffee."

James and I left at the same time, headed in different directions. I arrived at the Paoli train station just as the train was unloading its passengers, and Lissa spotted me immediately. She opened the car door and slid into the passenger seat.

"Good morning," I said.

"Morning," she replied. "Any word on those skeletons?"

"The FBI says that they're definitely old, at least two hundred years. What do I need to know about Chester County and its history? And whatever you've got on the land Wakeman owns specifically."

"I'll give you what I can. What are we looking for from the historical society?"

"Mainly, I don't want to tick off the administrators there by tramping all over their territory without at least giving them fair warning. I can explain that it was Wakeman's idea to pull me in — and I have no idea why he didn't go to them first, or maybe he did and didn't think they were up to the job — but I'm sure we'll have to work with these people long after this particular project is done, and it helps to keep things collegial."

"That makes sense. Have you ever visited the place?" Lissa asked.

"A couple of times, but not recently. I know the president, Janet Butler, slightly from regional cultural events, but I don't recall if I've ever had a real conversation with her. How about you?"

"I've checked out what they have, but the Society's resources are more comprehensive. They have a lot of good stuff from the Civil War in their collections, but not so much for the Revolution. They also have a separate genealogy library focusing on Chester County families."

I nodded. "That sounds useful. And you never know what you're going to find in unexpected places."

We followed the route we had taken before, driving past the Garrett farm on our way to West Chester. No sign of crime-scene tape or police guards; it looked idyllic, as if nothing unpleasant had happened there. I continued on into West Chester, just past

173

the center of town, and pulled into a parking garage across from the historical society just as my phone started ringing. I looked to see who it was and was surprised to see the logo for the Wakeman Property Trust. I didn't recall giving anyone there my cell number.

"Hello?" I said when I connected.

"Where are you?" Mitchell Wakeman barked.

"In West Chester. I have a meeting."

"I need to talk with you — now."

I checked my watch. "I can meet you at eleven. Where?"

He was silent for a moment. I inferred that my not jumping at his *now* surprised him. "At the site, down by the pond," he finally said grudgingly. "Press conference starts at noon." He hung up.

I turned to look at Lissa. "Okay, we've got about two hours to learn everything we need to know about Chester County."

At the historical society we were greeted by a woman I recognized vaguely, who must have been waiting for us, since she opened the door on my first ring. She held out her hand, "Hi, Nell, I'm Janet Butler — we met at one of those Philanthropy Network events in the past year, I think. Except you hadn't been elevated to upstairs then. You've had quite a year. And this is?" She looked at Lissa.

Lissa stepped forward. "I'm Lissa Penrose. I'm an intern working on a project . . . well, I'd better let Nell tell you about it."

Janet turned back to me. "All right. What's with all the rush-rush hush-hush? Is this about George Bowen?"

"Maybe. First, thanks for seeing us on such short notice, and under such vague circumstances. Is there somewhere we can talk? This may take a few minutes."

"My office is free. Coffee?"

"I don't think we have time," I said ruefully. Lissa and I followed her upstairs and to the back of the building. Janet settled herself behind her desk and pointed to the two guest chairs.

I cleared my throat. "Before I start, let me apologize up front and say that this whole approach was not my idea, and I'm in no way responsible for cutting you out of the loop. Mitchell Wakeman showed up at my office a couple of days ago and said he wanted the Society to do some research on a plot of land in Chester County, because he plans to build on it."

"The Garrett farm? No surprise there. There've been rumors floating around for months, although no public announcement.

I gather that the great Wakeman likes to keep his cards close to his vest. If he has history questions, why didn't he come to us? We've got all the records here."

"I don't know, and I agree that he should have. But he is who he is and I couldn't exactly tell him no thanks and send him to you."

Janet laughed. "I understand, believe me. So why are you here now?"

"Because we do need your help. I've been asked to act as figurehead for the press, but I don't know nearly enough about local history here, and I can't fake it. If you can help me out with a short course, I will be happy to share any credit that trickles down."

"Thanks, but don't worry about it," Janet said. "Will those other bodies turning up put a monkey wrench in his plans?"

"So you know about those?" Apparently there were no secrets in the suburbs.

"Of course. There's been a lot of traffic around the Garrett property these past few days, and I've got friends in Goshen. Although nobody's saying much about the details. What can you tell me?"

"They're not recent — more like a couple hundred years old. That comes from the FBI, not the local coroner, but don't spread it around."

I watched expressions flit across her face. The predominant one was excitement. "Wow! An old mystery!"

I had to smile at her enthusiasm. I resumed my spiel. "So you understand why this complicates things for Wakeman. I'll be the first to admit that the man probably has enough clout to sweep it all under the rug if those bodies turn out to be inconvenient for him, but he hasn't given me any indication that he plans to do that. I think he might have suspected that something like this would happen, and he wanted to be prepared. But since for the moment we're moving forward, and he brought us into the loop, Lissa and I can also use your help to figure out who they are, or were, and why George Bowen was interested in them."

"George? How'd he get involved in that?"

I didn't answer her question immediately. "Did you know him well?"

Janet bobbed her head. "Not on a personal level, but George was a real history buff. He'd been a member here for years, and he'd done some volunteer stuff here. I know he'd done research using our collections, too."

That was encouraging to me: if he'd looked at research resources here recently, maybe we could figure out what those were and then follow in his footsteps and figure out how he found the bodies. "It looks like George was at the burial site in the recent past. The police sent in dogs to look for the actual crime scene where he was killed, and they found more than they were looking for."

"Are you asking me to participate in an investigation?" Janet looked at me. "Does this involve anything risky?"

"I don't think so, but I've learned never to say never. I am involved in this investigation, if only in a peripheral way, and in part because I was there — as was Lissa — when George Bowen's body was found. So by some sort of transitive property, you would be, too. You now know as much about the situation as anybody else around here, including the police. You've got to admit you have a better idea of the local history than they do. You might be able to help sort out the identity of the skeletons, and what their discovery might mean. Tell me, was George a treasure hunter, hoping to find artifacts and make a big score on eBay?"

Janet shook her head. "Nothing like that. He just liked history. He liked living in the middle of where it happened. It was his hobby, after his kids moved out — that much he told me. Making money had nothing to do with it — which I think kind of annoyed his wife. In fact, she already brought over a couple of boxes of his artifacts. She wanted them out of the house."

"Could we see them?" I asked. In spite of the time pressure we were under, I was curious.

"I don't see why not. You know the drill — handle carefully, white gloves, etc. But from my first glance, I didn't see much that was very special. You want to see them now?"

Lissa spoke for the first time in quite a while. "Would you mind if I looked at your library and archives for a bit? We've got to leave soon, but it would really help if I could get an idea of what you have here."

"Sure, no problem. Nell will vouch for you, right? You won't be hiding valuable documents under your shirt?"

"Of course I'll vouch for her," I answered for Lissa. "But you should know that Lissa's technically working for Mitchell Wakeman."

Janet struck a dramatic pose. "Be gone, foul fiend of Satan!" Lissa looked startled, but Janet grinned. "Just kidding. Still, I don't want to see Wakeman plundering any historic sites under my watch."

A woman after my own heart. "Believe

me, neither do I," I said firmly. "So it's okay if Lissa looks around?"

"Sure — Lissa, I'll take you down to the library, and then, Nell, I'll take you to where we stashed George's artifacts."

"Thank you. Let me know if there's anything I can do to thank you."

"I'll think of something," Janet said cheerfully, standing up. "Come on."

She pointed out the library as we passed it, and Lissa disappeared into it eagerly. I followed Janet down a hall and through a couple of doors, until we came to a crammed workroom. No one else was there, but there were several banker's boxes lined up on a rough table in the middle of the room. Janet pointed toward them. "That's what Pat, George's wife, brought. She said there might be more back at the house. Do you know what you're looking for?"

"Not really. This may be telling tales out of class, but it looks like George was not only at the site where the bodies were found, but he was also poking around — the earth was disturbed, enough that he would have known the bodies were there. He didn't do any harm to them, if you're worried."

"Oh my," Janet breathed. "He must have been thrilled."

"So he didn't come straight here and tell you?"

"No, this is news to me."

"Can you think of who he would have told? His wife?"

"Maybe, but I doubt that she'd have cared one way or the other."

"Was he a whistle-blower type? I mean, would he have gone to some authority or other and tried to stop Wakeman's building project until the site had been fully investigated?"

"Again, maybe. Probably. Like all of us here at the society, he took our local heritage seriously."

My phone buzzed: Wakeman. I checked the time: I wasn't due to meet him for at least a half an hour. Why was he calling?

"What's keeping you?" he said without any niceties.

This was starting to get on my nerves. "I told you, I'll be there at eleven," I said, managing not to add something like *Keep your shirt on.*

"Make it fast." He hung up again. What a charmer.

Janet and I were both startled when there was a pounding on a metal door at the back of the room, which I guessed led to the staff parking lot. We exchanged glances, and she

181

went over to open it. Janet had barely pulled it open when a haggard-looking older woman shoved her way in, wrestling with a pair of stacked banker's boxes. After a brief glance at me, she addressed Janet.

"This is the last of them. I don't want them in the house. I don't want to see them again, ever. I've got people calling, and the kids are flying in, and there's a funeral to arrange, and I can't deal with any more of this. Do whatever you want with the stuff." She dumped the boxes on the table next to the others, and then, as if she had run out of steam, she dropped heavily into a folding chair. I realized there were tears running down her face. Obviously, this must be Mrs. George Bowen.

Janet took over immediately. "I'm so sorry, Pat. Of course we'll take care of it all — you have other things you need to worry about. Can I get you anything? Water? Coffee? Maybe you should just sit here a minute and catch your breath."

The woman just shook her head, but she made no move to get up. The tears kept trickling down her face.

I was torn. The woman was clearly grieving, and she faced a hellacious next few days. At the same time, I really wanted to ask if her late husband had said anything to her about a big discovery, and if not, who he might have told. But I didn't know the woman, and she didn't know me. I hadn't even known her husband.

"Pat, I know this must be hard for you, and you're under a lot of stress," Janet said to her, "but do you mind if I take a peek in the boxes and make sure there's nothing you'll regret having gotten rid of?"

"I don't care. Go ahead. Just don't hand it back to me. You can keep it or sell it or pitch it — I don't care."

"Thank you. Nell, do you want to help?"

"I think I'll keep Mrs. Bowen company." I could ask her some questions, I rationalized, thinking that such things might be kinder coming from me than from the police or the FBI. I looked at Janet and tried to convey all this without saying anything, which was kind of absurd.

But somehow she got my message, for which I thanked the stars. I looked around until I found another folding chair, then pulled it close to Pat's. "Janet tells me your husband was really interested in local history?"

"Interested — ha!" Pat snorted, then rummaged in her pocket and pulled out a used tissue and blew her nose. "Obsessed is more like it. Why couldn't he have taken up something like golf or bridge? But no, he had to go poking around in the dirt looking for God knows what. And then he'd bring me home his new finds and expect me to *ooh* and *aah* over them. Pieces of trash, as far as I could see. Bits of this, shards of that. I wouldn't let him keep them in the house — made him stash them all in the garage. He built a whole wall of shelves for them. He never got tired of looking — even up to this week."

An opening? I seized it. "Had he found something new?"

"I'd never seen him so excited — I mean, he was practically hopping up and down. After all these years, he said, he'd finally found something big."

"Did he tell you what it was?"

"If he did, it didn't make an impression on me. There was some dirty stuff spread out on his workbench in the garage. I just threw it all into one of those boxes. I don't know if it was what he was excited about, but it just looked like junk to me."

Janet and I exchanged another look, and Janet came over to join us, holding something small in her hand. "Is this what you're talking about?"

"Could be. I didn't look too closely."

Janet held out her hand toward me. "Does

that soil look fresh to you?"

I saw some small round items encrusted in dirt in Janet's palm. I nodded. "What are they?"

"Metal buttons."

I peered more closely and made out something stamped on at least one of them. "Can you date them?"

"I'm pretty sure they're from the Revolutionary War. And if I'm not mistaken, they might be British."

We looked at each other for a long moment. "Oh my," I said intelligently. "A British soldier buried in Ezra Garrett's woods? This really is going to be a mess."

"Are you sure you don't want them, Pat?" Janet said gently.

Pat shook her head. "You keep them. George would probably want you to have them." She stood up abruptly, nearly knocking over the flimsy chair. "I've got to go." She was out the door before either Janet or I could protest.

CHAPTER 15

I was still struggling to make sense of what Janet — or rather, George — had found when my phone rang again. I walked a few feet away to answer it.

"You're late." The ever-charming Mitchell Wakeman: no hello or anything.

I knew I wasn't late, but there was no point in arguing with him. "I'm on my way." I hung up on him. If he could be abrupt, then so could I. I turned to Janet, who had come up beside me. "I'm sorry to bail on you like this, but I've got a press conference to attend, and Wakeman wants to talk with me before we go on the air."

"Are you going to talk about . . . these?" Janet asked, pointing to the dirt-encrusted artifacts.

"I don't know, but I think they're important — take good care of them, will you? And do you mind speaking to the FBI about them?" I wondered if I was supposed to worry about chain of evidence or something like that, but I really didn't have time.

"Of course I don't mind. I'll see if I can find out anything else about them, maybe narrow down which group of soldiers they would have belonged to. And please let me know what's going on."

"Thanks, I will. I've got to go find Lissa and get over to the Garrett farm, like, immediately. I'll let myself out, okay?"

"Sure. Go."

I grabbed my bag and ran for the stairs. I located Lissa and all but dragged her out of the library and out to my car, and shoved her in, and we peeled out of the parking garage, heading for the farm.

"I know we're late, but what's the rush?" Lissa asked, after she had made sure her seat belt was buckled.

"George Bowen's wife Pat showed up with more artifacts. She said George came home all excited from one of his history hunts shortly before he died, but she had no idea why and really didn't care. She just dragged in everything he'd collected and dumped it on the historical society because she couldn't stand the sight of it. Janet found some bits and pieces that had fresh dirt on them, and it looks like they're Revolutionary War buttons, possibly British. I'm going to make a wild guess and say that they likely belonged to the bodies found up the hill, where we know the dead man had been poking around. Which means there's going to have to be a lot more investigation of the site. It could be those are the only bodies, or it could be the fields are full of them. Wakeman doesn't know about the buttons yet, but he's already called twice asking where we were. Which is why I'm in a hurry."

"Wow," Lissa said. "That's amazing."

"It would be if I didn't have to stand up at this press conference in about ten minutes and say something that won't tick off Mitchell Wakeman or the FBI and all the other cops."

"You think Wakeman won't be happy to learn that his new development property is an archeological site? In addition to being a crime scene?"

"What do you think?"

Lissa's mouth twitched into a half smile. "Can I stay in the car?"

We reached the Garrett farm in record time — good thing that most of the local cops were already there, or I'd probably have been busted for speeding on our way over. I pulled into the driveway near the old farmhouse and walked over to an unhappy-looking Mitchell Wakeman. "We need to talk," I said. I figured we had at least fifteen minutes before the newsies started tuning up their equipment.

"No time — I can't give you more than a few minutes," he replied curtly. He turned his back on me and resumed talking to someone I didn't recognize, alternating with a guy with a large camera hoisted on his shoulder. I recognized one of the daytime newscasters, a pretty youngish woman in heavy makeup, clutching a microphone. Once everyone was happy with the proposed camera angles, she said, "Let's get some background shots."

She and the cameraman stepped away and started panning the summer landscape. Wakeman turned his attention to me once again. "What took you so long?"

I swallowed a sharp retort. "You said the press conference was at noon. We've got plenty of time. And I've found some information that you need to know: those older bodies they found are probably from the Revolution, and it's possible that at least one was British."

"Crap," he said eloquently. "Don't say anything about it on camera."

He left me gaping at his back. And fuming. I was not about to go public with what

I'd just learned, not without making sure we all had the details right. Here was a scene of possible historic significance that might be connected to a recent murder, and he was telling me not to mention it? How dumb did he think I was? I reminded myself that I didn't work for him and we had no formal agreement, nor had any money changed hands. So I could damn well say what I wanted — but I knew better than to jeopardize this investigation, whether or not it involved Wakeman.

I checked my watch. Nearly twelve, and since this was a local event, I guessed it would come up somewhere in the middle of the broadcast rather than lead off, unless it was a really slow news day and the Phillies were slumping. I swallowed a smile. If the story led with "multiple bodies found in Chester County field" it might get moved up front, but Wakeman wouldn't be happy. If I were spiteful, I could probably ensure it went out like that on the five o'clock news, but that wouldn't be professional. I sighed. I knew I would wimp out and make nice for the cameras, because whatever my personal opinion of Mitchell Wakeman, he was still a major player in the region and it wouldn't be smart to antagonize him. I decided I would wait and see how he played it.

We assembled in a staggered row with Wakeman in front, flanked by people who seemed to be one of his employees and someone from the township, with me at the edge of the small group. Cameras came on, the news lady perked up and raised her microphone, and we were off. I was no stranger to being on camera, so I smoothed whatever I could, stood up straighter, and waited for my turn. When it came, I was pleased that they got my name right, and my job title, and then the newscaster lobbed a softball at me: "I understand that the Wakeman Property Trust has invited you in to assess the historic importance of this site."

I smiled. "Yes, that's correct. This area is rich in history, and Mr. Wakeman wants to preserve the integrity of any historic structures, such as the old farmhouse. I hope the Society will be able to provide documentation for him."

"What about the body found here this week?"

Ulp. Why hadn't she asked anybody else? Did I look like a softy who would spill whatever I knew? "I can't comment on that."

"Weren't you present when the body was found?"

Double *ulp*. "Yes, because Mr. Wakeman was giving me a tour of the site at the time."

"And haven't you been involved in more than one Philadelphia-area homicide in the past?"

I could feel Wakeman glaring at me as I was apparently hijacking his moment in the press sun. I was trying to figure out how to answer her when someone else on her crew started making hand signals that I interpreted to mean something like "wrap it up." The woman looked frustrated, but turned back to the camera and made some chirpy noises tying up loose ends. She didn't look at me. Did she need my permission to quote me? Or was I now "news" myself? That was a depressing thought.

Wakeman stalked over to me. "What the hell was that about?"

I wasn't in a mood to make nice. "Hey, if you'd done your homework, you'd know what she said is true. And I hate to tell you, but this is probably going to get worse before it gets better. The dead man knew where those bodies were buried. And it's likely that he knew *what* they were. The question is, who did he tell? You?" I glared at him.

His complexion reddened and his jaw clenched, but he didn't speak for almost thirty seconds until he got himself under control. "Nobody told me anything about all that. You thinking that's what got him killed?"

"The FBI just figured it out this morning. It could be a motive. And the authorities may think the same thing. So you'd better be ready for more questions."

"Ah, crap," he muttered. His vocabulary was a bit limited; I had a feeling he'd had a stronger epithet in mind.

I wasn't interested in coddling him at the moment, if ever. "Who are all these other guys? Did you invite them?"

Wakeman looked around him. The television crew had packed up and vanished, but there was still a small crowd of others milling around in the field, apparently not sure if they had been dismissed. "Couple of guys who work for me. The others are from the township."

"Introduce me," I said. "They might be able to help with our report."

Wakeman nodded his head, then beckoned the group over. They came quickly, like well-trained dogs: Wakeman's project mattered to them. "Guys, this is Nell Pratt, from the historical society in the city. She's doing some research for me. You want to tell her who you all are? And answer whatever questions she's got. Thanks." He turned and strode off, followed by his own employees.

I turned my attention to the remaining people. "Sorry — I should have introduced myself sooner, but things have been kind of rushed. As Mr. Wakeman said, I'm Nell Pratt. And you are?"

One man stepped up first. "Ms. Pratt, good to meet you," he said eagerly. "I'm Mr. Wakeman's project manager, Scott Mason. We'll probably be seeing a lot more of each other. Let me introduce you to the team from the township here. Marv?"

A slightly portly middle-aged man wearing rumpled khakis held out his hand. "I'm Marvin Jackson, Goshen Township manager. This guy here is Joseph Dilworth, who heads up the Goshen historical commission. Oh, hi, Eddie — didn't see you arrive." That was addressed to a short stocky man who had hung back. "This is Eddie Garrett — Ezra was his father."

Ah, one of the offspring who had watched their father sell the farm. "Hello, Eddie." I extended my hand, and he took it unwillingly. His grip was strong, his skin surprisingly thick and rough, and I remembered that until fairly recently he had been a dairy farmer on the land where we now stood. What was he doing now? Or had he inherited enough from his father that he didn't need to work anymore? "I'm glad to meet you. I'd love to talk to you about your father and the farm, if you have the time."

Eddie mumbled something vague and backed off once again to hide behind the group — not exactly a sociable guy. I wondered briefly why he had been the only Garrett to show up today and why he had shown up at all, since he was so clearly uncomfortable. I suspected that Wakeman had ordered, er, asked him to be there to put a right spin on the family's participation.

Having struck out with Eddie Garrett, I turned to Joseph Dilworth, a tall greying man in his early sixties. "Mr. Dilworth, you're head of the historical commission? Would you have time to speak with me?"

He glanced at his watch. "Want to grab a sandwich? And who's your colleague here?"

As Lissa slid up alongside me, I realized I hadn't even had time to introduce her. "This is Lissa Penrose. She's researching the history of Mr. Wakeman's property for us. But she's only just started, and I'm sure you could help point her in the right direction."

"No problem. The Salt Shaker up the road does good sandwiches. You want to follow my car? Marv, you want to come, too?"

"Can't do it, Joe," Marv said. "I've got budgets to go over. But if you want to talk with me, Ms. Pratt, give me a call. Happy to help." He held out a business card, and I took it.

"I'll do that, Marv. And we'd love to have lunch with you, Joe. Thank you." We all trudged up the hill to where the cars were parked, and I waited until Joe pulled out and turned down the hill, then followed.

"I hope you don't mind taking the time for lunch," I said to Lissa.

Lissa said, "Of course not. I'd be speaking with Joe Dilworth in any case, so it might be good to get to know him. That is, if I still have a job?"

"If Wakeman's smart he'll keep us on after this discovery, to make him look like a sensitive and responsible good citizen. But I'll let him work through that for himself. Actually, I'd be happy if you'd do at least a little more research anyway, to try to figure out who those skeletons are and what they were doing here. Because now I want to know. That's why we're having lunch with the guy from the township. Feel free to ask him anything you want."

"Because he doesn't work for Wakeman?" Lissa asked promptly. "I'm curious myself, about all these bodies. And I think I've got some ideas where to start."

We parked next to Joseph Dilworth's car in front of the Salt Shaker, and he waited for us before entering the small building. Once we were inside, it was clear that it was a local place; at least three people waved or nodded at Dilworth as he made his way to a table. The waitress came over quickly, and we ordered sandwiches and iced tea.

Dilworth rubbed his hands together and smiled. "So what can I do for you two lovely ladies?"

"Mr. Dilworth, as you heard, Mr. Wakeman approached me to ask that the Society undertake a thorough investigation of the former Garrett property, which he now owns. Obviously things have gotten a bit more complicated over the past few days, particularly with the most recent find." I'd had little time to think about what I wanted to know from him and what he might be able to tell me. "Tell me about your town here, and about Ezra Garrett."

That seemed to be enough to get him started. He proceeded to outline for us the entire history of Goshen Township since its founding some three hundred years before; referred to every building within a several-mile radius that had been standing for a couple of centuries; and pointed with justifiable pride to the small historic district that the township had established under his watch. Apparently Goshen was truly invested in its history, which I found admirable. I waited until he paused long enough to take a drink of his tea before interrupting.

"Where does the Garrett farm fit in all this, Mr. Dilworth?" I asked

"Hey, call me Joe. Garretts are an old family around here — they go way back. There were Garretts back when the first meeting house was set up, back right after 1700."

"They were Quakers?"

"Were and are. Ezra was laid to rest in the cemetery there — right across the street."

I followed his gesture. I hadn't realized that there was a cemetery there, but I knew vaguely that the Quakers preferred low, simple stones, which weren't visible behind the stone wall that surrounded the site.

"I met Edward Garrett briefly after the press conference. Are there other family members?"

"He's got an older brother, William, but he couldn't be bothered to come. Eddie doesn't like public events, but I'll bet Wakeman pressured him to come, just to have a Garrett face in the pictures." Exactly as I had thought.

"Mr. Wakeman told me that he had arranged the purchase of the land before Ezra Garrett passed on, but he allowed the family to stay until Ezra's death. Did everyone know about that?"

Joe Dilworth cocked his head at me. "What's it to you? If you don't mind my asking."

I phrased my response carefully. "Mr. Dilworth — Joe — it was Mr. Wakeman who brought me into this and asked me to research the place. Because of that, I was there when George Bowen's body was found, so I guess you could say I feel a kind of personal interest in it now. You've told me that the land was in the Garrett family's hands for centuries. Why did Ezra decide to sell? How did the rest of the family feel about that?"

"I'm sorry you had to see that. George was a good man, and he deserved better. As for what you're asking — William Garrett didn't want to have anything to do with dairy farming. What's more, he knew what the land would be worth, and I'm pretty sure Wakeman cut a fair deal."

"What about Eddie?"

Joe Dilworth signaled to the waitress that he wanted coffee; Lissa and I declined. He waited until the coffee arrived before answering. "Only thing Eddie ever wanted to do was raise dairy cattle. But he's not young, and he couldn't handle it by himself. I kind of guess Ezra overruled him, or Ezra and William together. Like I said, it was a good deal financially."

Poor Eddie. "What's he doing with himself these days?" I asked.

"I don't think he's settled on any one thing. He's kind of a lost soul."

Belatedly, I realized that Lissa had been shut out of most of our conversation. "Lissa, I'm sorry I haven't let you get a word in. Did you have any questions?"

Lissa addressed Joe Dilworth directly. "I do, but I think I should meet with Mr. Dilworth at another time. If that's all right with you?"

"I'm always happy to meet with nice young ladies who like history. Why don't you call my office, say, tomorrow, and we can set up a time?"

"I'll do that, thank you."

Dilworth looked at his watch again. "Shoot, I've got a meeting about ten minutes ago. Sorry to leave so fast, but it's been a pleasure talking with you both. Lissa, I'll be talking with you again. Ms. Pratt, nice to meet you." And he was gone — leaving me with the check. At least it was fairly reasonable.

When I'd paid, I told Lissa, "I guess we'd better head back to the city. And on the way we can talk about what we've learned today."

CHAPTER 16

We drove into the city, making good time because it was mid-afternoon. We reviewed what we'd heard from Janet and Joe, and Lissa was already scribbling down a list of things to look up. I parked in the pay lot across from the Society, mentally planning to bill it to Wakeman. When I reached my desk, Eric handed me a sheaf of message slips. "Did you watch the news at noon?" I asked.

"I did, on the computer. Is something funny goin' on?"

"Is that how it looked to you? The problem is, we're not sure what yet. Stay tuned for further developments. Unless, of course, Mitchell Wakeman has called and told me that our services are no longer required." I wondered if I'd be happy to hear that.

Eric smiled. "Haven't heard from him. You know, nobody ever told me this job would be so exciting."

"I wouldn't have believed it myself, Eric." I went into my office and sorted through the slips. A couple of calls from James. Since he'd called on my professional line, it was probably a professional question, and not urgent enough to use my cell. I called him back first.

"Nell," he said when he picked up.

"James. You called?"

"I saw the newscast. Your statement lacked a certain, uh, specificity."

"That was the plan. Look, I've got some new info for you. You want it over the phone?"

"No, I'll come by the Society. Half an hour?"

"Fine."

I returned a couple of more calls, then went looking for Lissa. I found her in the processing room talking with Ben, and they had some documents spread out in front of them.

"Hi, Ben," I said. "Lissa, Agent Morrison is on his way over here to talk about what we found out today in West Chester. I think you should sit in."

"Yes, I want to. I told you there were some things I wanted to check, and I asked Ben about one in particular. Turns out he knows a lot more than I do, and I'm guessing it may be relevant to the two bodies at the farm. I think he should join us — it might save time."

The more the merrier, apparently. Crime solving by committee. "Sure. Let's set up in the boardroom."

Ben rolled up a couple of the maps they had been looking at, then he and Lissa followed me to the boardroom. I kept going, so I could meet James downstairs. He was waiting in the lobby when I arrived.

"So, have you had any irate calls from Wakeman yet?" I asked, as we walked toward the elevator.

"Not that I'm aware of. I've kept Agent Cooper in the loop, so if Wakeman reached out to him, Cooper would have shot him down. After all, Wakeman asked us in to look at Bowen's death, but he can't demand we drop it now that we're in it. Finding the other two bodies grew out of that, although strictly speaking they're not our problem. Why? Is he complaining about you? The investigation?"

We'd reached the elevator. As the doors slid shut behind us, I said, "No, I wouldn't say that. He seems to be on edge, but he's not interfering. In any case, you probably won't be surprised to hear that the two discoveries are kind of connected."

James smiled. "What else could I have expected?"

We'd reached the boardroom, where Ben and Lissa were busy studying one of the maps again. They looked up when James and I arrived. "Hey, Morrison," Ben said.

"Hey, Ben. What're you doing here?"

"Lissa thought we might have something useful. If you don't mind us sitting in? I mean, we're not talking supersecret stuff here, are we?"

James dropped into a chair. "Not if Wakeman keeps insisting on holding press conferences. What've you got, Nell?"

"You remember that Lissa and I met with Janet Butler at the Chester County Historical Society this morning, as a courtesy to her and to keep her informed, since Wakeman's project is in her backyard. I apologized to her that Wakeman hadn't included her, which seems kind of rude, professionally speaking."

"So?" James looked impatient.

"While I was talking with Janet, George Bowen's wife, Pat, came in, bringing with her all the artifacts and stuff that her husband had collected over the years, saying she never wanted to see it again. Apparently she didn't share her husband's enthusiasm for local history. But she did say that he came home earlier in the week really excited about something he had found. Janet noticed that a couple of things still had damp soil on them, so we inferred that they were items George had found shortly before he died. It turns out that they were metal buttons that dated to the Revolutionary War, and Janet thinks they're British. I'd put money on it that they go with those skeletons, which mean they've been sitting there since the seventeen hundreds."

"I'd guess 1777," Ben spoke up for the first time. "Have you all heard of the Paoli Massacre? Also known as the Battle of Paoli? Because I think that's where they came from."

"That's what I wanted to check out," Lissa said triumphantly.

"The Paoli Massacre?" I asked Ben. "Shoot, I've been driving by that historical marker for years on the way to West Chester, but I don't know the details. The Garrett farm is only a couple of miles farther down the road."

"You have time for the full story?" Ben asked.

I glanced at James, who did not look relaxed. "Why don't you give us the high points?"

"Okay," he agreed. "You know the Battle

of the Brandywine?"

"Uh, I know where it happened — I go by that all the time, too, when I go to the museum out that way. But I don't know the details of the battle itself. I guess my high school history class didn't include it." I was not covering myself with glory as the representative for local history. "How do you happen to know so much about a local battle?" I asked.

Ben shrugged. "I was in the military, remember? I always liked military history. So you know that the British took Philadelphia in 1777, right?"

"Yes, that much I knew."

Ben settled himself more comfortably in his wheelchair. "All right, so in September of 1777, Washington's troops faced off against British troops at the Brandywine Creek — yes, the one next to where that art museum is now." Ben grinned at me, teasing a little. "The thinking was that the patriot troops would have an advantage, because there were limited places where the British army could ford the creek. They lost anyway and were forced to retreat. It was disastrous — Washington's troops were outnumbered and outflanked. He lost a lot of men and eleven cannons, and opened up the way to Philadelphia. But he was also lucky — he got away with most of his army intact, and for a number of reasons the British forces didn't press their advantage.

"Washington was going to go toward Chester, but instead he decided to keep his army between the British and Philadelphia, and he laid out his troops in position both to block the access routes and to protect their supply centers. The next confrontation took place on September sixteenth near Malvern."

I was beginning to see where he was going with this. "Which is next to Paoli."

"Right. The American army got lucky again — it rained so hard it flooded the Schuylkill River, which kept the British troops from crossing. Could have been a major battle, if it weren't for the nor'easter. But the downside was, all their ammunition got wet, so Washington had to go restock."

James was looking at his watch. "Can we fast forward here?"

"Just setting the stage for you, pal. Don't you want to learn something?"

"I'd like to learn who killed George Bowen and what his death might have to do with those bodies he found."

"All right, all right. So Washington stationed some troops in Paoli to defend the rear, while the rest of them went to resupply. He left about fifteen hundred troops under General Anthony Wayne, who you might have heard of. Wayne was a local, so he knew the area well. But the British snuck up on their encampment in the middle of the night and attacked with sabers and bayonets. It was one of the more vicious battles of the war — there was a lot of blood shed by the Americans. In PR terms the British strategy turned out to be a mistake, because they were so brutal that public opinion rallied in the Americans' favor. The attack was thought to be ungentlemanly, if you will, and unnecessarily cruel. Anyway, Wayne lost a lot of people, with even more seriously wounded; the British lost all of four. Then Wayne gathered his troops as best he could and fled west."

I finally saw the connection. "You're saying Wayne's men headed west along what is now the Paoli Pike? Which would've taken at least some of them right past the Garrett farm."

"Exactly. Of course, the battle was chaotic, and to this day it's not one hundred percent certain who fought and what happened to them. Often local militia men would show up for a battle, but they wouldn't be recorded on any official rolls — they were just fighting in their backyards. And remember, there were Loyalists in that area, so who's to say some of them didn't throw on a red coat and join the British?"

"So," James said slowly, "one could hypothesize that soldiers from both sides may have faced off on or near the Garrett farm during the retreat and died, and in the confusion nobody ever reported them as dead?"

"It could have happened," Ben said.

"Would this be important now, Ben?" Lissa asked.

"Depends on who got hold of that information — if it's true. It would make a good human interest story — you know, enemies lying together in a common grave for centuries, a footnote to a bloody battle. Which I guess might increase pressure to do a more thorough excavation, in case there're more bodies to be found. I mean, it would be a new story about an old event."

"But an excavation, if done right, would delay the development project." I said.

"Not my area of expertise," Ben said quickly. "And it wouldn't delay it forever — just slow it down a bit. If you're thinking about how Wakeman would react, he or his people might be able to spin it to his own advantage. You know, important historic site, treasured history, that kind of line —

all very open and public. Just as long as he isn't viewed as bulldozing our sacred heritage — or building a condo over the grave."

"Got it," I said.

"You need anything else from me?" Ben asked.

"Could you write up a brief summary for us history-challenged types?"

"No problem," Ben said.

I turned to Lissa. "Lissa, you can probably guess what else we need. Would you look into land records and find out who lived where back then? Who was on which side in the war? Work with Chester County if you want — I'm sure they've got plenty of local details. See if they have letters or family histories there. We should keep Janet in the loop. It would be great if we could identify who's who."

"Absolutely. Uh, maybe this is premature, but if I find anything worthwhile and put it together, would you mind if I published it?"

"I wouldn't mind, but we should run it by Wakeman, as a courtesy. I don't think he'd have any problem with it. Maybe the Society can help with publication. Great idea."

"I'll get right on it. Ben, you want to show me some more of your maps? Maybe we can pin down the path of the retreat more closely."

"Sure. Follow me." He wheeled his way out, followed closely by Lissa. I watched them go, and as they went down the hall, I said, "Is Ben involved with anyone?"

"What, you're playing matchmaker?" James said, with a laugh. "Not that I know of."

"Just checking." I turned to him. "So, what do we do now?"

"We?" He cocked an eyebrow at me.

I assumed he wasn't serious. "Hey, I brought you the details from the widow, didn't I? By the way, do you need anything more from her? You may not be able to interview her anytime soon — she's burying her husband this weekend, and the family is arriving. She seemed completely over-whelmed."

James thought for a moment. "Not right away. I need to know who George might have been close enough to on the township staff to tell about what he found. Any friends he might have shared this with, if he was really excited. His wife would know about either of those, but I agree — this is not the time to intrude on her with our questions. I wonder if your colleague Janet could help."

"How so?"

"Well, since she knew George, she has an

entrée — maybe she could go by after the funeral and thank the widow for her generous contribution of some old buttons and whatever else was in the boxes. That would get her in the door, and then she could ask some questions, like: who did George share his love of artifacts with?" James sighed. "Of course, I can't ask her to do it any more than I can ask you. But you know as well as I do that the longer a murder goes unsolved, the less likely it ever will be solved."

"I'm pretty sure Pat Bowen doesn't want to hear anything relating to those artifacts she was in such a hurry to get rid of. She may even think that they're somehow related to George's death. Have you or the local police interviewed the people he worked with on the township staff?"

"The local police have, at least on a preliminary basis. But most of the cops have known those local government guys for years, so it's hard for me to know what questions they asked — or how hard they pushed. By the way, good work with the widow."

"I was lucky to be in the right place at the right time, that's all."

"Do you mind kicking some ideas around now?"

I looked at him incredulously; he was

actually asking me? "About the murder? So now you're willing to share? Sure — I don't have any other commitments this afternoon." Not that there was much left of it.

"Thanks." He leaned back in his chair and studied the blank wall across the room. "Say you and Ben are right and the bodies in the copse were soldiers from the Revolution, at least one of them British, whose deaths were never recorded."

"That reminds me, do your guys want to look at the buttons? Janet still has them, but I told her you might want to see them."

"Eventually, yes. Anyway, George Bowen, amateur history enthusiast and artifact collector, stumbles on these bodies, maybe by accident or maybe because he's been prowling around the property for years."

"Janet did say he's been interested in local history for quite a while, and not because he wanted to sell his finds on eBay. He seems to have kept everything."

"Good. So Bowen finds the skeletons and he recognizes them for what they are, and he even brings back a button or two, just to confirm what he suspects or to try to look it up. He has to be excited, and he knows that his wife won't care. What does he do next?"

"Tell a friend? Janet says he didn't go to the historical society with his find, although he might have planned to soon."

James nodded. "Maybe. We'd need to find out who his friends were. And we need to know more about George. Option A: he tells someone he's close to, who shares his hobby or at least cares about it. Option B: he realizes the significance of his find and he runs to tell the township and/or the Wakeman Property Trust to tell them to hold their horses until the discovery can be evaluated."

"Okay, both make sense, and maybe he did both. But if it was someone at either the township or the trust, they haven't come forward about it. So, who did he talk to? And more important, who would have killed him because of what he found?"

James looked at me then. "That's the question. As we've discussed before, *cui bono*? Who benefits from keeping this a secret? Is there a time value? Wakeman already owns the land. Is he expecting a change in state or local administration? Does something else come due or expire? Are there new regulations that are going to take effect at some point? And who would know about any of those and their potential impact?"

"I'm glad we're just spitballing, because I

don't have an answer for any of these questions."

"But I'm not off base, am I?"

"No, I don't think so. The question is, what does the FBI do next? Who do you talk to? Do you hand this off to the local authorities? Do you pull rank and do it yourself? Do you go hand in hand with the police?"

He sighed. "All of the above? Or none? The local police resent the interference, and they kind of close ranks against an outsider. I understand that, and I'm not saying they aren't good at their jobs. And to be fair, the victim was one of their citizens. Wakeman has to tread lightly because he needs the goodwill of the township to make his project work — he doesn't want to fan any local resentment."

"He's the one who called you in, remember. He can't have it both ways. Do you know what approvals he needs, locally? Is there a single person who controls permits, like the zoning officer — and now they're going to need a new one — or if there's something that has to be approved by a committee, like the historical commission? Or, heck, if something this big has to be approved by local ballot."

James looked at me approvingly. "That's a

good question, and I have no idea. But I can find out. Nell, why do you know about local government when I don't?"

"I live in the suburbs. I read the local paper, and I see notices like this all the time announcing zoning meetings or committee meetings or ballot initiatives."

"Good call. And I can delegate the task of finding all that out to someone junior in the office. Nobody's feathers will be ruffled if we're looking at zoning codes — that's public information."

"How much pull does Wakeman have at the FBI?"

"Officially? None, of course. We're a neutral government agency, and we aren't even dependent on keeping the local politicos happy, just the national ones. Off the record? It never hurts to have a friend in high places, so if we can accommodate someone like him without bending any rules, we will. Does that answer your question?"

"It's more or less what I expected."

He looked down at his hands. "Look, Nell, I've got some business to see to tomorrow morning, but maybe after that we could go over some property listings?"

It took me a moment to figure out what he mean by listings: a place to live. Together.

Why was I avoiding thinking about that? "On paper or online? Or in person?"

He looked at me then. "Whichever you want. I think we need to move this forward. Don't you?"

Yes. Maybe. "Fine. Tomorrow is good for me."

I could swear he looked relieved. "That's great."

Maybe. I wasn't sure. Maybe if we looked at places that were neutral, new to us, with no history and no associations, it would be easier. I hoped. What was *wrong* with me?

"Where will you be tonight?" I asked.

"My place, I assumed. You want to join me there? Or, no, I can meet you out at your place, since I've got some people to interview out that way."

I wasn't invited to that party. Of course, there was no reason why I should be; I was representing the historical community, not law enforcement. Still, I felt shut out, just a little. "Why don't we meet up at my place tomorrow?"

He stood up; I stood up. We were at my workplace, so no lingering good-bye kiss. And it looked like I'd be going home alone tonight. That was what I wanted, wasn't it? Some space? Some time to take a long hard look at my place and decide what I liked about it and what didn't work? That's what I told myself. "I'll walk you to the elevator."

After seeing James off, I went back to my office. I was surprised when Eric handed me a message slip from Janet Butler. "Did she say what she wanted, Eric?"

"No, just said she needed to talk with you."

"Nell, thanks for getting back to me," Janet said somewhat breathlessly when I called her back. "Look, this may sound really weird, but Pat Bowen wants to talk to us."

"Us? Did she say that?"

"Yes, she did — both of us."

"Isn't she in the middle of planning a funeral for her husband?"

"Yes, that's on Sunday. But she said it was important. Can you meet me here in West Chester tomorrow morning?"

"Sure, no problem. Nine?"

"Nine is great. See you then." Janet hung up, leaving me wondering what on earth Pat Bowen thought was so important that it couldn't wait until after the funeral.

CHAPTER 17

I went home — alone. I threw together a skimpy dinner and ate it — alone. Was this place more quiet than it used to be? As I ate I studied my onetime carriage house, with its tiny kitchen carved out of one corner, and the fireplace I had insisted on adding as a pure indulgence. I liked my fireplace. Its light and warmth struck some fundamental, even primitive, chord in me.

All right, I wanted a fireplace in our new place. But not some stark, architectural construct with lots of glass and angles or — heaven forbid — a switch to turn it on and off; I wanted a fireplace that belonged, that was integral to the structure of a building, inefficient and messy though it might be. Which, I reminded myself, wasn't likely to come with a modern apartment. Okay, back to the list. Fireplace. Closets. A bigger kitchen. A garden? No, neither of us seemed much interested in land or lawn. But definitely space for each of us to be alone, which meant at least three bedrooms, or at least two plus a study. This hypothetical place was growing by the minute. And it looked like it would have to be a house. City row house? Something on the fringes of the city? I hadn't looked at real estate listings for years, but it seemed I was going to. That seemed like such a big leap forward. Living together — okay, I was getting used to the idea, sort of. But buying something together? That was — yes, I had to use the word — a big commitment. Financially it made sense, I had to admit: rents in or near the city were wicked, and a mortgage would probably be no higher. But whose name would go on the documents? I (and my bank) owned the little house where I sat. I liked that. I could call the shots, make any changes I wanted. I was responsible for it. I didn't have to negotiate everything with someone else. I felt I was in uncharted territory. James and I had seen each other under pretty much the worst possible circumstances and survived; handling day-to-day living should be a piece of cake, right?

Nell, what is your problem? Easy: I was scared. I'd been married once when I was young. It hadn't worked out and had just kind of ended, without recriminations or hurt feelings. I'd thought that it was good that we'd been so civil about it, but Marty had told me, not long ago, that I should be troubled by how the marriage had dissolved with so little pain. Had the marriage meant so little to me? I wasn't sure how to respond to that. I had long since chosen to see that split as specific, not symptomatic — but it was hard to hold to that rationalization when I hadn't managed to find another serious relationship since.

Until James. With James it was different. Of course, I was older, and James was older than my husband had been when we married. I had my own life and I had thought I was happy, until we'd been thrown together. Now I had to rethink a lot of things. Why was I so reluctant to face this head-on? I loved him, he loved me. But where did that take us?

As I headed to West Chester the next morning, I struggled to understand why Pat Bowen would want to see me as well as Janet. She'd met me only the one time, and I didn't think we'd exactly bonded. Janet she knew only slightly better, and Pat had professed nothing but contempt for her late husband's historical interests. So why talk to either of us at all? At least I knew why I was headed to West Chester: it was possible that Pat held information that could point us toward who might have wanted her husband dead — information that both the police and James wanted. But if that was the case, why hadn't she simply told the police? Had they asked? Why call in the historical society and near-stranger me?

When I arrived and rang the doorbell at the CCHS, Janet pulled the door open immediately. "She's not here yet."

"I'm early," I replied. "I thought we should talk before Pat gets here. You still don't know why she's coming to see us? Or why she wanted me here?"

Janet shook her head. "Not really. It's not like we're close — I knew George better than I know her."

"Maybe she's got something she didn't feel comfortable telling the police," I speculated. "After all, she's almost too close to them, since they all live in the community here. We're more neutral."

"I can't believe she'd have anything worth hiding, although I suppose she might be feeling guilty about not sharing George's enthusiasms. Look, let me get right to it: Do you think George was killed because of something he found? On the Garrett farm?"

"I think it's possible. George had been

poking around here for a number of years, right? Nobody seemed to care. Suddenly he finds something that might actually be important, and he's killed pretty quickly after that. Maybe that's circumstantial, but I think it's suggestive."

Janet nodded. "I agree. Poor George — he finally found something and he never got to enjoy it. So who would care about two very old bodies enough to kill George?"

"Wakeman is the obvious suspect, because he wouldn't want his pet project to be derailed or held up. But I have trouble getting my head around that because, first, he came to me to ask to do a full historical analysis of the place. I told him up front that I wouldn't be party to any cover-up if we found something he didn't like. He said he was okay with that."

"Maybe he knew there was something to find and wanted to be prepared," Janet suggested.

"Maybe. But if he knew, and he suspected it would become public, why kill George? Plus, he's the one who called in the FBI from the start. If he'd wanted to hush things up, he'd have done better leaving the investigation to the local guys. Heck, he could have paid them off to keep quiet."

"So you think he's really not involved?"

Janet asked.

"Based on what I know about him, and what he's done, I do. I don't think he had anything to do with George's death."

"Then who?" Janet asked.

We were interrupted by the ringing of the doorbell. "That'll be Pat — I'll go let her in. Why don't you wait here?"

I sat and thought about what I'd just said. I didn't believe that Wakeman was implicated in this crime. Sure, he was rough around the edges, but he had a solid public reputation. He'd taken charge of more than one floundering local project and made it happen, usually on time and on budget. Would he sacrifice the reputation he'd built over the years for the sake of one small suburban development? Unlikely. I thought he was more of a realist than that.

Janet returned with Pat in tow. "Would anybody like coffee? Tea?"

"Can we just get this over with?" Pat said. "I know I'm the one who asked to meet you, but I've got a house full of relatives, and I've got to get back soon."

"Of course, no problem," Janet said. Janet's office was like mine in that it had a settee and a couple of chairs, so the three of us settled into a rough circle. Pat took a deep breath before jumping straight in.

"You must think I'm crazy, what with George's funeral tomorrow and all. But I had to get out of the house. It's bad enough having the kids and grandkids around, much as I love them, but then there are all the people in the neighborhood who keep showing up with casseroles, and then I have to repeat the same damn details, over and over. I mean, it's wonderful that he had so many friends, but I needed some space." She paused to collect herself. "I've been thinking of what we talked about before, about the stuff George liked to collect. I'm sorry I dumped it all on you and ran, Janet, but I wanted to get it out of my sight. I couldn't bear to see it sitting there in the garage."

She turned to me. "Ms. Pratt, I've read about you in the *Inquirer,* and I know your Society is one of the best of its kind in the country, and I want George to have the best. If he found something important, I want him to get the recognition he deserves for it."

She shut her eyes for a moment, fighting for control, and when she opened them, she began again. "George always loved history. When the kids were little he dragged us on every tour within a hundred miles. We even took the kids to see Gettysburg, where they were bored silly. Williamsburg, one vacation. He'd always hoped to visit Monticello, but we never found the time. Then the kids grew up and left home, and I really didn't care about all that stuff, so the trips stopped. But George still cared. Don't get me wrong — we'd been married a long time, and I had my own interests and George had his. And one of his was roaming the countryside looking for bits and pieces of history. You know, foundations of old buildings he'd read about, or just tracing the paths of battles. He had plenty to keep him busy around here. I didn't pay much attention after a while, although he'd keep coming to me with his latest treasure, all excited. Even up to the end . . . He was so wound up, and I just ignored him."

She looked down at her lap, trying to hold back tears. "And now you regret it?" I said gently.

"I do." Then Pat looked up again. "Was this obsession with collecting old stuff what got him killed?"

That seemed to be my territory. "It's . . . possible. It looks like George had been where those older bodies were found shortly before . . . we found him, so it's pretty likely he discovered the bodies, and took a couple of small items with him as proof. They were in those boxes you brought in. Do you know if George spent time on that farm?"

Pat nodded. "Oh, sure — he'd known the Garrett family all his life. It's kind of rare that you find a place that's been in the family as long as that one had, until Ezra took it into his head to sell it."

"Why did he decide to sell?" I asked. "I mean, did he want the money, or did Wakeman sweet-talk him into it somehow?"

Pat shook her head. "George and I talked about it. It wasn't anything complicated. Ezra Garrett had two kids, and only Eddie — the younger one — wanted to stay on and keep the dairy business going. His brother, William, didn't want anything to do with it. Anyway, selling it made sense financially. Once Ezra decided to sell, he planned ahead. He didn't want to see a ticky-tacky housing development there — we've got enough of those already — so he decided he'd sell it before he died. He did his research. He didn't want another corporate park, either, but he saw something about Wakeman's plans for a structured community, and they got to talking, and he finally sold it to Wakeman's company for a nice piece of change. The kids got their share. And I'll give Wakeman and his people credit — he's been taking his time, getting to know people around here. He's smart. I think he'll make a good job of it. Of course, I may not stick around to see it. Now that George is gone, I'll probably sell the house and move closer to our kids. I'd hate to have to drive by that pond every time I want to get groceries."

"I can understand that," I said. I thought for a moment. "So, from what you're saying, it doesn't sound as though your husband posed any obstacle to Wakeman and his project, at least, not in the long run."

"Not to Wakeman, no. Maybe some of the guys who worked for him. Heck, you know what the economy's been like these past few years. People want jobs, sooner rather than later. This is going to be a big project, spread over a couple of years. Maybe Wakeman's people didn't want to wait around while the boss admired the views and took the township people out to lunch."

"And someone thought George's discovery would interfere with their timetable? Janet, you'd know better than I would," I said, turning to her.

Janet answered quickly. "You know the whole Duffy's Cut mess?" When I nodded, she went on, "There was a lot of argument over that when it was found, like between the railroad and the archeologists and historians. The railroad wouldn't let the historians finish excavating the site because they had to keep the trains running, so who knows how many other bodies are buried there, really. So let's say those people who wanted to see the dig done right last time around and didn't get their way are all primed to fight now if somebody says, 'hey, there's a historic burial ground here,' what're they going to do? Shouldn't somebody check it out before this Philadelphia guy sticks a parking lot over it?"

Which was why I had been brought in, to provide at least a veneer of historical respectability to the project. "I can't say I blame them. Once history like that is lost, it's gone forever."

"Nell," Janet said, "you know the man. Would Wakeman condone a cover-up, literally in this case, to speed up the construction process? Or at least, look the other way?"

I shook my head. "As I said before, I can't see it. Of course, I haven't met any of the people who work for him. Look, Pat, there's something we need to know."

"What's that?" Pat asked, rousing herself from her misery.

"Who else besides you would George have told about what he found, or thought he

230

found? He didn't bring it to Janet here. Did he have friends who shared his interest? What about the township?"

"That's more than one question," Pat said. "Friends? Not so much. He was kind of a loner, liked to ramble around with a pocket full of maps, maybe a GPS locator so he could mark where the finds came from, maybe some binoculars and a camera. I don't think he knew anyone else who wanted to do that in all weather. Now, the township's another question. You see, George was zoning officer, so he would've had a legal and a moral obligation to inform them if he'd made a significant historical find."

"And had he told them, do you know?"

"I don't know. I mean, if he had found those bodies, it was pretty recently. And the lines of communication around here are kind of blurry, anyway. Like, there are official meetings, schedules, that kind of thing, and he would have had to submit something in writing. But that doesn't mean he didn't run into someone else from the township at the hardware store, and take him aside and give him a heads-up about what he'd found."

"Was he close to anyone in particular?"

"He wasn't exactly buddies with anyone.

He got along okay with them. But he'd gone to work for the township because he thought it was his civic duty, not because he wanted to hang out with the guys."

"Who would he have had to report this to?" I asked.

"As far as official reporting, I think he'd have to tell Marvin Jackson — he's the township manager — and maybe the historic commission. Like I said, I don't know if he'd gotten around to it, or if he had time. He'd only just found . . . the bodies, I guess." She stood up abruptly, her motions jerky. "I'd better get back before people worry."

Janet stood up as well and, after a moment's hesitation, gave her a quick hug, which surprised Pat. "Pat, thank you so much for coming to us with this," Janet said. "I know it can't be easy for you, especially right now."

Pat impatiently brushed away more tears. "I had to do something. I mean, I laughed at George's little hobby, but I never thought it'd get him killed. That's not right. He was a good man, a good father, a hard worker. He didn't deserve to die in that muddy puddle, so close to home. If I know something that can help you find whoever did this, I want to help." She glanced at her watch and stood up. "I've got to go. I'll be tied up for the next couple of days, as you can guess, but if you think of anything you need to know, call me, okay?"

"Of course. Thank you again." I wavered for a moment: I barely knew this woman, and I'm not a hugger by nature, but she'd just lost her husband and she wanted to make it right — and if anybody looked like they needed a hug, she did. So I reached out to her, and she leaned against me, just for a moment.

"Thank you," she said in a small voice. Then she turned and left quickly, with Janet trailing behind her to let her out.

Janet was back a minute later. "Well." She dropped back into her chair. "What do we do now?"

"I . . . I'm not sure. I suppose I'll start by telling the FBI what Pat told us about George and his relationship with the township, and who he might have told about his find."

Janet nodded, with a smile. "You're tight with that agent, right?"

There was no point in arguing. "Yes, and he'll want to know. I know it's not exactly evidence, but it gives us a clearer picture of what could have happened. I'll see him this afternoon. But I could use your insights about approaching the township."

"What do you mean?"

I tried to gather my thoughts. "I don't come from around here, so I don't know who's who or even what problems the township is facing. It would help to know things like who the players are, how they get along. Do they usually agree or are there a lot of battles? What kind of financial shape is the township in, and what would this development project mean to it, in terms of jobs and tax revenues and stuff like that? Who would think it's important that it go forward ASAP, and who would like to slow or stop it, see it go away completely?"

"You don't ask for much, do you?" Janet said in a sarcastic but not unkind tone. "I don't live in the township, so I can't answer you directly. But I can find out who does know, and who'd be willing to talk to you or your agent friend."

"That would be a start. How good are you at diplomacy? Subterfuge?"

She looked blankly at me for a moment, and then her face brightened. "Oh, you mean asking who knows what without being obvious about it?"

"Yes, sort of. Don't make it look like you're pumping them for information. We can't lose sight of the fact that somebody killed George, and it was probably over this. And it wasn't even in the heat of the moment, because that person moved George after he was dead, most likely to divert attention from where it happened and what was there. I can't ask you to put yourself at risk."

"Message received, and I will be careful. But I guess I have to say that I want to help, too. I liked George. He was a decent guy, and made a point to chat with me for a minute when he visited here. I'm sure he never figured his hobby would be dangerous."

Now I was checking my watch. "I'd better go too. Take care, okay?"

"I will. Thanks, Nell. Good luck."

CHAPTER 18

James was sitting in his car reading something in a file when I pulled into my tiny
driveway. "Am I late or are you early?" I
asked when I climbed out of my car.

He smiled. "Neither. Both. No big deal.
My interviews went more quickly than I
expected."

I fished my keys out of my bag and headed
toward my door, and he followed. "Are they
something you can talk about?" I asked,
opening the door — then crossing quickly
to the other side of the room to open
windows. It was getting stuffy in the August
heat, but I didn't leave the air-conditioning
on when I wasn't around.

"Maybe."

I waited for him to ask where I'd been,
but he didn't, so I volunteered. "I may have
something useful. Have you eaten? I think I
have cold cuts and stuff. I haven't done
much shopping lately." *Mostly because I've*

been spending a lot of time at your place.

"Fine." He pulled off his jacket and draped it over a chair.

He came up behind me as I was peering into the rather empty depths of my refrigerator, and turned me around to face him. "I haven't said hello." He then kissed me thoroughly, and I wondered if we were going to skip lunch altogether. But he was the one to break it off. "We've got things to do, so let's eat."

"Right. Food. Bread, turkey, some kind of limp lettuce. There's beer." Which I kept only for him, since I didn't like the stuff much.

"Whatever," he said. "Mind if I plug in my laptop? I've bookmarked some sites."

"Sure, go ahead." I assembled a couple of sandwiches on bread that I didn't dare examine too closely, found a miraculously unopened bag of potato chips, and presented him with a loaded plate, then took my own and sat down next to him.

He pushed the laptop aside to focus on his sandwich. "You said you had something new?"

I chewed for a moment, then swallowed. "After I talked to you yesterday I got a call from Janet Butler at CCHS, and she said George Bowen's wife wanted to talk to us."

"The dead man's wife? I thought you said she'd be tied up with funeral arrangements and the like."

"That's what I'd figured, but I think she feels guilty about blowing off George's hobby and wanted to make it right." As we ate I proceeded to fill him in on what Pat Bowen had told Janet and me about who George might have told about his find. "So, in my humble opinion, you need to talk with Wakeman's senior staff, and as I've said before, with some of the guys at the township. And in the case of the township, maybe without the local police getting in the way."

"I do know how to do my job, Nell," he said.

"Of course you do, but you don't know local politics or who's buddies with who. I asked Janet to nose around and see if she could find someone you could talk to. You need someone who's willing to share the internal stuff."

"What, you'll actually let me take part in your investigation?"

I had to check to make sure he was joking. "Hey, I'm just trying to help. You're the one who can dig into phone records and financial backgrounds and all that stuff. I'm looking to work out the local dynamic and that takes some insider information. My big question now is, if George comes home all excited about his big find, who does he tell? You can ask everybody he's ever known, or everybody in his address book or on his Christmas list. I asked Pat directly, and she wasn't sure."

James held up both hands. "I surrender. You're right."

"Music to my ears." I grinned at him. "Look, I'll let you know if Janet comes up with a contact for you."

"Please do. So, are you ready to look for a place? Unless you'd rather not?" He looked at me as if challenging me to back off.

"No, no, we should do this." I stood up and took our few dishes into the tiny kitchen. "Do you want to lay out the basics? Size, location, number of bedrooms, all that stuff?"

He sat back in his chair. "You go first."

He wasn't going to make this easy, was he? "Okay. I don't think we'll find an apartment that would work. And there's something about the term *condo* that makes me think of plastic. I've told you before, I like living in the suburbs — it keeps work and home separate — but I can see that might be difficult for you. I'm not wedded to the idea of a large house — a row house in a nice neighborhood would work. And I want a bigger kitchen and more closets. Your turn."

He was smiling. "So far we're pretty much on the same page. You're right about the burbs — I hate to waste time commuting, although keeping two cars in the city may be difficult, or at least expensive. What do you think of Marty's place?"

Marty lived in a nice, tree-lined neighborhood within walking distance of the Society. Her row house was narrow but had high ceilings. Still, from what I'd seen of it, I remembered it as cramped, and that was with only her living in it. "Why, is she selling it?"

"No, I'm just holding it up as a model."

"Not big enough for the two of us," I said firmly. "We'd be bumping into each other all the time." Neither of us was what you would call a small person.

"Okay. You want wider?"

"Yes. And maybe more windows, more light. I like it here because there are windows on all sides. And I want more elbow room if there are two of us. Don't you?"

"Yes. I wasn't sure if you would. More stuff to keep clean."

"We'll hire someone," I replied. "I hate housework. We're busy people, and we can afford it. What about condition? You into rehabbing a place?"

James skewered me with a look. "You seriously think either of us has the time to mess with woodwork and painting?"

Of course, older houses — which I preferred — always had something that needed fixing, but he was right. "Good point. So, how do we do this?"

"As I told you, you can take virtual tours of almost any place online these days. Of course, they're set up to make the place look good, so they don't show you the highway running right over the house, or tell you that you're in the airport flight path."

"I'm not going to decide on a place by looking at a two-inch picture."

"You don't have to. Tomorrow's Sunday — there should be plenty of open houses. Pick out some you like and we'll go look at them. I've already bookmarked a few."

We looked at the online listings. There were plenty to choose from, but many we easily eliminated for one reason or another. One looked too dark, even from the thumbnail pictures. Another had no parking. This one was too close to a major road; that one was too expensive, even with our combined incomes. After a while I was beginning to feel like Goldilocks, complaining that none of the porridge was "just right." "Am I being unreasonable, James?"

"I think we should walk through a few together. Things don't always look the same in reality."

"Okay. Maybe we should go through a house that we know we'll hate, too, just to get the patter right."

"Not a bad idea. Like a dry run. Are you into role-playing? Do you want to walk through and play happy homemaker and gush over the perfect cabinets and the cute bathroom tiles?"

"No. But if I did, you'd have to make manly noises about where you'd put your woodworking tools and the chain saw."

He shut his laptop with a snap. "I think we've passed the point of constructive virtual searching. We can put together a short list of three to five places to look at tomorrow. Deal?"

"Okay," I said hesitantly. "Can you take time off to go house hunting in the middle of a case?"

"Nell, I'm always in the middle of a case, usually more than one. But I'm allowed to have a life. Besides, half the people I need to talk to will be at George Bowen's funeral tomorrow. There's nothing that can't wait until Monday."

"All right then, we'll let it all wait." We

passed the rest of the day in companionable fashion, doing nothing more significant than grocery shopping. It felt nice.

The next morning James pulled out a couple of maps of the city and its environs and spread them all out on my dining table, then booted up his laptop and started plotting. I left him alone because he seemed to be having so much fun. I was willing to go wherever he chose, since I had no idea where to start and I was trying to keep an open mind. I plied him with coffee and store-bought crumpets until he declared that he had a plan.

"I think I've got five that are worth a look. More than that and they'll start running together in your head."

"Okay," I said amiably, finishing my second cup of coffee.

He gave me a sharp look but didn't say anything. Was I not acting eager enough?

We set off on our house odyssey about eleven. James was a surprisingly patient driver and seldom got lost, so I felt free to watch the neighborhoods we passed through. It was interesting to see how quickly they could change, even within a block or two. I could also trace some of the city's history just by looking at the transitions, from sturdy row-houses to modest individual homes to stately stone mansions or the other way around. I paid attention to where the public transit stops were and where the nearest amenities, like grocery stores and pharmacies, were located. And I felt a little out of my depth; it was hard to imagine actually living in any of these areas. I kept reminding myself that even Bryn Mawr had been unfamiliar once.

We toured all five places. The Realtors burbled on about school districts and property taxes, and I nodded and smiled — and didn't fall in love with any of them. There was always something wrong: too small, too dark, too inconveniently located. Not that I'd expected to hit the ball out of the park on the first try. After all, this was just an exploratory trip. But I was finding far more elements I didn't like than those that I did.

At four we called it quits and found a quiet coffee shop to recharge our batteries.

"What did you think?" James said carefully.

"There was nothing that wowed me," I admitted, stirring the foam of my cappuccino. "This is harder than it looks. How about you?"

He shrugged. "About the same. But there's more out there, if we can find the time to look."

"When's your lease up again?"

"End of the month. I can always flash my badge and lean on the rental agency, but I'd hate to do that. They'd miss renting to the returning students."

Not a lot of time to make a big decision, although that didn't seem to be troubling James. "No pressure, right?"

"Nell, if you're having doubts . . ."

"No, it's not that. You know, something's been bothering me about Pat Bowen."

James seemed startled at my abrupt change of topic. "About the murder?"

"Not so much that. But she said that she and George had kind of grown apart. He had his interests — in this case, local history — and she had hers, and they didn't seem to have anything together. Now she feels bad because he's gone and there's nothing she can do about it, except try to find out what happened. It's like she's lost him twice. How do couples avoid that? The drifting apart?"

"Nell, I don't know. I don't have a lot of experience in this. But — what's the expression? Don't borrow trouble? The Bowens must have been married for thirty years or more. You and I, we've got a long way to go before we get bored. Don't we?"

"I hope so." I reached out for his hand across the table, and we gazed meaningfully into each other's eyes until the busboy came over and grabbed our empty cups. We weren't very good at mushy.

He finally said, "So what now? Are you going to see Wakeman anytime soon?"

"We don't have anything planned, but he kind of makes up his own rules. I've got Lissa looking at the early history of the area, so maybe she can figure out who the old bodies were. The FBI still has them, right?"

"We do. It's not quite clear what we're supposed to do with them. Bury them somewhere nearby, I suppose."

"It would help if we know who they were — there might even be family around here somewhere. Anything else you need me to look for?"

"Not that I can think of. Just stay safe, will you?"

"I try, honestly. Things keep happening."

He gave me a look but didn't say anything more on the topic, and our parting was sweet but short when he drove me home. I waved as he left and returned to my small, lonely home.

CHAPTER 19

Bright and early Monday morning I was seated at my desk at the Society with a steaming cup of coffee in front of me (on a coaster, of course, to protect the mahogany) when Eric answered the phone, and called out, "Mr. Wakeman is here."

Without an appointment. I sighed. So much for a quiet time to gather my thoughts for the coming week. "Can you bring him upstairs, please?"

"Will do." Eric headed quickly for the elevator, while I tried to figure out what Wakeman could want from me now. Maybe he wanted to end our informal agreement? I was starting to think that would be fine with me. I still believed he should have gone to Janet Butler first, and I was glad she didn't hold it against me that Wakeman had more or less ignored her and her institution and gone straight to me and the Society.

When Wakeman arrived, striding ahead of

Eric, he was not alone; he had with him a young man I thought I recognized from the press conference. I stood up to greet them.

"You've met Mason here?" Wakeman nodded toward the man next to him.

"You were at the press conference, weren't you?" I said to him.

"Scott Mason," he said, extending him hand and flashing a smile with a lot of white teeth, and we shook. "I'm the manager for the Paoli project."

I had to assume he liked saying that, because I'd heard it before. Of course, he had probably forgotten we'd already met. "Well, what do you need from me today? Do you want me to call Lissa in?" I wasn't sure she was in the building, but if it involved the history of the site, she should hear it from the horse's mouth.

"Nah, you can fill her in later," Wakeman said. "Listen, is that FBI agent any closer to solving this Bowen thing?" he asked bluntly. Not one to beat around the bush.

"No. Frankly, I'm not sure why you asked the FBI to participate. It only annoyed the local police, by implying that you didn't think they could do the job."

"Not sure they can," Wakeman answered. I wasn't going to comment, since I had no direct knowledge of that police force, but I was pretty sure having an FBI agent forced upon them by someone who didn't even live in the community did not sit well. He went on, "Look, I'm not here to argue police procedures. Mason here thinks we can move forward on schedule in spite of this murder problem. But we don't want to look like jerks, like that guy dying doesn't matter. It does, of course, and we want to get that message out. What I want from you is to get this story together fast. You know, the history of the property, the history of the battle — real local color. Check with the township, find out what other historic projects they've supported — isn't there an old mill or something they restored? Or was it a blacksmith shop? Anyway, check those out. Make it clear that they're on board with us going ahead. If you find anything good, we can name a road after one of the dead guys or something."

I kept a smile plastered on my face and silently counted to ten. Wakeman was crude and rude, no question. But I had to add *shrewd* to that list. No matter what his real feelings were about history and the Revolutionary War, he was first and foremost a businessman, and he had a project to advance. Waiting cost money and momentum. He wanted me to put together a pretty story about the poor fallen dead, lying there in that field for a couple of centuries. I could do that, couldn't I?

"When do you want this, Mr. Wakeman?" I said sweetly.

"End of the week?" he said. He might have smiled, for maybe a tenth of a second. Had he expected me to refuse?

"I think that can be managed," I replied. It was Monday — that at least gave us a week. Then a thought occurred to me: here sat the project manager in front of me. I needed to talk to said project manager, and see if I could figure out if he had anything remotely resembling a motive for wanting to silence George Bowen. I turned to him. "Mr. Mason —" I began.

"Scott, please." He smiled eagerly. He didn't look much past thirty, but maybe that meant he was extra hungry to prove himself and impress his boss.

"Scott," I corrected myself. "Can I assume you've spent time on the site or in the township and you know the people involved there?"

"Of course. Why?"

"It might be helpful to us if you could fill me in on their personalities, their roles within the community. Then I'd be able to pitch what we write more accurately, to be more effective." That might be BS, but that didn't mean it wasn't true. "That is, if you can spare him for an hour, Mr. Wakeman?"

"Yeah, sure. Scott, you stay. But don't forget that meeting at eleven. Thanks, Ms. Pratt." He stood up and strode out the door, and Eric raced to catch up to escort him out.

Scott and I were left alone with each other. "I hope you don't mind, Scott," I said. "I live in Bryn Mawr, not that far from Paoli, but I won't pretend to know the local personalities in Goshen Township. Have you been involved in the negotiations with them from the start?"

"More or less. Well, Mitch has had his eye on that property for a long time, but he waited until he knew he had it locked in before starting any real planning. That's when he brought me on board. You know much about the town planning process?"

"I can't say that I do." I thought for a moment. "Listen, do you mind if I see if our researcher, Lissa Penrose, is in the building? I'd like her to hear what you have to say, and then you wouldn't have to repeat yourself. I'll have to go look for her, but if she's here, she should be right down the hall. Would you like some coffee while I go get her?"

"Uh, okay," he said.

"Great. Be right back." As I passed Eric's desk, I said, "I'm going to find Lissa. Could you get Mr. Mason some coffee?"

"Sure thing," Eric said.

I hurried down the hall, past the elevator, and into the processing room. Luckily Lissa was there, deep in conversation with Ben — again. "Lissa?" I called out.

She looked up, said something to Ben, then came over. "You need something, Nell?"

"Yes. Wakeman was just here again and he wants a historically accurate account about his project site — and the old bodies — by the end of the week. I've got the project manager in my office now, and I'd like you to sit in while we talk. And then you'll have to hit the ground running, I'm afraid."

"I can handle it," Lissa said calmly. "Ben's been filling me in on a lot of the details on the history and the battle, which will save me time."

"Great. Let's go. Oh, and if some of my questions seem a little, uh, oblique, just go with it, okay?"

"You're still looking at the murder?" she said, raising one eyebrow.

"Yes, kind of. I can't be too direct, but this man might know something that would help." Or he might be a killer, for all I knew, despite his fresh-faced appearance; he certainly had a strong motive for seeing this project continue. But I was on my own turf, surrounded by people, and I thought I could be tactful if I tried. I just didn't want Lissa to put her foot in anything by accident.

I led the way back to my office and introduced Lissa and Scott. We settled ourselves on the settee and flanking chairs, and I prompted Lissa to describe what she had done so far — in less than a week! — and what she planned to do next. Scott seemed pleased, nodding enthusiastically.

When Lissa had about wrapped up, I broke in. "Does that sound like the kind of material you had in mind, Scott?"

"It does, precisely. I have to say, this has been kind of an intriguing process. How much do you know about Mitchell Wakeman?" Scott asked.

I guessed he was itching to talk about his boss, who he obviously admired. "Mainly what I read in the papers. How long have you been working for him?"

"Since I graduated from college. I have a degree in architectural engineering, but Mitchell Wakeman likes everybody to get his hands dirty, so I've done a lot of things since I started working for him. This project is different, though."

"How do you mean?" I asked, honestly curious.

"Well, he's done a lot of big important buildings in the city, as I'm sure you know. He's made his name, and he's made a lot of money — he's not shy about either one. And he's given a lot back to the community, too."

"So what is special about this project?" I prompted.

"It's kind of like he wants to distill everything he's learned in his career and create this kind of ideal community, you know?"

I nodded. "I think so. The way he's described it to me, it would include homes for a range of lifestyles, from condos to fairly large freestanding houses, plus communal areas for the residents and basic amenities like shops. Have I got that right?"

"More or less. But he doesn't want it to be an insular community, closed off from the established local community. He wants it to be welcoming for area residents, too. Like with a small concert hall or movie theater, to draw other people in. It's not like a gated community, all closed in. He took a long time to pick his site, and he thought about it carefully. If you live in the suburbs, I'm sure you're aware of urban sprawl."

I had to laugh. "Yes, I've seen that even in the decade or so I've lived around here."

"It's certainly true in Chester County. Mitch wants to slow down that growth and create something that harmonizes with what's already there, while at the same time make it efficient, green — all that good stuff. It's a multiyear plan, and so far you've probably seen only the first phase."

"Wow," Lissa said. "This really sounds Utopian. And he thinks it can work? I mean, is it financially viable?"

"We think so." Scott nodded. "Again, he's been moving carefully. We've run the numbers, and we keep doing it as circumstances change. He's got enough contacts in and around Philadelphia — not to mention quite a few landmark projects that he's brought in on budget — that he was able to line up really solid funding. I know, it's rare, but if anyone can do it, Mitchell Wakeman can."

"I am impressed," I said, and I meant it. Now for my big question, for which Scott had given me a perfect opening: "So, tell me, Scott — does this discovery of these bodies, both new and old, throw a wrench into the project?"

"I'll be honest: I don't know. We have always intended to preserve the historic and physical integrity of the site to the greatest extent possible. I'm sure that there are many things yet to be discovered all around the area, and relics pop up all the time. Will it delay ground breaking? I don't think so, or if it does, not for long. Did Mitch show you the spot where they were found — before he knew they were there, of course?"

"I think we saw every square foot of the property, but I can't say I know where those men were buried," I replied.

"You probably went past it when you came in. It's a cluster of old-growth trees, on the side toward Paoli. Of course, we wouldn't be callous enough to build a home over that particular place, but we never intended to. We always planned to retain that as a buffer or screen between the homes and the road. So, to get back to the point, what we want from you here at the Society is perhaps above and beyond what is necessary: we want to learn more about these poor soldiers, if that's what they were, not cover them up. If they were local we want to know it. If they were Hessians or something, we want to know that, too. I'm not a historian, but I don't believe we should ignore our history, especially when it's right under our noses like this."

I had to admit, Scott gave a good speech. I really wanted to believe Scott Mason. Was there any reason why I shouldn't have? "Will a historic discovery of this kind upset any of the funders?"

"I don't think so. We haven't spoken with them directly yet — we were waiting to see what you people found out first — but they take the long view, and they've seen things like this before."

Check that point off the list. "What's it been like, working with the township staff?"

"I'm not surprised you ask, Nell," Scott said. "Again, we approached this cautiously — we didn't just ride in roughshod and tell the local government that we were building a whole new development in the midst of their township whether they liked it or not. That's not the best way to get things done, and we do value their cooperation."

"I assume you need township approvals of some sort? Have you run into any opposition? Any naysayers?" I wondered what George had thought about the project.

"We are well on the path to obtaining all necessary permitting. We've met no substantial obstacles. After all, we're becoming a part of their community. We need their infrastructure — water, sewer, power, schools, snowplowing. The whole range. And they need to know that those will not impose any new financial burden on the current citizens of the township. The tax revenues generated by this project will be far higher than they've been historically for the dairy farm. It's a win-win situation for everyone."

I was getting kind of overwhelmed. This sounded like the best of all possible worlds, a thoughtful and conscientious project intended to be fully integrated with the existing community and to actually improve the quality of life there. He almost had me sold.

"Scott, it all sounds wonderful, and I'm glad you came to us for help. Tell me, is there any township employee you've dealt with more than the others?"

"Well, the township manager, Marvin Jackson. He's a paid employee of the township. Then there was George Bowen — he was the zoning officer and also sat on the board of supervisors. That's an elected position. It's a small group, so there's a lot of overlap among the committees. Why do you ask?"

Because I'm investigating George's murder. I didn't say that. But now I knew that Scott had known George and had obviously worked with him to some extent. "I'd like to learn if there have been other historic discoveries within their boundaries and how they've handled them. Archeology has changed, and public opinion swings back and forth. If Mr. Wakeman wants us to make the strongest case for this project, then we need to know what's happened in the past."

"Of course. Was there anything else? Because I should leave for that meeting Mitch mentioned."

"Did you have any questions, Lissa?"

"I think you covered it, Nell. I really would like to see the details on how the township set up the historic district — it could be a good model."

"No problem." Scott beamed. "I'm sure the township sent us a copy for our files. I'll fax a copy over as soon as I get back to the office."

"Thank you, Scott," Lissa said. "That's all I need for now."

"So I think we've covered it," I said firmly. "We'll definitely have something for you by the end of the week. And thank you for taking the time to talk to us."

Scott stood up and smiled. "Nell, I really believe in this project, and I'm proud to be part of it. If you need anything else, just let me know. Lissa, it was nice to see you again."

"Same here," Lissa said.

"Let me walk you out." I escorted him downstairs and to the door, then made my way slowly back to my office. His story hung together, and I knew of nothing that contradicted it — but didn't explain why the body of George Bowen had ended up in the pond. James could look into the financial aspects of it, in case Scott had been lying when he said the funders weren't troubled by finding a few old skeletons. If it turned out that Mitchell Wakeman had strangled George himself and somebody had a video of it, it might be a different scenario, but that seemed more and more unlikely to me. Wakeman was a rare bird: exactly what he appeared to be, an honest businessman, even if he was a bit rough around the edges.

When I got back to the office, Lissa was chatting with Eric. "You were pretty quiet in there," I commented.

"I didn't think that township management was relevant to what I'm supposed to be looking for. I'd be happy to explore any earlier historic projects in Goshen. I'm sorry if I misunderstood what you wanted."

"Don't worry about it — if Wakeman and his people keep dropping in unannounced, it's hard to plan. But if we get a meeting set up with the township officials, I'd like you there. Who knows — maybe there were historic projects they *didn't* pursue, for lack of funding or interest or whatever."

"I'd be happy to come, thanks. You know," she said, "I'm beginning to get really excited by this project, if it lives up to its own publicity. And of course, now it's personal — I really do want to know who the skeletons were. I'm glad Wakeman doesn't plan to mess with that part of the site."

"Me, too — and I'm glad he knows he shouldn't. Well, you've gotten a lot to get done in a short time. Let me know what you come up with and we can go over it before you put the final draft together. Okay?"

"Sure. I'm looking forward to it."

CHAPTER 20

No sooner had the dust settled from Wakeman's departure and that of his henchman Scott than Marty Terwilliger showed up. *So much for my getting anything done this morning.* "Hi, stranger!" I greeted her. "I haven't seen much of you lately."

Marty dropped into a chair in front of my desk. To my eye she was looking a bit sleeker than I'd seen her before.

"I've been, uh, busy," she said, trying to stifle a smile.

"With a certain professor?" I countered.

"Yup. I was going to tell you about it — since I guess I figure I owe you, what with James and all — but like I said, I've been busy."

"I'm glad," I said. Marty had been on her own for a while now, and I thought she deserved somebody in her life — other than her dead ancestors. And she needed to get out of the Society now and then, get some fresh air. "So, are you just touching base, or do you need me for something?"

"Both. Maybe. Let's start with this murder thing out your way, on that piece of land Wakeman owns."

I'd long since given up asking how Marty knew about everything that happened in Pennsylvania and half of New Jersey; the answer was usually from one of her relatives. "What about it?"

"Wakeman asked you to look at the history of the land, right?"

"Yes," I said slowly.

"And that's right down the road from the Paoli battle site, right?"

"Yes again. Look, is this a Terwilliger family thing?" Marty's ancestor John Terwilliger had played an important role in the Revolution in and around Philadelphia, and Marty had been sorting through his extensive family papers for years, only a small part of the Terwilliger Collection she had Rich working on.

"Sort of. Do I have to explain about General Wayne?"

I held up one hand. "No, I think I've got that covered. I've been doing a little research of my own on the battle, although Lissa's been handling the bulk of it. It seems like Wayne was not a happy camper after the battle and wanted to prove the dismal failure was not his fault. Right?"

"Close enough. It was one of the nastiest battles of the war, and Wayne was caught with his pants down in a place he knew well. He insisted on a court martial to prove he was right, and he was in fact cleared."

"So what's all this got to do with the murder? Wait — how much do you know about that?"

"Jimmy's filled me in on the bare outline. We'll come back to him. Anyway, you find a dead guy in the pond — you know, you've got to cut that out, Nell — and it turns out he had found a couple of bodies himself not far away, except those were old enough that they could have been soldiers from that battle. Jimmy's people are running the forensics on that. Right so far?"

"I guess." I couldn't see where she was going with this, apart from her usual tendency to stick a finger in every pie she could.

Marty seemed to be enjoying herself. "You could count the Brits' casualties from that battle on one hand. They made sure everybody knew how well they'd done — although that kind of backfired on them, because the patriots got peeved that the redcoats had pulled off a sneak attack and gotten away unscathed. But anyway, if it turns out that there's a dead British soldier involved, and he was part of that battle, it would kind of change history, just a bit."

"And George Bowen, who was a history buff, would know that," I said, almost to myself. "Wait — why are you asking if there was a British soldier?"

"I heard about the buttons," she replied smugly. I didn't bother to ask how. "So if that's the case, it kind of ups the ante, doesn't it? So what would George do next?"

"That's what we've been trying to figure out. Quite possibly, if I were him, I'd do a little in-depth research on the battle, and then try to find out who the dead soldiers were. If that's even possible. Sounds like the records for that battle are a little sketchy."

"I agree. Have you talked to the Chester County Historical Society people?"

"Yes, of course I have. They knew George there, but he didn't bring this to them before he died."

"Huh. Maybe he didn't have time. But the logical conclusion is that he must have told somebody, and that somebody must have been pretty unhappy about it, and most likely that got him killed."

"Marty, James and I have already gotten that far. The question is, who would care enough to kill him? Who stood to gain anything? Wakeman's project doesn't sound like it's going to be affected, so I don't think it's related. Doesn't that more or less clear his people?"

Marty sagged just a little. "That's where I get stuck, too. You and Lissa come up with anything about the land?"

"Not yet, but we've barely had time to get started. Although Wakeman was here this morning, and he wants results by Friday, so I'm guessing we'll know a whole lot more by then."

"That'll be the old stuff. Bowen was killed last week, and not by a ghost. Who're you looking at for it?"

I tried not to laugh. "Marty, that's not my job, remember? That's the local detectives', and the FBI's, at least in part."

"Yeah, but you're the interface between the history of the place and the modern investigation. You're in a unique position. Tell me you haven't thought about it!"

"Of course I've thought about it."

"And?" she challenged.

I tried to line my thoughts up before I spoke. "I don't think the list of suspects is very long, since it's unlikely this is a random killing. Wakeman has a stake in it — he's been planning on developing this property for a while, and I will say his plans sound pretty impressive, from what I've heard. But he said to my face that he thinks things will go forward regardless."

"I've always heard that he's a straight shooter, and I can't see him killing anyone over this, even if it is his dream project. Next?"

"Unless George's wife, Pat, took out a large life insurance policy on him a couple of months ago, I'm inclined to think she's in the clear." James had no doubt already checked out things like insurance policies and the family's finances. "Of course, maybe George brought home one too many pieces of muddy junk that pushed her over the edge."

"Unless she's built like a linebacker, she couldn't have carried him and dumped him in the pond — that would have taken a man. Next?"

"Wakeman's project manager, Scott Mason, is young and eager. Maybe he saw George's discovery as a threat to the project and thought he'd do his boss a favor by covering it up and eliminating George?" Even if he was wrong, he might have believed it.

"Maybe. Keep him on the list. Who else?"

"There are the people at the township

who could have a motive. I met a couple of them at that press conference the other day. It's their town, and I'm sure somebody there must have some negative feelings about Wakeman's plans."

"Anybody want to see this project shut down?"

I shook my head. "Marty, I don't know. I haven't talked to any of them, or at least, I haven't asked them that kind of question."

"Can you get to them?"

I was about to say no when I remembered that Scott had said he planned to meet with them. "The project manager said he'd be talking with them about past projects in the township that had historical significance. You know, see how they presented the idea to the public, how they found the funding — that kind of thing. I'm sure he'd be willing to include me if I asked. It's no doubt in public records, but it would be easier to get it directly."

"So ask."

I was beginning to feel pressured. "Fine, I will. Marty, why does this matter so much to you?"

"Because I want you and Jimmy to get on with your lives."

"You think a murder investigation gets in the way of that? Heck, for us, that's business as usual. And what happened to your no-meddling policy?" This seemed to be a discussion we'd had before.

"I got tired of waiting. Are you even looking for a place?"

"Yes," I said, hating the defensive note in my voice. "We looked at a few places yesterday, but nothing's been right. Can't we get through this investigation first? With Wakeman pushing, it shouldn't be long."

Marty made a rude noise. "And then there'll be another investigation or something else in the way. Jimmy's a very patient guy, but you've got to move forward, Nell. He's not going to wait forever for you to figure things out."

"I know. I get it. Can we take this conversation in some other direction, please?"

She gave me one more searching look, then reverted to her favorite subject, the Terwilliger Collection and the status of its cataloging. It was nearly noon by the time she stood up, and said, "I'm going to go check on Rich in the processing room and see what's he's accomplished while I've been . . . busy. See you later." And she was gone, as abruptly as she'd arrived. Apparently her relationship with Ethan hadn't mellowed her all that much, or maybe she was saving all her directness for me.

"Eric?" I called out.

"Yes, ma'am?" he responded quickly.

"Do I have any meetings scheduled for the rest of the week?"

"Nope, all clear."

"Then I'm going to try to set up a meeting in Goshen, so I'd be out of the office whenever I get it scheduled. I'll let you know." I picked up Scott Mason's card from my blotter and punched in his number. It went to voice mail, but I left a message saying I'd like to be included in any meeting he held with the Goshen township officials. Then I dug back into the pile of paperwork that seemed to multiply on my desk when I wasn't looking.

I had just pulled out my file on the Wakeman project and was searching for the phone numbers I needed when Shelby stuck her head in my door. "You busy?" she asked.

"Always." I smiled to soften the comment. "You need something?"

"I need lunch, and I feel like I haven't had a conversation with you for about a month. Wanna go get something to eat?"

"It couldn't have been that long," I protested, flipping through my daily calendar. No, not a month, only a week. And I was hungry. Dealing with Mitchell Wakeman was hard work. "Sure, as long as we don't take too long. Where?"

"The sandwich place down the street is fine. It's not the food, it's the company, right?"

I gathered up my bag and led the way out of the building. As we walked the block or so to the restaurant, I said, "You know, you're right — I haven't seen much of you for a couple of weeks. It's this Wakeman project thing — you've heard the rumblings about that?" There was nothing secret about it anymore.

"Of course, but you can fill me in."

"Well, the result has been that I've been spending a lot of time out in Chester County rather than here at my office. I hope that won't last much longer."

"What's the man like?"

"I'll tell you over lunch." We entered the restaurant, ordered sandwiches, and settled in. As we ate I told her about Wakeman and Goshen and the recent murder (George) and the earlier, more mysterious deaths (soldiers?) and how the FBI had come to be involved, and suburban housing in general, and the state of the union, and . . . The next time I looked at my watch, an hour had passed. I couldn't remember if Shelby had said more than ten words. "I'm sorry, I've been babbling on. Everything okay with you?"

"No problems. Fundraising is always slow in summer, since all the people with money are out of town. I'll be busier by September. How's the house hunting going?"

I looked at her quizzically. "Did Marty put you up to asking? You're tag-teaming me now?"

"What? No, of course not! I haven't seen much of Marty, either — usually she pops in at least once a day. It's been a lonely few weeks. But from where I sit, it looks like you've been dragging your heels with Mr. Agent Man. He wants you to move in together. You don't want to?"

"No, it's not that." Was it? "But we've both been busy, and we haven't decided what we're looking for, and we've seen a couple of places but they just weren't right —"

Shelby cut me off. "Listen to yourself! I've never heard such a lame string of excuses. The man's a catch and he's in love with you. What's your problem?"

I faced her squarely. "Shelby, I don't know. He's a terrific guy. We're good together. But I'm stuck. I mean, I've spent years building a nice life for myself, but it never included somebody else. It's kind of hard to turn my head around overnight."

"It's not overnight, lady — you've been seeing each other for months. It's a wonder he hasn't kicked you to the curb by now."

I sighed. "I know. What do you think I should do?"

"Bite the bullet. Buy a house. You can't get an insurance policy for Happily Ever After, but you've got to try. If it doesn't work, you'll be back to where you are now, only a couple of years older and with a few more wrinkles. And no James."

It was not a pretty picture. "I get it. And I appreciate your honesty. Don't hesitate to beat me up anytime you want to."

Shelby stuck out her tongue at me.

"I'd better get back — I've got calls to make. And I'll get the check, since you provided the free psychotherapy."

"Anytime."

Chapter 21

I settled back at my desk and started making phone calls. A couple of hours later, the office phone rang and Eric poked his head in the door. "A Ms. Butler on the phone for you?"

"Oh, right, from Chester County. I'll pick up."

When Janet came on the line, she said, "Hi, Nell. Are you going to be out this way anytime soon?"

"I'm trying to plan something out there for this week, actually. Why?"

"I've been going through some stuff, and I found a few things I think you ought to see. Nothing earthshaking, but they might be relevant. But you don't need to make a special trip just for those."

I trusted Janet's judgment on anything related to Chester County history. "I'd love to take a look at them. Let me see if I can get this other meeting scheduled and we'll firm up the date. And thanks for calling." After I'd rung off, I reflected again how glad I was that Janet was willing to work with me rather than resenting my involvement. I resolved to make sure that Wakeman acknowledged her contribution to whatever solution we arrived at eventually.

Scott Mason returned my call after three. "Sorry it took me so long to get back to you, but that meeting ran on and on. I've got an appointment in Goshen tomorrow morning. Your message said you wanted to talk with the township people — you want to meet me at the township building at, say, ten?"

"That sounds fine. Who's the meeting with?"

"Marvin Jackson, the township manager, and Joseph Dilworth, who's on the historic commission."

"Sounds good. I've met both of them, but only briefly. Thanks for including me. I'll see you there." I debated a moment about involving Lissa, but decided that with a looming deadline she'd be more useful staying at the Society and pulling together the research on the Garrett farm. I could report back any important details, and she could talk with them at greater length later. If there was a later.

Then I hit the speed dial button for James's private line. He answered quickly. "What's up?"

"I'm meeting with Scott Mason at the Goshen township offices tomorrow morning to talk to Marvin Jackson and Joseph Dilworth about their past historic projects. So I should probably head home again after work tonight." I realized I wasn't sure what message I was sending him: did I want him to join me there or not?

There was an infinitesimal hesitation before he answered. "All right. Dinner tomorrow?"

"Sounds good. I should get to the office sometime in the afternoon." I debated briefly about mentioning Marty's lecture, and decided that would be better handled in person. "Oh, by the way — have you FBI types looked at the backgrounds for the township employees?"

"I can't talk about that, Nell."

Another topic for tomorrow night. At least then I'd know something more about the people involved, face-to-face. "Okay. I'll call you tomorrow when I get here and you can let me know where you want to meet."

"I will. Take care." He hung up first. I'd driven in, and I arrived home while it was still daylight and grabbed my mail on the way in. Maybe most of the commuters were down at the shore — I wasn't going to complain. I dumped the mail on the dining table, where it joined at lot of other unsorted stuff, and went upstairs to change into something grubby and comfortable. Back downstairs I wandered aimlessly to the kitchen. Spending so much time in the city with James had wrought havoc with my grocery shopping, and I didn't feel like getting in the car and going out to find food. I petulantly told myself that if I lived alone I could eat cereal and ice cream for dinner whenever I wanted, so there. Very mature.

Instead of cereal I made myself some marginally more grown-up scrambled eggs, and sat at my table and looked through the mail while I ate. Mostly junk mail and solicitations — as a former fundraiser I sympathized with the senders, but I didn't write checks to them — but one letter caught my eye: it was from the group of psychologists who owned the "big house" for which my little building had once been the carriage house. I opened the letter with some trepidation. Was the group telling me that they had sold the front property to someone else? I wasn't sure what that would mean, but the area was kind of transitional. The grand old houses now held a shifting mix of multifamily residences and discreet commercial offices such as those of "my" psychologists. I didn't see whoever handled zoning in Bryn Mawr loosening the restrictions anytime soon, but odd things could happen.

The letter was a preliminary offer to buy my little property. It seemed that the practice was prospering and they wanted more space, and had decided that my ex–carriage house would make an excellent site for group sessions. The price they preemptively offered made me blink and look again: it was more than twice what I had paid for the place a decade ago, admittedly before a lot of fixing up, and it was more than fair by current market standards.

Was this a sign from above? Had James somehow exerted pressure on the group to buy me out? I smiled at that paranoid thought. My first impulse was to call him and tell him about the very nice offer, but after a moment of consideration I decided to sit on it overnight and see how I felt about it in the morning. I could talk to James about it at dinner tomorrow. At the rate that list of topics was growing, it was going to be a very long dinner.

The next morning I slept in, since I didn't need to be in Goshen until ten and it was a relatively short drive away; I'd even scheduled lunch with Janet. But I found I was restless. After I'd washed up my few breakfast dishes, I kind of drifted around my small home, looking at it with a new eye. A decade ago I'd transformed it from a badly renovated rental unit to a comfortable home — for one. I'd been happy here, though — or had I just been kidding myself? What did it mean, that I'd built myself a home with room for only one person?

Finally, I couldn't stand fidgeting any longer and decided to leave early. I could sit in my car in the parking lot and make notes of the questions I wanted to ask, if I arrived with time to spare. Since I was driving against traffic headed toward Philadelphia, I took Route 30 to Paoli and then turned onto the Paoli Pike, following it to the Goshen township building, a sturdy, modern brick structure. Scott Mason was already waiting, ever the eager beaver.

"Good morning," I called out as I got out of my car. The air still felt pleasantly cool, although it promised to be hot later. "Are you an early bird, or do you live near here?"

"Hi, Nell. I live in the city, but I thought I'd allow myself plenty of time for traffic. I forgot it would all be going the other direction, so here I am. You have any questions before we go in and meet with the guys?"

"Tell me about who we're seeing?"

"The township manager, Marvin Jackson — he's an outside hire, but he's been here for a while — and the head of the historical commission, Joe Dilworth. He's local. That's a seven-member board, and advisory only, but they do carry some weight in decision making. Other people said they might drop by — like the township engineer and the township solicitor, but they've already been involved in plenty of meetings, and they're on board with the project going forward. Nobody's raised any new issues. So my main goal today is to touch base with the manager, bring him up to speed on what impact the death might have on the plans, and talk about strategy with the historical commission. As you may know, not too many years ago the township did a thorough renovation of the old blacksmith shop not far from here, and there's also a small historic district — I sent Lissa the details on all that before the end of the day yesterday. Both have been well handled and the community has responded positively to them. You may have noticed as you drove over here that even the corporate park you passed maintains a lot of green space and a couple of the old stone buildings. That's the feeling Mr. Wakeman is aiming for, maybe even a little more private with the addition of some more greenery over time."

"It sounds lovely. So you've been working with the township staff from the beginning?"

"I have. They're a good bunch. And what's more, old Ezra laid the groundwork well. He made his plans known to the township well before he passed on, so everybody had time to get used to the idea. He was a supervisor for the township for decades and was always respected, so people listened to him. It's been a pleasure to work on this, and everything has gone really well — at least, up until George Bowen's unfortunate death." He looked quickly at his watch. "We should go in now."

I followed him into the building, where a pleasant receptionist escorted us to a well-lit conference room. Three men were already there. They greeted Scott, and then he introduced me — again, as it turned out, since we all recognized each other from the press conference. Coffee was offered and accepted. While we poured from the carafe on the table, Scott handed out copies of stapled documents.

"As you can see, this is simply an update on documents you already have," he explained. "The numbers have held remarkably steady, and we're ready to proceed along the lines of the original schedule."

"What about the murder?" The township manager, Marvin Jackson, said bluntly. "You going to wait until the cops have figured that out?"

"We're hoping that won't take long, Marv. After all, we have the best minds of the local police working on it, plus FBI assistance. You knew George, didn't you?"

"Sure did. Good guy, did his job well. He really cared about Goshen." The men observed an awkward moment of silence.

"How did George feel about this project?" I asked.

The township men exchanged a glance. "I think it made him sad to see one more parcel lost — we've already got that corporate park up the road. But he knew what it would mean for the township."

"What exactly was his job?" I went on.

"Zoning officer. He made sure local codes were enforced. We're not that big a township, so people who work here kind of wear different hats. George kept an eye on most building projects, even things like rebuilding a chimney or installing lawn sprinklers. Anything that needed a permit, really. He liked it — he enjoyed talking to people, and he wasn't hardnosed about it. If somebody was having problems getting a home repair project done, he'd cut them some slack. But he didn't forget about it, either — he'd nudge people gently until it was finished and he could sign off on it."

"People must have liked him."

"Yeah, they did. Last person I would have expected to be murdered. I don't know anybody who ever said a bad word about him."

Scott seemed to be fidgeting, no doubt impatient to move the meeting along and get back to the city. "Joe, tell Nell about the historic district."

Joe smiled at me, then sat back in his chair and proceeded to outline the entire forty-year history of the Goshen historic district, now a national historic district. A variety of buildings had been moved there from different parts of the township, but had been carefully integrated so they looked as though they had always been there. It had proved a mildly popular local attraction over the past decade or so.

"Upkeep comes out of the township budget, right?" I finally said, when Joe seemed to be winding down.

"Sure does." He nodded. "We contribute some basic maintenance for the buildings, but there's always more. You should know all about that."

I smiled at him. "I sure do. Did the township make any effort to acquire the Garrett property?"

Marvin addressed that question. "Unless Ezra had decided to give it to us free and clear, there was no way we could have afforded it. He'd cut a deal with Wakeman before we even thought about it, but he made sure there were some restrictions about what could and couldn't be done on it. He brought it to the township as a courtesy, since he had every right to sell, but we couldn't find anything to object to."

I filed that away for future thought. "Mr. Dilworth — Joe — you said that the Garrett land had been in the family for a long time?"

"Since Goshen was first settled," Dilworth replied. "That's why we were so glad that the land wouldn't be chopped up. There's a lot of history there."

"I look forward to learning more about it. It sounds as though Ezra Garrett was an impressive man."

"That he was. He's been gone for a while now, but he's still missed."

"What about his sons? How did they feel about their dad selling the place?"

"Will and Eddie? Heck, there was no

future in a rundown dairy farming operation, and they weren't about to hold on to a prime piece of real estate out of sentiment, even if it has been in the family for centuries. Wakeman gave Ezra a fair price, and the kids inherited the proceeds. To be honest, I'm kinda glad Ezra handled it the way he did — at least Wakeman is keeping the parcel intact, and he's promised to make this a classy development, not a bunch of ticky-tacky houses. Right, Scott?"

"Exactly," Scott agreed. "Mr. Wakeman knew and liked Ezra, and they worked it out between them. We intend to follow through in that spirit." He hesitated a moment. "Look, would it be in bad taste if we named something after George Bowen? A street, or maybe a community center? You know the people around here better than I do."

The township men were nodding thoughtfully. "Might be a nice idea. Let us think about it, okay? Nobody has to decide this right now."

Scott looked relieved. "Of course not. You can ask around, see what the response is."

Marvin rubbed his hands together; he looked like he was eager to end the meeting. "Anything else we can help you with today? Ms. Pratt, you and your people are looking at the history of the place, right?"

"We are. Does anyone here know anything about those older bodies found on the land?" I asked, curious to see how they would respond.

Marvin deferred to Joseph, who seemed happy to answer. "Ms. Pratt, we're sitting on a lot of history here. We turn up musket balls and old tools and bottles all the time. No bodies until now, but it's not really surprising. If you know anything about the Paoli Massacre, you know it was a mess. Who knows how many other bodies might have met the same fate?"

"I've read a little, and I can see your point." I didn't mention that the timing of the discovery seemed a bit odd. "In any case, we aren't planning a scholarly study. More likely we'll give Mr. Wakeman something that he can use to help promote his development to prospective buyers. You know, 'live in the midst of history,' and so on. I hope he'll share it with you."

Scott bounced to his feet. "Well, gentlemen, I'll let you review the handouts when you have time, but I think it's safe to say there are no surprises. We hope to break ground in the fall, as planned. Please call me if you have any questions or concerns."

I seemed to have no option but to follow

Scott's lead, but I couldn't think of any more questions myself. "Thank you for seeing me. May I get in touch with you if I have any questions about the history of the town?" I handed each man one of my business cards.

"Sure, no problem," Marvin said. "But Janet Butler over in West Chester probably knows as much as we do."

I laughed. "And I'm meeting her for lunch today."

"Thanks again, guys," Scott said, shaking hands and all but pushing me out the door.

I followed meekly, but once in the parking lot, I asked, "Are you in a hurry?"

"What? No. But this was mainly a courtesy call — there really wasn't much new. Did you get what you needed?"

"I think so," I said, although I wasn't sure what I had hoped for. I'd confirmed that everybody had liked George, but that wasn't a surprise. Nobody seemed to want to stop the project from going forward. So why was George dead? Maybe he'd found something more than a few old buttons when he was snooping around. Maybe the bodies had been buried with a carefully wrapped diary written by George Washington, or General Wayne's battle plan, and George Bowen's killer had snatched it from him. "You're headed back to the city now?"

"Yup. You said you were meeting Janet Butler at the historical society?"

"Yes." I stopped short of telling him that Janet thought she had found something I needed to see. It could be nothing or it could be important, but Scott didn't need to know about it. "I assume I'll be talking with you later in the week, when the Society puts that report together for you."

"Great, thanks, Nell. See you!"

I watched him pull away, and then I got into my car and headed in the opposite direction, toward West Chester — a route that took me by the Garrett farm yet again. It still looked green and peaceful; there were a few ducks bobbing on the small pond by the road. It seemed an unlikely place for a murder. Or two, or three.

CHAPTER 22

I arrived at the Chester County Historical Society a few minutes early, but Janet was free, and came down from her office to meet me. She looked excited.

"Thanks for coming on such short notice, Nell. I know you must be busy."

"I'm happy to be here, especially since this Wakeman thing has leapfrogged to the top of my priority list — not by my own choosing, may I add."

Janet's eyes twinkled. "The man can be a bit, uh, peremptory, can't he?"

I laughed. "That's putting it kindly! Did you want to show me what you've found, or should we get something to eat first?"

"Are you hungry?"

"I'm always hungry. Is there someplace nearby we could walk to?"

"Sure — right around the corner. Follow me."

I didn't need much encouragement. It was

a lovely day, and I liked West Chester — it felt about the right size, and it had a real center, not just shops flanking a too-busy local highway. High trees arched over the street, keeping the downtown cool. We strolled without hurrying, arriving at a corner brewpub on the nearest corner in a few minutes. Once seated inside, we each ordered the brew of the day and sandwiches, and settled in to talk.

"I am so glad you brought me in on this," Janet began. "This is really exciting, especially since I think I can help."

"I'm glad to hear it. And I'll do my best to make sure your participation is recognized somewhere, and not just in a footnote. After all, you're putting a lot of time into this. Do you have any staff who can help?"

Janet waved her hand dismissively. "Sure there's staff, but I knew George, and I find this whole thing with the old bodies fascinating. Why should I hand the research off and miss all the fun?"

We talked about professional matters through our sandwiches, and I noted that we shared a lot of the same problems, setting aside the difference in the respective sizes of our institutions. The sandwiches were generously sized and tasty, and the local brew was good. If I hadn't had to go into the city later, I might have been tempted to play hooky and get to know West Chester a little better. But now was not the time.

"Let me pick up the tab," I volunteered. "I'm pretty sure I can pass it on to the Wakeman Trust, or whoever he decides is paying the bills."

"I'm not going to argue with you."

With the bill settled, Janet and I emerged from the restaurant and walked the few blocks back to her society. "You know," I began tentatively, "I feel like I'm here on false pretenses. I'm not really a historian — I started out as an English major and then ended up as a fundraiser. I'm president of the Society kind of by default. So I'm willing to bet you know a whole lot more about the history of this area than I do."

"I suppose I do," Janet replied. "I've lived here most of my life. I started out as a docent at the society, leading tours, which kind of shifted into researching the collections, and things kind of happened from there. As I'm sure you know quite well."

"I do. It's been a strange trip, and nothing that I'd planned."

"Are you enjoying it?"

"I am. I won't say it's always a pleasure to be an administrator, but I do believe in the institution and what we're doing, and if I can keep it moving forward in this increasingly digital world, I'll be satisfied." *I'd like it even better if I could concentrate on the job and stop finding crimes under my nose,* I reflected silently.

"There's still nothing like the real thing," Janet said firmly. "I love being able to handle the original documents."

"Amen to that!" We'd reached her building, and she held open the door for me to enter. "So, what've you got to show me?"

"Follow me." Instead of leading me to her office, we went back to the shabby working area at the rear of the building, where several archival boxes sat on the long table, along with a few pairs of white cotton gloves lying beside them.

I looked at Janet and waited for her to explain.

"Have a seat," she said, waving at one of the folding chairs next to the table. I sat, and she took another chair opposite and pulled on a pair of the gloves. "When Ezra Garrett reached ninety years old — still in full possession of his faculties, let me add — he decided to go through all the family documents. That must have been about the same time he started talking to the Wakeman people. Since the Garretts had been living on the farm for over two hundred years, and since they seem to have had a gene for hoarding, if there is such a thing, you can imagine the scope of what Ezra and the family had assembled over the years. Well, maybe that's not overstating it: his ancestors hadn't gone in much for papers. They were farmers from the beginning, and Ezra and his son Eddie were the last of them, once William washed his hands of the place. Let's say that what was preserved was very succinct, but valuable to any social historian. And to anyone interested in the history of Chester County, like me."

"Believe me, I understand. What did you find?"

"I'm getting there. Ezra got started, but his energy wasn't what it used to be, so after a bit he turned it all over to us."

"As a gift, or only for processing?"

"He gave it all to us, with the provision that we make it accessible to any of his family members who wanted to see it, and eventually to the public, once we'd cataloged and conserved it. And, yes — I can see you thinking — he left money to cover that work. But as you might guess, we don't have a lot of staff, and there was no apparent rush to get the processing done. Ezra had made a first pass and seen whatever he wanted to see, so he wasn't pressuring us to hurry. And then he died, and since nobody had requested access to the documents, we've been taking our time with the cataloging, kind of dipping into it a little at a time whenever somebody was interested. We've had a couple of interns from the university here, but most of them don't know anything about local history, so they're just going through the mechanics of cataloging."

I understood what she was telling me, but I wondered when she was going to get to the point. Here we were sitting in front of Ezra Garrett's family's historical collection of documents. I guessed that she had found something that she wanted to share with me, and I hated to begrudge her the pleasure of telling her tale, but I still had to get into the city sometime today. "Did the Wakeman deal prompt you to work any faster?"

"To be honest, no. You've got to remember that a lot of the discussion about the disposition of the land went on behind the scenes, and nobody came to us for anything. It was really only when you were called in that I sat up and took notice. That's when I hauled out these boxes and took stock of where we were in the cataloging."

"And?"

"I know, you're getting impatient." Janet grinned at me. "Okay, I checked our rough list, and then I focused on the Revolutionary War period, say, 1770 to 1790. There wasn't a lot, as you might guess, but I was lucky to find that Edward Garrett, the owner back then, had kept sort of a daybook. He mainly kept notes about farm issues, like the weather and which cows had calved, and major expenses, like replacing the roof or adding on to the house. But he did mention the battle."

Aha, now we had finally gotten down to it. "What did he say?"

"Not as much as I'm sure you'd like. He was a Quaker, which was a difficult thing to be during the Revolution because nobody really trusted a group of people who refused to fight, or even to pick sides. I'd guess the family kept pretty quiet about it, but that's only by inference, since they held on to their land and there were no public complaints about them."

"I assume that means they didn't take part in the local militia?" I asked.

"Not officially, at least. Anyway, as you must know by now, the Battle of Paoli took place just up the road from the farm, so it would have been hard to ignore it entirely. Then these two bodies turn up now, and evidence suggests that they died somewhere around the same time, and at least one of them must have been wearing a British uniform, because of the buttons that George found. Anyway, long story short, Edward makes a rather cryptic mention of the event. Here, it's easier to show you. But please, put on gloves first!"

I had already reached for the cotton gloves. I took the small volume Janet offered me from her hand and studied it briefly: worn leather binding, pages in surprisingly good condition, ink browned by age but still legible. I leafed through it carefully, noting the intermingling of financial notations, comments on planting cycles, even the occasional note of someone's death.

"I marked the pages," Janet said, watching me.

I turned to the place she had marked, and read. Edward, if he was indeed the writer, had summed up the battle in two lines, but had given a little more space to the chaos of the retreat. There must have been people milling around all over the roads that dawn, the American soldiers torn between rallying to defend themselves and retreating as fast as possible to regroup and assess what they had left. And Garrett's farm had been smack in the middle of the path. I looked up at Janet. "This is fascinating from a historical point of view, but what's it got to do with the bodies?"

"Look at the next page."

I turned the page, and read, " 'We laid the two dead men to rest where they fell. God grant them peace.' " The handwriting was the same, but shakier, as if the writer were upset; it returned to normal by the next page, where the entry was about shoeing a horse.

"So you're assuming that those are the two bodies that George Bowen found?"

"Wouldn't you? It's not a burial ground — all the Garretts are buried behind the meeting house nearby. But the conditions at that moment must have been awful, and I've read that most of the casualties during that war were buried where they fell. But there's another possibility — and this is pure speculation on my part, mind you: What if the two dead men were indeed from different sides? How were the Garretts supposed to return them to the right people? Think about it — no matter which way they turned, somebody would have been angry at them, and might possibly have taken it out on good Quaker Edward. Maybe it wasn't right to simply bury them and say

297

nothing, but in the heat of the moment it was the easiest thing to do, and safest for the Garretts. And things in the region stayed pretty unsettled for a while — maybe there never was a good opportunity to fix things. Does that make sense to you?"

I nodded slowly. "I think it does. Tell me, did George Bowen ever look at the Garrett papers?"

Janet tilted her head. "He may have. He's someone who would've had an interest, out of sheer curiosity. He was in and out over the past few years, not that he always stopped to chat with anyone. We probably don't keep track as scrupulously as you do, and he may not have filled out a request. He had kind of free rein with the collections, because everyone knew him and trusted him."

"I was wondering if he knew he was looking for bodies, or if he just happened to stumble on them. I don't suppose it matters, since it's pretty clear that he found them. Who would George have talked to first?"

"I'm still not sure. I think he would have told us, sooner rather than later, but he might have gone to the township first."

"Somebody on the historical commission, maybe?"

Janet considered that. "Like Joe Dilworth? I . . . don't know. I'd like to say that George's commitment to history outweighed his sense of duty to the township, but he was a conscientious man, and it could have gone either way. I really can't say. Poor George. He must have been torn."

And now he was dead. Had he picked the wrong person to tell?

"Does this help anything?" Janet asked.

I sighed. "Janet, I don't know. I think there could be a great story in there to give to Wakeman, and I'll tell Lissa about it, because I'm sure she'll want to see the book. Whether it tells us anything about who killed George, it's not clear. I need to think about this, maybe share it with someone." Like James, for instance. "Take good care of this book, though. Is there anything else in there that you think I should see? Or anything else about the farm in that era that may tie in?"

"I'll go through it more carefully, particularly the part that comes right after the war. I can't believe they just left those poor men in the field there, but I guess I can understand their thinking. Where are the bodies now?"

"The FBI took custody of them — they have the best forensics lab around. I'm not sure what they can tell us, but at least they're looking at them carefully. Listen, I've got to get into the city this afternoon, but thank you for sharing this. Wakeman wants a short report by the end of the week, and if we find anything that either corroborates or contradicts your theory, I'll let you know."

"Thank you — I'd appreciate it." She stood up. "Let me see you out."

Stepping out into the bright sunshine after being closeted in a dim room with documents from another century was a bit of a shock. "I'll be in touch," I told Janet, then walked over to the parking garage where I'd left my car. It was early enough in the day that I didn't have to contend with traffic as I drove toward Philadelphia, but I still had time to think about what Janet had shown me. Had Edward Garrett had mixed loyalties? Shouldn't he have told either the patriots or the redcoats, or both, about the two dead men, if in fact they had fought on different sides? Telling no one sounded politically expedient but not exactly honorable. I decided that I needed to know more about Edward Garrett before I made a final judgment.

And I wondered if the FBI forensic team could tell me any more about the bodies. I would have to ask James, over dinner. Another romantic conversation: *What's new with those skeletal corpses we found?*

CHAPTER 23

I arrived in Philadelphia about three and was lucky to find a space in the lot across from the Society. Not much was left of the workday, but I was looking forward to seeing James later.

On my way upstairs I made a detour to look for Lissa. I found her in the third-floor stacks, sitting cross-legged on the floor reading an old book, so completely absorbed that she was startled when I spoke. "Hey, Lissa. No, don't get up." I paused by a sturdy bookshelf and listened for a moment but didn't hear any other human sounds near us. I leaned down toward her. "Listen, I found out something today from Janet. Edward Garrett kept a daybook during the Revolution, and he mentions burying two bodies on his land after the battle at Paoli."

Lissa sat up straighter, her eyes bright. "Really? Did he say who they were?"

"Nothing like that. In fact, it's barely more

than a sentence, but I think it corroborates our guess about how those bodies came to be there."

"It's too bad that Edward Garrett didn't identify who he buried."

I smiled. "That would've been too easy, eh? He might honestly not have known them — after all, there were soldiers from all over the place running around in that battle. Or, since they may have fought for different sides, maybe he simply didn't want trouble, and burying them was the easiest solution." I straightened up. "I want you to check everything about Edward Garrett and the farm around the time of the Revolution, please. I'm sure you're itching to get a look at that daybook, but you probably won't have time before Wakeman wants his report."

"I was hoping to look into the Garrett family in more depth a bit later. I'm not a genealogist, and since the land stayed in the family all along, there wasn't a lot of reason to look at all the wills or deeds."

"Could you do that now? We may not need to give all that information to Wakeman, but I'm curious about a couple of things." I stopped her before she could ask for particulars. "No, I don't want to give you any hints — just assemble the basic facts and give them to me tomorrow sometime. How's the rest of it coming?"

"Good, I think. You had lunch with Janet today, right?" I nodded, and she went on. "Did she find that reference to the bodies while you were there?"

"No. She told me that Ezra Garrett gave the Chester County society a big batch of family papers before he died, and they're not fully cataloged, so she's been slowly going through them and came across this. If you exhaust what we have here at the Society, you might want to take a run out there and look. Of course, all this has to be in presentable form by Friday."

"That's barely three days!"

"I know, I know," I replied, laughing. "Do what you can, and we'll see where that takes us."

"Gotcha," Lissa said. "I'll get back to you."

With only a couple of hours of the working day left, I hesitated to start anything new. I called James to confirm our date, then took care of the messages from the day and signed a few papers that Eric had left neatly stacked on my desk for me. Then, feeling restless, I got up and wandered down the hall. I hadn't talked to Ben recently, and I felt badly about that, since he'd kind of been thrown directly into the deep end. I saw that Latoya was in her office and went over and knocked on the doorframe.

She looked up, startled. "Nell? What can I do for you?"

"I wanted to see if you've been keeping an eye on Ben Hartley. You know, giving him a helping hand when he needs it."

"I have made sure to speak with him at least daily. He does not appear to acknowledge that he might need help. I only hope that he doesn't assume that to ask for help is a sign of weakness."

"Duly noted. He has a lot to prove, to himself at least, but he still doesn't know collections management. What do you think we need to do to modify his physical space appropriately?" There, I was asking her opinion.

"He seems to have settled into the processing room. It may be that's a better location than in the cubicle outside this office that has been used by prior registrars."

We talked about furniture options for a few minutes, and in the end, I stood up, and said, "Why not just ask him what he wants? If he's touchy, he's going to have to get over it, here or at any other workplace."

"A good point, Nell. We are all trying so hard to be politically correct that we miss the obvious."

We parted ways amicably.

I didn't mean to invade Latoya's turf, but since I was close by I decided to drop in on Ben and make sure he was doing all right. I felt guilty for not thinking of what he might need. Of course, I often felt guilty that most of the staff had to make do with elderly desks and rickety chairs; and then I felt guilty because I had the nicest furniture in the building. But that was for impressing important people, not to keep me happy.

I located Ben in front of a computer in the processing room.

"Hey, Ben, how's it going?"

"All right, I guess. I'm somewhere halfway up the slope of the learning curve, maybe."

"Don't worry. That's to be expected."

"Hey, can I ask you something?" he said.

"Sure, go ahead."

"You think I can find a better desk, or modify this one? It's not exactly wheelchair-friendly."

Just what I'd feared. "I'm sorry. Tell me what you'd prefer and we'll see what we can do about getting it."

Ben actually laughed. "Hey, don't get bent out of shape about it. If you're okay with it, though, I may know some people I can ask to help. I assume the budget is nonexistent?"

"Close to. But we'll work it out. Does that mean you're thinking about sticking around long enough to use the new-and-improved furniture?"

"Yeah, I think so. I'm enjoying it. Nice place, nice people. Why would I leave?"

"Dusty history isn't for everyone. Oh, and thanks for your insights on the Battle of Paoli. I look at that site in a whole new way now, every time I drive by it. Of course, it's always amazed me that anybody managed to conduct a battle in those days. How did the military communicate with each other on the field? And if the original plan fell apart, did all the commanders have a plan B, or did everything just fall into chaos?"

"Some of each. That particular battle is a good example. And add to the mix that any local militia that took part had precious little military training, and not necessarily with large units. The Brits really did have the advantage there — they were better organized and equipped, and they had more experience."

"Well, I have to say it becomes a lot more real when you're standing on the spot where it took place. I'll let you get back to work. Contact whoever you want about the desk and let me know what you come up with."

As I left I reflected that I hadn't asked

him anything about the technical aspects of what he was supposed to be doing, but at least he was proving to be a true history enthusiast, and that counted for a lot.

I left the office at six-thirty, assuming — correctly — that I'd run into city traffic on my way to James's neighborhood. I was lucky that it was still summer, which meant I found parking easily, since the Penn students hadn't yet returned to the nearby campus. I let myself into the building and into James's apartment to find he hadn't arrived home. That gave me time to look critically at the place — and at what it said about him. Sure, I'd spent plenty of time in it, especially over the past month, but I'd never really paid attention to it. Actually, the simplicity of the place had made the caretaking part of the job easier: I could concentrate on nursing rather than housekeeping, not that I ever gave much energy to the latter in any case. But once James was on the road to recovery, we kept colliding with each other. The space had worked for him; it did not work for the two of us.

I heard his key in the lock, and James walked in with a couple of bags that smelled wonderful. He dropped them on the kitchen counter quickly, then turned and kissed me. "I missed you."

"Me, too," I said. "I keep thinking of things I want to tell you. I should start keeping a list."

He finally let me go and started pulling containers out of the bags. "I got Greek for a change. What sort of things were you thinking about? Houses or dead bodies?"

"Both, I guess. How much of the case can you talk about?"

"Depends." He pulled plates out of a cabinet. "Wine?"

Did I plan to go back to my place later? No, I decided quickly. "Sure."

He handed me the plates and I took them to the small round dining table while he filled two wine glasses, then joined me. "Business before pleasure?"

"The case, you mean? Let me go first. Today Scott Mason and I met with Marvin Jackson and Joe Dilworth and the other Goshen Township people. Have you talked to them?"

He shrugged, chewing, then said, "Not yet, or not personally. What did you make of them?"

I looked at him curiously. Was he fishing for something? Was there something I should have noticed? "They seemed nice enough. They said the right things about George Bowen and his death. Joe told me all about the local historic district and how it came about. What are you looking for?"

"Just between us, Nell, Marvin Jackson's bank accounts show that he's stretched very thin."

"Why does that matter?"

"Because it's possible he's been dipping into township funds to cover his personal debts. Wakeman's project would help him refill the coffers before anybody had to take notice officially at the end of the fiscal year. Bowen's discovery might have delayed things enough to make that an issue."

"Huh." Funny how little we know about what goes on behind the scenes in any community, large or small. "Would that give him enough of a motive for silencing George? Even if George told him about finding the bodies right away, Marvin should have known that George would talk to someone else, like the county historical society."

"But did he?"

"Not that I know of, actually. I had lunch with Janet in West Chester today, and she said George hadn't gotten around to telling her people about it. But that's not to say he didn't tell *someone* at the township. Can you tell me anything significant about Joseph Dilworth?"

"Dilworth's been having an affair with

George's wife," James said bluntly.

I gaped at him. "How do you find out these things? And this is just scratching the surface for you guys at the FBI? You scare me."

"Phone records, mostly. Let's not get into that. But it does mean that, while Dilworth might not have any reason to interfere with the historical aspects of this project, he might well have had a personal reason to want George out of the way."

I tried to remember what Pat Bowen had said when I'd talked to her. "Pat hates history. Or maybe it was only how much of George's attention it consumed. Joseph isn't a burly guy — heck, Marvin is beefier — but could he and Pat together have hauled George's body to where it was found?"

"Possibly."

"Great. So you haven't eliminated anyone? What about Scott Mason, the eager young assistant?"

"He has no alibis for the relevant time periods. Nor does Wakeman, officially, for that matter — he volunteered that he was home with his wife of thirty-five years and whichever of his eight kids are still living at home. I haven't confirmed that with any of them, but I'm inclined to believe Wakeman and leave it at that."

"What about phone records? Did Scott and Wakeman exchange any calls at the right times?"

"Nell, we don't have enough evidence to request a subpoena for Wakeman's records. I don't supposed you 'borrowed' Scott's phone to check his call list?" He hurried to add, "Just kidding." He took a sip of wine. "Was there anything else?"

"Well, as a matter of fact, Janet did show me something interesting. Ezra Garrett left all his family papers to the county society before he died — I guess he wanted to be sure they stayed together and were well looked after — but Janet and her staff hadn't gotten around the cataloging them yet when all this started. They have even less staff than we do, so recently Janet took a look at them herself. She found a daybook kept by Edward Garrett — that's Ezra's Quaker ancestor who owned the farm at the time of the Revolution."

James interrupted me. "What's a daybook?"

"Kind of a daily journal that covers administrative and financial things about running the farm. Not a personal diary, mostly business details. Anyway, there's a short entry right after the battle, where he mentions burying two bodies where they fell.

What're the odds that those are the same two bodies that George found?"

"I'd say it's pretty likely. I'd hate to think there were more bodies scattered around the place — or anywhere else for that matter, but from what Ben told us about the battle, it wouldn't surprise me. I don't suppose that book mentioned who they were?"

"No. It was a very terse entry. I got the impression that Edward would rather not have mentioned it at all, but maybe he thought it was important to leave some kind of record. It does seem to be the only mention of bodies we've found so far."

"Did Ezra know about them?"

"How am I supposed to know that? From what Janet said, he just showed up one day with several boxes full of family books and papers. Who knows if anybody in his family ever read them? Janet said no one has shown any interest in them since Ezra dropped them off — that's partially why they haven't exactly rushed to sort through the contents. Maybe some of Edward's offspring, if they were still involved in running the farm — they might have looked back to see how he had done things. Or —" I stopped myself and realized what had been percolating in the back of my consciousness, and what had prompted me to ask Lissa to look more closely at Edward Garrett and his family. "What if the family *did* know?"

"Know what? That there were two bodies on their land?"

"Well, maybe they kept quiet about it. Maybe Edward hid the book — he couldn't bring himself to destroy it because it was the only evidence of those two bodies, vague though it is. How do we figure that out now?" And then another thought hit me. "James," I said slowly, "have you done a DNA analysis on the bodies?"

"Looking for what?"

"Maybe Edward Garrett did know who the dead men were. And maybe one of them was related to him."

James sat back in his chair. "I never thought of that. It's not standard operating procedure for an FBI investigation, but I can get a quick-and-dirty DNA test done, for a price. I suppose Wakeman would foot the bill. But who am I comparing it to?"

"Ezra's two sons, William and Eddie, still live in Chester County. I'm sure you could persuade one of them to provide a DNA sample."

"Wait a minute — you're suggesting that one or both of the dead men are related to the Garrett family? That's a heck of a big jump."

"I know that. But it might explain why that first Edward never said anything about the bodies."

James thought for a moment, staring into space. "I'll look into getting the DNA work done. But even in the unlikely case that it was a Garrett who killed the soldier, how do you get from there to killing George Bowen now?"

"Maybe if you keep a secret that long, it becomes a force of its own. Maybe somebody didn't want it to go public."

"Maybe. I'd still be more comfortable with finding someone with a financial motive, like Jackson, or a personal motive, like Joseph Dilworth and Pat Bowen."

"Well, it would certainly be easier to make a case."

We'd finished eating without my even noticing. "So," James began, "I've got some more listings for us to check out." He looked at me expectantly.

"I, uh," I fumbled, then raised my chin, determined to feign enthusiasm if I needed to. "Okay, show me."

He permitted himself a small smile, and it hurt — I'd made him happy, and it had taken so little. He stood up to fetch a slim stack of printouts, and snagged the bottle of wine on the way back, refilling both our glasses before sitting down. He took the chair next to me, rather than sit across the table. "I kind of like this one," he said, shuffling the stack and handing me a page.

I barely glanced at it. "Mmm, nice. Where is it?"

As we went through the stack, I made polite noises. But it's hard to fool a trained FBI agent. After a while James backed up his chair and looked at me. "What's wrong, Nell?"

"Nothing. Well, not nothing, but I don't know what it is."

"You don't want to move in together."

"I do. Really. But . . ." There was nothing to come after the *but*. Either I did or I didn't, and if I didn't know by now, when would I? I took another sip of wine, stalling. "James, you know I love you. I want to be with you. I hate not knowing from day to day if I'll see you, or where we'll be. But something is holding me back, and I don't even know what it is. And I can't seem to get past it." He started to speak, and I raised a hand. "It's not that I'm afraid it won't work out. I know the statistics. I know we're both reasonable, intelligent people, and we should be able to talk about this. I know we're not young, and if this is going to happen we don't have the luxury of drifting along for years. We've even had a sort of trial run these last few weeks, under challenging conditions, and we came through it with flying colors. So I don't understand why I can't seem to move forward." His gaze had never left my face, and I wanted to cry. How could I be doing this to him?

Then his expression changed, just a bit. "Nell, I have an idea. No, don't say anything — I've got a few details to work out. But will you hold tomorrow night for me? Or, no, better make it Thursday, in case something comes up."

"You mean, like finding another corpse or two?" I pulled together a wavering smile. "Thursday sounds good for me."

"All right, then. Are you staying, tonight?"

"I've had a few glasses of wine — I shouldn't drive. So, yes."

He gave me a quizzical look, no doubt questioning my lukewarm response. We really did need to work this out — just as soon as I figured out what my problem was.

CHAPTER 24

The next morning, I woke up early and studied still-sleeping James. He still looked a bit thinner since he'd been attacked, but he claimed there were no aftereffects from the concussion, no more headaches or dizziness. The long scar on his arm was fading slowly, but it would always be with him. He didn't remember those awful minutes when I was trying to stop the bleeding and wondering if I could — and wondering if he was going to die under my hands. *Cheerful thoughts for an early morning, Nell!* He'd survived, I'd survived, and the whole thing had shoved our relationship to this new level — where it had stalled. Now he was back at work and ready to resume a normal life, and here I was dragging my feet. Clearly I was an idiot, as my friends kept telling me.

I slid carefully out of bed and went to the kitchen — more like a kitchenette — to make coffee. What was on my calendar for today? No board meeting looming yet, and the next major social event at the Society was still a few months away. Shelby had the planning for that well in hand, and it promised to be fun: we were celebrating the life of the great nineteenth-century actor Edwin Forrest, whose larger-than-life personality lent itself to over-the-top festivities. New registrar Ben seemed to be getting a handle on his job, and despite, or maybe because of, the limitations to his mobility, he appeared to be a calm, stable presence — exactly what we needed. I was looking forward to seeing how he interacted with Latoya once he got his bearings.

Lissa, with a little help from me, would be cobbling together a report on the history of the Garrett site in Goshen to present to Wakeman by Friday, a deadline barreling toward us way too fast. I believed that if we made him happy, it could mean good things for the Society, maybe in the form of money, or maybe as some in-kind contributions for the building, like an updated HVAC system, or even a new roof. That would be a trifle to the Wakeman Property Trust, but it would mean a lot to us. If we disappointed him . . . no, I wasn't going to think about that. The Society had one of the best collections of historical material in the country, particularly on Pennsylvania history, and with Janet's help we could fill in whatever gaps there were. And I had enough experience with fine-tuning pitches to present a streamlined and concise story that would appeal to the public and the press alike. All good.

The coffee was ready when James emerged from the bedroom freshly showered. I handed him a cup and, said, "Want an English muffin?"

"Sure." He sat down at the table and watched me exercise my expert toaster skills.

When I'd set a plate in front of him and brought mine over to the table, I said, "What's next on your plate with the Wakeman — or should I say Bowen? — investigation?"

James sighed and sipped his coffee. "I really don't know. We're waiting for the final forensic details on the old bodies. The local police have interviewed everyone with a connection to George Bowen and they've sent on the reports to us. But in reading through them, it's clear that their prior knowledge of the people and the situation interferes with their objectivity to some extent. And maybe they haven't asked the right questions. But the FBI can't muscle in and redo everything."

That made sense to me. "Wakeman's not getting in your way?"

"Nope. He's getting the investigation he asked for. You have any suggestions?"

"You're asking me?" I thought for a moment. "James, we've worked together on a few cases now, and I think what I bring to the table is a different perspective. I know more about the people involved, and you deal with the facts. And I can ask questions that you can't, because I'm not official. Does that sound about right?"

"It does," he said. "And don't think I don't appreciate it."

"Thank you. To get back to the point, I think it still comes back to those two Revolutionary War bodies. We do agree that that's what they are?" When James nodded, I went on, "George Bowen found them, whether or not he was looking specifically for them. George told somebody about them, although we still aren't sure who. That person had what he — or she — thought was a motive to silence George. Does that sum it up?"

"It does. That's why I'm glad you're on this with me. And as you were saying, it may be that some of us don't appreciate that something that happened over two hundred years ago can matter so much to someone today."

"But you *can* work your forensic magic on the old bodies," I pointed out.

"We're working on it."

"Are you going to talk to anyone in Goshen today?"

"Maybe. I'd like a word with Jackson, and maybe Pat Bowen. What about you?"

"What am I doing? Going to work. Lissa's only got two days to put together that preliminary report for Wakeman, and I need to vet it first."

"How's she working out?"

"Very well. She's smart and she knows quite a bit about local history. Too bad the Society can't hire her, but it's not in the budget. Maybe I can talk Wakeman into endowing a position for a project historian, assuming he's pleased with what we give him. And then she can keep seeing Ben."

James smiled. "I'm not taking that bait. You aren't going to interfere, are you?"

"Why would I do that? My only concern is that Ben is now my employee, so I have some responsibility for him. Latoya and I haven't really had time to assess his professional capabilities. I was just wondering, in case I should say something to Lissa."

"They're both adults — let them work things out." He stood up and carried his dishes to the sink. "I'd better get going.

Don't forget, we've got a date tomorrow night," he said.

"Oh, right. I might have to make another run out to Chester County, either today or tomorrow, so I'll check in with you later. And I'll have to see how much progress Lissa has made on that report for Wakeman."

"Tomorrow." His tone didn't permit any argument. He gave me a serious kiss and headed out the door.

It didn't take me long to dress; the scant closet space didn't allow me to keep much at James's place, so I had few choices for work clothing. Then I drove into Center City and parked across from the Society. The day promised to be a warm one, but as usual the interior of my building was cool and serene. "Hi, Bob," I greeted our gatekeeper.

"Mornin', Nell. Busy day yesterday, and looks like it might be busy again today."

"All those summer genealogists, right? But that's what keeps us in business." I headed for the elevator and my office.

Eric had already arrived. "I'll get your coffee, Nell," he said as soon as he saw me, and went down the hall to the break room. He returned a minute later. "There you go."

"Thank you, Eric. I promise I'll start getting in earlier soon, so we can share coffee duty. How're things going? What with all this running back and forth to Goshen, I feel kind of left out of the loop. Any crises? Excitements?"

"Things've been pretty smooth this week. How's it going with your bodies?"

"The new one or the old ones? I think they're connected, but I still don't know how. We haven't heard from Mr. Wakeman yet today, have we?" I knew Wakeman had my cell phone number and wouldn't have hesitated to use it if he'd really wanted to reach me.

"No, ma'am. A couple of calls from his project manager."

"Scott?"

"That's the one. I don't think it was urgent."

"As long as Mr. Wakeman can find me, I think we're okay. Have you seen Lissa this morning?"

"Sure have. She came in real early."

Even as Eric spoke, Lissa appeared in the doorway behind him. "Hey, Nell. I've got some stuff I want to show you. Oh, hi, Eric."

"Hey, Lissa. You want some coffee?"

"Already helped myself, thanks. You make good coffee, Eric."

"Thank you! Then I'll let you all get down

to business." Eric retreated gracefully to his desk.

When he was gone, I gestured toward a chair. "Sit down. You look excited — you've found something?"

"Maybe. Hey, don't worry, I'll have a draft of that Wakeman report for you by tomorrow afternoon at the latest, so you can review it. But you asked me to look more closely at the genealogy of the family, right? Edward, the one who owned the land during the Revolution, and the rest of his family?"

"I did. What've you learned?" She must have thought it was significant, because she was almost bubbling with excitement.

"Well, as I'm sure you know, records are a little patchy back then. We've got the 1790 census, after the dust from the war had settled, and there's a 1774 list of taxable inhabitants in Goshen, and Edward's on it. If you're interested, he had two horses, three cattle, and three sheep at the time. Married to Hannah, and they had seven kids, four daughters and three sons, Charles, William, and Thomas. Thomas was the youngest boy. Edward left a will, and Thomas inherited the property when Edward died. So that made me wonder — what must've happened to Charles and William?"

CHAPTER 25

It took me a moment to grasp what Lissa was suggesting, and then another moment to see the connection she had made. "You're saying that you think that either or both of the two bodies found on the property were Edward's sons? That's a pretty huge leap of logic. Tell me why."

"Okay." Lissa picked up the thread dimpled, her enthusiasm undimmed. "It's kind of hard to prove a negative, but hear me out. When I started digging into the sources from after the war, I couldn't find any mention of Charles or William Garrett anywhere, not near Goshen or even in the commonwealth. Not in Edward's will, as I've just said, and no marriage or death records anywhere. They didn't leave wills, at least not in Pennsylvania, although I can't say I've looked beyond the state. No mention of widows or offspring for either of the sons. What is interesting is that William

shows up in the Goshen militia company —
there are some Sons of the American Revolution applications that refer to him."

"But wasn't he a Quaker? I thought they
were pacifists."

"Yes and no. Quakers are basically Chris-
tians but historically they've been very toler-
ant of individual beliefs. George Fox, who
founded the Religious Society of Friends in
England back in the mid-1600s, said that
Quakers should refuse to bear arms or use
deadly force against other humans or participate in any wars, but there have been
Quakers who've fought. They were and are
willing to fight for peace and freedom, if
that makes sense to you, but mostly they're
a very quiet group that avoids violence. The
Goshen Meeting was founded in 1702 or
1703 —"

"And is close to the Garrett farm. I know.
You've looked at their records?"

"Not yet. They're in the Friends Historical Library at Swarthmore College and in
the Haverford College Quaker Collection.
They're available for research, but I haven't
had the time to get there, and only the
catalog is online, not the documents themselves."

I sat back in my chair and thought. "So
how do you get from there to two dead men

buried secretly on the Garrett farm, one with a British uniform?"

"I'm getting there. You might guess that being pacifists put a lot of Quakers in difficult positions during the Revolution, because they weren't supposed to officially swear loyalty to either side, much less fight. Some remained Loyalists, and others sided with the patriots — and they could be disowned by their meeting for either. In Pennsylvania almost a thousand Quakers were disowned for bearing arms. Anyway, the result was that *nobody* trusted the Quakers around here."

I was beginning to see her logic. "And you're guessing that the Garrett family, in the confusion after the battle, found the bodies and buried them quickly, to avoid any problems?"

"It's possible, isn't it?" Lissa nodded eagerly. "The local Quakers had very mixed feelings about which side to choose and whether or not to fight, and besides, tempers run high in any war. Maybe Edward just wanted to avoid any difficulties."

I was intrigued, but she was really going out on a limb with her theory. I played devil's advocate. "If that was the case, why would anyone want to silence George Bowen? If anything, it would be kind of an intriguing archeological find, wouldn't it?"

Lissa's face clouded. "That's where I hit a wall. And that's why the missing heirs are important. What if one of them killed the British soldier? Or was killed by him? And maybe his brother helped cover that up, and then left, so no one would ask him about it?"

"It's possible, maybe. But why wouldn't Edward have resurrected his son, so to speak, when the war was over, and had him buried properly at the meeting?"

"That's why I'd really like to take a look at the original records at Swarthmore. Maybe the brothers are mentioned there, but I haven't had time to check, and we're running out of time if we're going to meet Wakeman's deadline."

Lissa fell silent while I digested what she'd told me. Finally, I said, "I guess the question is, if it's true — and that's still very much an *if* — then how did the family manage to keep the secret for all this time?"

Lissa shrugged. "You told me that Ezra Garrett made a point of giving the family documents to the historical society before he died. I wonder: do you think he knew?" Lissa said.

Something I couldn't answer. "Well, either he wanted to make sure the documents stayed together and were well cared for, or he knew there was something in there that probably would or should come out sometime. Maybe he didn't trust his own family to preserve them. I think maybe we need to know a bit more about family relations there, and I'll bet Janet can fill in some of the blanks. I wish we had more time to figure this out. How much can we take to Wakeman?"

"You're asking me?" Lissa laughed. "From what I understand, he wants a nice report to help sell his homes and condos. We don't have any proof about these conjectures, no matter how interesting a story it might make for him. I suppose we could say something like 'The Garrett family had a long and troubled history on their homestead . . .' And the bodies would be quietly reburied somewhere and never identified."

I shot upright in my chair. "But there is a way we can prove it!" While she looked at me, bewildered, I picked up my office phone and hit James's number.

"Morrison," he said automatically, then, "Nell? Why are you calling on this line?"

"Because this is official business. I'll be quick. Do you remember that we talked about DNA profiles for the old bodies from the Garrett property? How long would it

330

take to get them done? Remember, this is for Wakeman. Money is no object." I hoped that was true. If we got the story right, he might have something really interesting to include in his promotional material. It seemed worth trying.

"If our lab does it, you might see results in a couple of weeks. But I know the guys at the Jersey lab that takes our overflow. They can probably have something for you tomorrow — for a price. Why the hurry?"

I smiled to myself. "I'm working on a theory, but I don't want to prejudice you. I'll tell you when we get the results."

"All right. I'll call if there's any problem with getting the lab work done."

We hung up at the same time. I looked up to see Lissa grinning at me. "DNA tests, huh? Like, overnight? So we'll know if one of the bodies was related to the Garretts?"

"Only if we get a sample from a living Garrett. So we have to figure out how to get a sample from one of the surviving ones."

"Can you ask?"

"They might want to know why we're asking."

"Why can't we just tell them the truth? If you say it's to help with the murder investigation, won't they be willing?"

"Maybe. I don't really know any of them.

And, as far as I know, neither William nor Eddie has shown much interest in this investigation. Of course, they don't own the land anymore. I think we need to talk to Janet again. Do you have time today, or should I go alone?"

"If I can take my laptop along, I'd love to go. I can work on the report in the car. Maybe I can even get some pictures while we're out that way."

"Deal. I'll call Janet and see if she's free this afternoon."

"Great. I'll check back with you later."

Lissa left, and I spent a few minutes gathering my thoughts. Two dead men in the woods; two corpses in a copse. The buttons pointed to the Revolutionary War; a major battle in that war had taken place only a short distance away from the farm. The land had been held continuously by the same family since before that battle, up until Ezra Garrett had sold it to Mitch Wakeman. Had Ezra known about the bodies? If so, he must have realized that Wakeman would most likely discover them in the course of construction. If there had been no dark secret, any member of the Garrett family could have reported the bodies at any time over the past two centuries; ergo, there had to be a dark secret.

What was it, and who had known?

Or maybe the Garrett family had simply forgotten about the bodies; the story had not been passed down. The fact that the copse had never been disturbed was merely a coincidence. And George had been killed by a crazed stranger in the dark.

Which was more likely? Too many coincidences. My vote was for the first option.

I picked up the phone to call Janet Butler and luckily found her in her office. "Hey, Janet," I said. "It's Nell. Look, Lissa and I have some more questions about the whole Garrett history, and you know we've got a Friday deadline. Would you mind terribly if we came out and talked to you this afternoon?"

"Uh, sure, I guess. Does two o'clock work for you?"

"Fine. And thank you. I promise we'll stop bothering you soon."

Janet laughed. "Hey, this is more excitement than we usually get here. I'll see you at two."

Lissa and I left the city at one, and as I drove she read out loud pieces of the text she had assembled for the Wakeman report. I was pleased to find that she wrote well, striking a nice balance between accurate

333

historical fact and readable, entertaining style. Since traffic was light at mid-day, we arrived slightly early.

Janet was waiting for us in the lobby. "Welcome back, you two. Come on up to the office and we can talk." She led the way to her office, and I made sure the door was shut. As I did that, she gave me a curious look. "What do you need?"

I took a deep breath and started in. "Lissa has been doing some basic genealogy research on Edward Garrett and his family, and she turned up something odd. Edward had three sons, and the youngest one inherited the farm. The other two vanished from any records, just about the time of the Battle of Paoli."

Janet was quick to arrive at the same conclusion we had. "And you think they're connected to the two bodies that George found in the woods?"

"That's our working theory at the moment, but we need some help to flesh it out, if you'll pardon a bad pun. We know that Edward Garrett knew about the bodies, from his daybook, but he didn't identify them there, or anywhere else, as far as we know."

"But I still need to look at the Quaker records," Lissa said, then went quiet again.

I went on, "We been kicking around a theory that one of them was Edward's son. Would Edward have had reason to hide the death?"

"What an interesting idea. I can't say for sure. If I'm not mistaken, the records for the Goshen Meeting can be found in the Friends Library at Swarthmore College."

"Lissa will follow through on that, of course," I added. "She did find a record that says that one of the sons was listed as a member of the Goshen militia, which you know would have been relatively unusual. Add to that the buttons that George found, and it suggests that one of Edward's sons may have killed a British soldier on the family property, and then they died together and were buried right there, without ceremony or recognition. And then nobody said anything about them until Wakeman showed up."

"This is amazing!" Janet said. "Sounds like a soap opera."

"It does, but it's a strong possibility that George Bowen died because he found the bodies. At least, that's the only explanation that makes sense. Tell me, what was the timing of Ezra Garrett's gift of the family papers in relation to the start of the Wakeman project?"

"As I told you, about the same time. Of course, the announcement of the Wakeman project didn't go public right away, but there were hints coming from the township guys. Obviously Ezra and Wakeman had been talking about it for a while before that. I just figured Ezra handed over the papers because he was settling his affairs. He must have known he didn't have much time left. He was already ninety."

"What if he was worried that someone else would find the papers? Maybe even destroy them?"

Janet looked bewildered. "His family must have known about them, and they'd probably had access to them all along."

"What if the family didn't know?" I pressed. "Or what if it didn't matter until it became public that Wakeman was going to develop the site and would probably find those bodies?"

"I'm still not following," Janet said. "Why would anyone care now? Whatever happened, happened a long time ago. What's it got to do with the present?"

"That's what we don't know. As I'm sure you've seen, family traditions have a way of hanging on long after the people involved are gone. Like 'We don't talk about Aunt Hattie's first husband,' because he turned out to be a swindler — things like that. It's only when there's an outside eye looking at these things that the family members are kind of jolted out of their rut and take a different view. Say Edward did not want it known that his son was buried there, and swore the son who inherited to secrecy, and that information got passed down from generation to generation. So nobody touched that piece of land. They couldn't have known that the bodies and other bits and pieces would be so well-preserved."

"All this is kind of built on straw, isn't it? It could have been two strangers fleeing from the battle who happened to cross paths right there and died."

"Of course it could. That's why I've asked the FBI to do a DNA analysis of the remains."

"Oh-ho!" Janet replied, nodding. "So you'll know if one of them was a Garrett. But you still need a sample from a living Garrett, don't you?"

"That's where you come in."

CHAPTER 26

"Janet, is there some way to get a sample from the two sons?"

Janet smiled. "You mean, without asking them?"

I almost laughed. "That would be too easy. Do you know either of them well enough to ask? Where do they live?"

"Huh — let me think. I think both of them are still around West Chester, or at least in Pennsylvania. The younger son, Eddie — yes, the name has been passed down — lived on the farm until his father died and Wakeman took over the property. He never married, and he must be sixty now. He's a member here, but only because his father gave so much that we made him an honorary one. So I guess I know him, but he's not exactly a regular customer here. I do know him better than his brother, William, but that's not saying much. I don't think I've ever seen William in here."

"I met Eddie at that press conference," I said, "but he left as fast as he could. I had the impression he wasn't comfortable with that kind of attention. I'm sure the brothers have been interviewed about George's death and the bodies and the whole history of the farm." But who had interviewed them? I wondered. Odds were that the interviewers were local good ole boys who'd known the Garretts all their lives. Had the interviewer asked the right questions? Would that person have known if he was being lied to by one or another or even all of the Garretts? "It might look odd if someone came around now asking for a cheek swab."

"You want to break into their houses and steal a toothbrush?" Janet said, with a glint in her eye.

"That only happens on television. Look, if we want to prove our theory, we need to get serious. Janet, do you think you could ask them to come here?"

"I could come up with an excuse, I guess, at least for Eddie, since he's a member. Maybe a question about the family papers?"

"Has Eddie shown any interest in the past?"

"Not really, but he has to know that we're looking at the papers now, given everything that's been happening."

"But we don't have much time," Lissa said. "Even if Eddie comes in right away and you get DNA from him, it'll take a couple of days to process that to compare to the other samples. So the whole investigation has slopped over into next week already."

"At least it would be progress," I said. "No other agency has come up with anything. We ought to have preliminary DNA results for the bodies by tomorrow, and if we have to wait for a sample from Eddie to compare to, so be it."

Suddenly I really wanted to talk to James. I was out of my depth here. I had no idea what constituted evidence of anything or how to go about getting it even if I knew. I could end up doing more harm to the investigation than good. Heck, Eddie could probably sue someone if we tricked him into giving a sample.

Lissa's voice interrupted my thoughts. "Nell, how do you want me to spin all this for Wakeman's report?"

"I don't think he'll want wild speculation. If it turns out to be a good story, we can add it later, but I'd rather have the basic story of the land in his hands than give unsupported guesses about possible murders."

"So, what do you want me to do, Nell?" Janet asked.

"Call Eddie Garrett and ask him if he can come in to talk about the family papers. That's an innocent and appropriate request. Don't make it sound urgent — tomorrow would be fine. Then if he shows up, offer him a cup of coffee or tea or whatever then make sure you save whatever he drank out of."

Janet laughed. "Okay, I can do that. But I think you've been watching too much *CSI*."

"Probably." I stood up. "We've already taken too much of your time. Let me know if you reach Eddie and if he'll talk to you."

"You want to sit in, if I do talk to him?"

"If it seems natural. It might look odd if I was there. You know the Garrett material well. Oh, you are taking good care of the daybook, aren't you?"

"Yes, I put it in the safe. And I won't mention it unless Eddie brings it up."

"Good. Who knows, it may turn out to be crucial. Lissa, you ready to go?"

Janet escorted us to the front door. Outside it was still hot, even on the tree-shaded street. I dropped Lissa off at the Paoli train station and headed back to Bryn Mawr. We had cobbled together some shaky theories with very little to back them up, and if we told someone and we were wrong, we'd look very foolish. I parked behind my house and let myself in, then I went upstairs to change into something cool. Downstairs again, I checked the time: only four-thirty, so James would still be at work. Well, I had work-related things to discuss with him, so I called him.

"Again?" he answered, but with a hint of humor.

"Yes, again. I wanted to report on my meeting with Janet Butler. That's business related, right?"

I could hear his sigh. "Before you ask, I don't have the DNA results yet."

"I didn't think you would. But Janet and Lissa and I talked about our theory." I decided not to mention that we were going to try to get yet another DNA sample for him to run. I wasn't sure how legal or ethical it would be if we tricked either Garrett male to obtain the sample. And it was a pretty weak theory to begin with.

"Who've you got?" he said, all business.

"Both of Ezra Garrett's sons still live in the immediate area. Both are members of the historical society in West Chester but spend very little time there, if any. Janet is going to call and ask Eddie Garrett if he could come in to discuss the family papers that his father left to the society. And then maybe she can segue into asking him if he knew about the buried bodies on the land, since it was recorded in the family records." *And somehow get a DNA sample.*

"You think he's involved?"

"I have no idea. I barely know the man — I shook hands with him at Wakeman's press conference and that's it — and Janet knows him only slightly better because he's used the historical society's resources. I'm sure the local detectives have interviewed him, but they don't know as much about the family history as we do now. Besides, if something has been a closely guarded secret for two centuries plus, then it's likely to stay a secret, right? He may know something he hasn't told."

"Pretty thin stuff, Nell."

"You have anything better?"

"No. Where are you?"

"Home. But we're getting together tomorrow night, right?"

"Yes, we have plans for tomorrow night," he finally said enigmatically. "I'll meet you at the Society, unless something else breaks. Six?"

"Good. And then we'll have the whole weekend to look at places, right?"

"Yes. I'll hold you to it. See you tomorrow." He hung up, endearments conspicuously missing. I knew he was at work, but still. Why was I doing this to him? *Well, free single woman with no strings, what are you going to do with yourself tonight?*

I ended up playing on the computer, trolling through search engines, sticking in the name *Ezra Garrett* just to see what came up. Bits and pieces, including a nice obituary. Ezra sounded like he'd been a great all-around guy, a solid member of his meeting, an elected township official for decades, a supporter of worthy causes, a former school bus driver and a fox hunter — how did those last two go together? He'd been a good custodian of his land and his history. Had he known about the bodies? Had he handed over the family documents knowing that eventually the daybook would send someone looking for them? Who in Goshen would have pointed a finger at a pillar of the local community like Ezra in any event?

I kept searching idly, coming up with different versions of the same information. But then I found something new: a small news article from a local newspaper a few decades back reporting the death of a *third* son of Ezra Garrett's, who had died at the age of twelve in an unfortunate accident involving one of his father's guns. Details were vague, probably to protect the one who had pulled the trigger, but I thought I could read between the lines.

I felt chilled. I had my own history with weapons, one that I tried my best to avoid thinking about. Generally that worked, but what had happened when James was injured and nearly died had brought it barreling to the forefront again. I was still processing my own feelings about that, and I hadn't even told James the whole story, although I knew he needed to know. Add one more item to the list for dinner tomorrow. But at the very least, I could empathize with the family's tragic loss — I knew all too well how much pain that could cause. So now I knew that Ezra's long and productive life had not been without tragedy. It made me sad. Or maybe I was just sad in general: if I was honest with myself, I would have rather have been with James tonight. What would it be like to come home to each other in the same place every night? I was used to being alone; could I adapt to being half a couple all the time?

With a man who people shot at?

With a man who I loved?

Fish or cut bait, Nell. Get off the fence and commit to one side or the other. All you're doing now is making the two of you miserable.

CHAPTER 27

I woke up early, feeling anxious even before I opened my eyes. Today was Thursday, and Wakeman wanted his report tomorrow. I was confident that Lissa could put together something appropriate, but George Bowen's unsolved murder nagged at me. It had to be connected to those older bodies, didn't it? My mind wandering, I pondered what to wear. James and I hadn't made detailed plans for the evening, but I assumed I'd be staying over, which suited me fine, even if we spent the night looking at property listings.

It was only when I went downstairs to make breakfast that I noticed that the light on my landline phone was blinking. I didn't check it often because few people called me on that line, and most of those were telemarketers or people asking for money, and I preferred to not answer rather than try to come up with yet another polite way to say

346

no. I punched in numbers and retrieved my message, which turned out to be from Eric, informing me that Janet Butler had managed to set up a meeting with Eddie Garrett for ten o'clock this morning and he hoped I'd get the message before I came all the way into the city.

Why hadn't he called me on my cell phone? I checked it and realized I'd turned the sound off. Had I been subconsciously trying to avoid talking to James? During our last conversation, at the end of the workday, he'd sounded a bit cool, and I hadn't wanted to make things worse. But I scrolled through the messages and there were none from him last night, although I did find one from Eric, which was identical to the one he'd left on my home phone.

I thought for a moment, and then I realized I was tired of tiptoeing around the murder. I wanted some answers, and Eddie Garrett might have them. If he didn't, I'd rather know now so we could move in another direction.

So it looked like I was going to West Chester rather than to Philadelphia this morning.

It wasn't even eight o'clock yet, so I decided I'd wait until nine to call Janet to strategize. If she wasn't answering by then,

I'd just go over and sit on her steps and wait for her. That would still give us a little time to figure out how we should approach Eddie at ten.

In the end, that's what I did, and I was sitting in the shade enjoying watching the morning bustle of the town when Janet walked up to the building. "I take it you got my message!" she said. "But I didn't expect you in person."

"I decided I'd rather sit in on it than not. My presence won't intimidate Eddie, will it? We've already met, so he knows who I am. I thought you and I should talk before Eddie arrives. Did he think there was anything strange about you inviting him over?"

Janet was working her key into the front door. "No, or not that I could tell, but he's not one to waste words. Come on in." She led the way through the cool interior, flipping on a few lights along the way, and into her office. "You want coffee?"

"Always, but I'll come along with you so we can talk."

"Great."

I followed her to a space barely bigger than a closet, which held a single-cup coffeemaker and a sink and a small fridge and little more. "I should have given you my home number or my cell number yesterday," I said. "I guess I figured it would take you longer to set up something with Eddie."

"He more or less retired when the farm was sold, so he has plenty of time on his hands. How do you suggest we approach him?" Janet handed me a cup of coffee and then started one for herself.

"You've had conversations with him in the past, haven't you?" When Janet nodded, I went on, "You can start with telling him about how you've been going through Ezra's bequest since all the attention on the Wakeman project started up, asking him if he could tell us more about the family papers. That should give an opening to talk about the daybook, if he's seen it. Then see how he reacts. If he knows about the bodies, he should show *some* sort of reaction. But be tactful, of course."

Her coffee made, Janet turned to me and leaned against the mini fridge. "Nell, what do you really think we're going to find out?"

I thought I owed her an honest answer. "I don't know for sure. Let's just talk to him and see where it goes — he's one more piece of this puzzle. If you're okay with that?"

"That I can do. I really do think we need to get to the bottom of this. I know a little about Eddie, and I have a hard time visualizing him harming anyone. But I'm glad you're here, anyway — I'd probably put my foot in my mouth without you for backup. Let's leave the coffee in my office and go down and meet him in the lobby."

The building was slowly coming alive as staff came in and turned on more lights. Janet and I stood chatting in the lobby until Eddie Garrett walked in. I paid more attention that I had the last time I'd seen him: he looked older than what I knew to be his sixty-plus years, his face weathered, his hands still rough from many years of manual work; he was also taller and broader than I recalled. Dairy farming must be hard, and he'd put in a lifetime doing it. He hovered hesitantly, looking from one of us to the other.

Janet stepped forward with a warm smile. "Welcome, Eddie! I'm so glad you could make it on such short notice. You remember Nell Pratt, right? I asked her to join us because she's the local expert on historical documents, and I'm sure she'll be interested in your family's records. Please, come upstairs where we can be comfortable."

"Hello, Miss Pratt. Yeah, I remember you from that press conference." We followed Janet back to her office in silence.

"Would you like some coffee?" Janet asked.

"Don't trouble yourself," Eddie said.

"Oh, it's no trouble with these modern machines. Won't take a minute." Janet darted down the hall, leaving Eddie and me to sit in awkward silence.

I fought to break it. "We didn't have a chance to talk much at the press conference. From all that I've read or heard, your father was quite a noteworthy figure in Goshen. He was involved in a lot of different things, wasn't he?"

"Yeah. He liked to keep busy. Course, he had me to look after the farmwork."

Did I detect a hint of bitterness in his tone? "Did you handle it all on your own?"

"We had some hired help. Herd was too big for one man, even with the fancy modern machines. And there was always some new regulation coming along. Hard work. Then he sold the place to that damn developer. Oh, sorry." Yes, definitely bitter.

Janet returned and set a mug filled with coffee in front of Eddie. "I didn't know how you liked it, so I brought sugar and creamer."

"Black's fine." Eddie picked up the mug and sipped once, then set it down again, looking at us expectantly. Time to talk: I sat back and let Janet take the lead.

Janet gave him a smile that didn't betray any nervousness. "Eddie, I can't tell you how happy we are that your father entrusted us with his papers. Since all this recent trouble, I thought we should go through them sooner rather later, so I pulled out the boxes and I've been doing some preliminary sorting. Awful thing about George Bowen, wasn't it? Did you know him?"

I wondered if Eddie would notice the abrupt change of subject, but all he said was, "Met him now and then at the township. Wouldn't say we were friends."

"He was a member here, too — really took an interest in local history." Janet's glance darted briefly toward me, but I didn't interrupt her.

"Plenty of that to go around," Eddie said. "What do you want from me?"

"I thought you might be familiar with the papers that your father donated, since they involve many generations of your family, and maybe you could give me some guidance about where to start? You know, which documents might be the most interesting? Maybe we could put together a small exhibit, timed to coincide with the opening of the Wakeman development."

Eddie's expression didn't change. "Not

much to tell. Family settled on the place seventeen-something, and we were still there until Pa sold it to that Wakeman guy."

"Kind of an unusual transaction, wasn't it?" I asked. "Did all the family agree to that? Or would you rather have stayed and kept the dairy farm going?" I wondered if he would think I was being rude, asking such a personal question.

Apparently not. Eddie shrugged. "Pa had his mind made up. My brother, William, went along with it, so I didn't have much choice. The money offered was good, and the dairy business isn't what it once was. It seemed for the best."

Given what I'd seen of him so far, I had to wonder if Eddie had put up much of a fight, no matter what his preferences had been. "It must be hard to leave a place where you and your family had so much personal history."

"I've moved on." Eddie didn't add anything else. I wondered where he was living now.

I heard my cell phone ringing in the depths of my bag. When I looked at it, I saw it was James. "Excuse me — I have to take this." I walked out of the office and into the hall before I answered.

"Where are you?" James said.

"In West Chester, talking to Eddie Garrett. Why?"

"The DNA results are in."

"And?"

"I don't know what you were expecting, but it turns out that the two dead men were closely related, probably brothers. You're betting they were also both Garretts?"

I was stunned into silence for a moment; that was one item I had not been expecting. "You are very good at your job. Yes, I am." More so than ever.

"And you're going to ask Eddie Garrett for a sample?"

"I . . . don't know. Depends on what he says. It may not be necessary."

James was silent for a couple of seconds. "Do you think he had anything to do with George Bowen's murder?"

"Maybe. It makes sense, in a way."

"Nell, be careful. Tell Janet Butler to be careful. You're interfering in a police investigation."

Not for the first time, I wanted to say, but didn't. "I will. See you later." I hung up before he could lecture me any more. And turned off the ringer.

"I apologize," I said as I returned to Janet's office. She raised an eyebrow a discreet eighth of an inch, and I nodded, just a bit. I hoped she had gotten the message, that there was more to tell. "Did I miss anything?"

"Eddie was just telling me about how proud his father was of the history of the farm."

"Do you share his enthusiasm, Eddie?" I asked, hoping it sounded like an innocent question.

"About history? Not much. There was always too much to do around the place — I didn't have time to mess around with old stories and papers and stuff. My brother went to college, got a job where he wears a suit. I ended up looking after the farm with Pa."

I nodded, mainly to encourage him to talk. "Let me tell you, people like Janet and me, who work at institutions like this, we're always thrilled to find original documents. It makes history seem so much more real, and then we get to share that feeling with the public. What did you think when those two older bodies were found? Obviously they'd been there for a long time."

His expression hardened. "I was as surprised as the next man," he said.

"Do you know, there's something in one of the documents that suggests that those bodies had been there since the Revolution," Janet said brightly.

Eddie's gaze swiveled slowly from me to Janet. "Is that so."

"We think they might have taken part in the Battle of Paoli," I added. He didn't rise to the bait, so I went on. "I thought it was curious that the part of the farm where they were found was never used as pasture."

"Pa never wanted to — said he liked to keep some trees around the place. Cattle need shade now and then." Eddie's tone was neutral, giving nothing away.

"Still, it's surprising that nobody found the bodies before now," I said, watching him.

"Like I said, lots of history around here." If he'd been a cat, I thought his tail would be twitching by now.

Time to lob my little bomb. "There's something even more interesting about those bodies, Eddie. It turns out they were brothers."

Eddie's head whipped back toward me. "How would anybody know that?"

"DNA," I said. We held each other's eyes for several beats.

He stood up suddenly. "Janet, I've got a . . . an appointment I've got to be at. Can we pick this up some other time?"

Janet had come to her feet when he stood.

"Of course, whenever you like. I really appreciate your help on this, Eddie."

"Yeah." He turned and left abruptly, too quickly for Janet to follow.

She sat down again slowly. "Well, that was interesting. I take it that call was from the FBI, about the DNA test?"

"Yes. I certainly didn't expect that result. We have to rethink our theory, if it was brother against brother." And only one of them in a British uniform. "What an awful thing."

"It is," Janet said softly.

We were silent for a few beats, and then I said, "And if you handle that carefully" — I nodded toward Eddie's coffee mug — "you'll have a Garrett sample to compare it to. He was definitely spooked we knew that the bodies were related, which makes me think he must have known."

"But why would he care so much?"

It was all coming together. That so-polite article I'd read the night before? The boy with the gun had to have been Eddie, even though he wasn't named. "I think it's something personal." I described the old news article to Janet. "I think it's possible that Eddie was involved in the shooting accident that killed his older brother, even though the article didn't say so outright, since they were both children and the family was respected in the community. If that's true, then the idea of brother killing brother would have a lot more meaning to him. He might think that if it came out, the old story would be dredged up again and people would know what he'd done all those years ago. But of course, that would also mean he knew who the bodies were."

"Oh God, how sad. Poor Eddie."

"Poor Eddie may have killed a man to keep his secret," I reminded her. "The article I saw online was pretty vague, and Eddie would've been young at the time, so the reporter was probably protecting him. But I'd guess Eddie didn't want the story of how his brother died to become common knowledge, which is in fact what is probably going to happen now that the old bodies have been discovered. News coverage has changed a lot, and I don't think they'd respect his privacy now."

"What the heck do we do now?" Janet asked.

"I really don't know. All we've done is establish a potential motive for George's murder: Eddie wanted the bodies to stay buried, and he knew George would talk. That makes Eddie the most likely suspect. We don't know if George went to Eddie to tell him, or if Eddie just happened to cross paths with George right after he'd made his big find. But there's nothing remotely resembling proof of any of this. Still, you should be careful. If we're right, he's already killed one person."

"But he has to realize he can't keep a lid on this now."

"Still, just watch out. And don't tell anyone else what we suspect for the moment."

"I'll stick close to my husband — that should make him happy. What about you?"

"I'll be in the city, so I'm not worried." Not with my own personal FBI bodyguard. "I'll take that mug with me and give it to the FBI." I stood up, retrieved the mug with a tissue, and retraced my steps to the break closet, where I carefully poured out the coffee, then slipped the mug into a large clean envelope I'd gotten from Janet — feeling absurdly foolish all the way — then stuffed the mug into my bag.

Janet walked me downstairs. "Well, this has been interesting. Is your job normally like this?"

I laughed. "More often than you might guess. I hope this will all be wrapped up soon. I think your cover story about a small exhibit was a good one, by the way. We should talk more about it, when all this is settled."

"I'd like that. Thanks for everything — let me know if you need anything else."

"I will, Janet. Take care."

I retrieved my car and set off for Philadelphia with my bag of evidence.

CHAPTER 28

I arrived in the city not long after noon. The drive gave me time to think — always risky. I had to wonder how I kept finding myself in the middle of situations that involved murder and mayhem — and now I was dragging other people, like Janet, into them as well. It wasn't that I went looking for trouble, or that I thought I was some super sleuth, wiser than the police, the FBI, and anybody else who might be looking at a crime. What I did bring to the table was a different perspective: I knew history. I'd be a fish out of water in the investigation of a domestic killing or a street-corner drug shooting, but anything that had deep roots in the greater Philadelphia area and its history was my turf. Sure, I would have said it was unlikely that the discovery of the remains of two men who had fought and died in the Revolution — and oddly, I could name the precise day they had died — could point to the culprit in a killing that had taken place only a week or two earlier, but there it was. I'd be happy to be proved wrong. Maybe George Bowen had been killed by his wife's lover or a random stranger.

But I doubted it. In any case, my heart ached for Eddie Garrett.

Once I was back in my office, Lissa appeared promptly and handed me a sheaf of papers. "This is the draft. You want me to go away while you read it?" she asked anxiously.

"In a minute. First, come in and close the door, will you?" When she had, I said, "I met with Janet Butler and Eddie Garrett this morning in West Chester. While I was there, I got a call from James, who said that the DNA samples from the two bodies shows that they were brothers. So I think you got it right: they were the first Edward Garrett's sons and died in the aftermath of the Battle of Paoli. I've got a sample of Eddie's DNA in my purse. But I think Janet and I more or less showed our hand when we were talking to Eddie."

Lissa seemed to take my statements in stride. "So he knows what you know?"

"Sort of. We didn't spell it out, but I think he knew what we were saying."

"But why on earth would he kill anybody?"

"I think I can guess. I was doing some research on the Garrett family online last night, and I found an article about the death of a third Garrett brother, when he was a child. Apparently it was an accident involving a gun. Back then reporters were pretty discreet, but it seems all too likely that somehow Eddie was responsible for his brother's death, or at least believes he was. And if that's true, then finding the two bodies now must have brought it all back. He probably couldn't face having all of his own family history dragged out and examined, so he lashed out to silence George. But remember, this is still just a theory. We don't have proof."

"That poor man," Lissa said softly. "No wonder it was such a sloppy murder. And he must have moved the body to draw attention away from that burial, but he didn't count on the police bringing dogs in."

"Criminals are not always smart people, and Eddie may have panicked, believed that silencing George would be enough to keep all of it quiet. George could have come to him first with his discovery, out of courtesy, since it had been his family's farm. Maybe he hoped Eddie would know something more. Poor George."

"Wow," Lissa said. "I never thought historical research could be so dramatic. What do I do with the report?"

"Hang on a moment." I went around my desk and opened the door, then asked Eric, "Have Wakeman's people called?"

"Sure have," Eric replied. "About four times. You're on for two o'clock tomorrow."

"Thanks, Eric." I went back into the office, shutting the door carefully behind me. "We have until two tomorrow to sort things out. I'll read what you've put together, and then I'll see James tonight, and I'll let you know in the morning if I think we need to make any changes. But we may not have enough information to include the full story of the two dead soldiers. Maybe you could include a brief discussion of that in your final draft, and we can decide tomorrow whether to present it to Wakeman. Sound OK?"

"That's fine. I'll get out of your hair now."

After she'd left I read through what she'd given me. It was good, and I had few suggestions for changes. As it was currently structured, we could either skirt around the Revolutionary War graves entirely, or we had the option of making them a prominent talking point. That decision was up to Wakeman and his crew, though I had a feeling the timing would depend on whether any arrest was imminent.

I threw myself back into the ordinary business of running the Society for the rest of the day. It was a good distraction. Signing begging letters was seldom a life-or-death issue. It was close to six when I went downstairs to the lobby to find James already there, deep in conversation with Front Desk Bob. I tended to forget that Bob was a retired police officer, which is what gave his quiet presence such authority when it came to arguing with cranky patrons. That made him a colleague of James's, sort of.

"Am I the last one to leave?" I asked Bob.

"Just about. I'll do a check after you go, and lock up."

"Thanks, Bob. Good night."

Out on the front steps, I looked up at James. "Where to?"

"We walk."

"We're going out for dinner?"

"Yes." He didn't elaborate. I didn't press.

We strolled amiably for a few blocks. A public sidewalk was not the place to discuss a murder investigation — or anything else of substance, for that matter — so we made chitchat in a desultory fashion. It was warm and humid, but occasionally we caught a breeze from the Delaware River.

After several blocks we stopped in front of a restaurant I had walked by countless times but had never been in. "This is where we're going?" I asked.

"It is. Have you been here?"

"No, but it smells wonderful." Behind a high iron fence I could see tables scattered around a courtyard surrounded by nine-teenth — or even eighteenth? — century buildings. Tea lights flickered on the tables, illuminating the small vases filled with fresh flowers. It looked lovely — and I was re-minded that I'd never eaten lunch.

We went through the gate, and James had a quiet word with the maître d', who nod-ded and escorted us to a table in a corner with an ivy-covered brick wall behind us. He held my chair for me, and I glared at him when he made a move toward my napkin; I was perfectly capable of unfolding a napkin for my lap, thank you. "Something to drink, perhaps?" he said.

James looked at me. "Wine?"

"Fine."

James conferred with the maître d', who nodded and retreated quickly toward the kitchen.

When he was gone, I said, "Don't let me forget that I have a DNA sample for you in my bag."

James cocked an eyebrow at me for a moment, then burst out laughing. "Here I try to create a lovely romantic evening, and this is what you say?"

He had a point, and I backtracked quickly. "I apologize. This is delightful, and I was hoping to get business out of the way so I could enjoy it." *Good save, Nell.*

"All right, I will remind you later. And before you ask, I have no new information on that case to offer. Do you?"

"No, not since I talked to you this morning. Although I think we spooked Eddie Garrett."

"What was your impression of him?"

"Sad. Taciturn. Bitter. Physically strong, since he's done farmwork his whole life. Do I think he's a killer? I'm not sure."

The maître d' reappeared with a bottle of wine in an ice bucket, and he and James went through the ritual of opening and tasting. Ultimately the waiter was allowed to pour us two glasses, then he distributed menus. Poring over the menus took another two minutes and some consultation, but finally we conveyed our orders and were left in peace.

I distracted myself with carefully buttering a roll (warm from the oven, and the butter was unsalted), because I had no idea what to say. I had the strong feeling that he'd set up this lovely dinner with a purpose in mind. I knew there were things I *didn't* want to say, but I also knew that at some point I had to say them. I loved James — that much I knew. But I still wasn't sure how much I wanted to change my life for him. I knew he wanted more, and a part of me did, too. So what was my problem? I looked up to find him watching me, and his expression broke my heart; it was so vulnerable, so uncertain. I wanted to fall back on a challenging *What?* but I knew what.

"I'm sorry," I said softly. "I'm not being fair to you. About us, I mean."

"So you're not apologizing for inserting yourself in the middle of yet another criminal investigation?" His mouth twitched, so I knew he wasn't serious.

"I don't go looking for them, and you know it. But I'll concede that they're a distraction."

"That they are."

A waitperson appeared and silently slid our appetizers before us. They looked too pretty to eat, but that didn't stop me.

Between bites I said, "You aren't going to go all macho on me and tell me to tend to my knitting and stay out of police and FBI business, are you?"

"Heaven forbid. I know it wouldn't work anyway. And I acknowledge that you do bring a unique perspective to certain cases."

"Thank you. I'm glad you feel that way. I'm also glad I can help — I couldn't just sit by when I thought I knew something that might make a difference."

"And I wouldn't ask you to. But know that I worry about you, about your safety."

"And you don't think I worry about yours? Your job is a heck of a lot more dangerous than mine."

"Most of the time, anyway," he agreed.

The appetizer plates were whisked away, to be replaced by our entrees. I took one look at my plate, and said, "Can we table this discussion until we've finished eating? This looks incredible, and I'd hate to waste it."

"I agree. And there's no hurry."

We ate. No, we more than ate: We savored. Reveled. Wallowed. Gorged. I ran out of verbs. How had I never known about this little gem of a restaurant, mere blocks from where I'd worked for years?

"How did you ever find this place?" I asked James, all but licking the plate to capture the last few smears of an exquisite sauce.

"Marty."

"Marty doesn't do food."

"But she knows about it."

"Marty apparently knows about everything in a two-hundred-mile radius. But I'll thank her for this. Did Marty know we were coming here?"

"Yes."

I pondered that for a moment. Maybe Marty was trying to nudge — or given Marty's lack of subtlety, shove — our relationship forward. I opened my mouth to speak, and the server appeared again. "Dessert?"

I looked at James, and he looked at the server. "Espresso. Two."

The server collected our plates and disappeared. I love dessert; I always order dessert. James knew that. But tonight I *didn't* want dessert — and James knew that, too. I looked around the charming courtyard, filled with happy couples enjoying the food and one another's company. The sun had sunk low, although it was still light, and there were shadows in the corners. I felt tears pricking my eyes.

I turned to face James squarely. "Are you ending things with me?"

He looked shocked. "What? No! Of course not. Why the hell would you think that?"

His vehemence attracted a few curious looks from people at nearby tables.

"Because this would be the perfect setting. You know I wouldn't make a scene. You've softened me up with good food and fine wine. Now you're supposed to say something like 'Nell, I don't think this is going to work.' "

"How could you think such a thing? Nell, I love you. Maybe we've hit a couple of speed bumps, but nothing serious. I brought you here because I thought you'd like it. And . . ."

"I do like it, very much. What's the *and*?"

"This restaurant is attached to the hotel there. I took a room for the night."

That I had not expected. "Why?"

"Because I thought we needed neutral ground — not your place, not my place — if we're going to make some serious decisions. We have things to talk about, yes, but it's not about ending this, it's about moving forward."

"Oh. Well, then. Good idea." James was one smart man.

The server appeared with our espressos. We finished off the last of the wine in the bottle, then drank our coffee silently. But it was not an ominous silence.

No bill appeared, so James must have arranged to have it added to the hotel bill. "Are you ready to go?" he asked.

"I am." And I followed him into the building.

CHAPTER 29

Worried though I was about whatever was to come, I was impressed by the boutique hotel. I guessed that it had been built as an elegant home for a prominent family in the eighteenth century, and any changes made since were discreet. The rooms were scattered over three floors above the ground floor, one or two rooms off each landing with a curving stairway connecting the floors.

Clearly James had taken care of all the details earlier. He nodded toward the concierge at a desk in the small lobby, then pointed me toward the stairway and guided me to a door on the third floor, which he opened with a key he pulled from his pocket. I walked in to find, first, a miniature sitting room with a short settee and a small desk, on which were a vase of flowers and an ice bucket with another bottle of chilled wine. Beyond that lay the bedroom, with a small bathroom — obviously a later addition, but nicely done — shoehorned into the corner adjacent to the sitting room. The windows overlooked the restaurant courtyard, but they were well insulated and I couldn't hear anything from below.

My mind was working slowly, and eventually it occurred to me that I didn't have any night things or clothes. "I don't have . . ." I began.

"Yes, you do," James said, nodding toward a bag tucked in a corner.

"Marty?" I guessed. He nodded.

"So, what now?"

James took off his jacket and hung it neatly over the back of a chair. And then he took off his holster and his gun. No matter how often I saw James armed, it still threw me. After what had happened earlier this year, I was grateful for his weapon, but it was still unsettling.

"Is that . . . ?" I pointed. I hadn't actually looked at his gun since he'd gone back to work. The sight, the presence of that weapon, disturbed me, made me edgy. And it looked especially incongruous in this lovely antique room.

"The same weapon? Yes, it was returned to me." Then he looked at me more closely. "Yes, that's the one you fired. You know, we never talked about that."

I quailed inwardly. "Well, there really wasn't a good time right after, and then things just moved on . . . Are you going to open the wine?"

Yes, it was a distraction, but I needed it. I followed James into the front room, where he was filling two glasses. He handed me one. "What's wrong?"

A good observer was Special Agent James Morrison of the FBI. "I owe you that explanation. Can we sit?"

He sat on the mini settee. I sat on the stiff side chair by the small window, not touching him.

I hesitated, unsure of how to begin; I knew this would be hard for me, but it had to be said. "About the gun thing — there are some things you need to know. I've been handling weapons — handguns, shotguns, the whole gamut — since I was in high school. My father taught me. It was one of the bonding things we did — I was an only child, and I think he would have preferred a boy, but he took me along to the range one day, and when I turned out to be a pretty good shot, it helped. We used to go regularly on Sundays, just the two of us."

James was watching me intently, but he made no effort to interrupt. I took a deep breath and went on. "When I realized that I could get my hands on your Glock that day, I acted without even thinking."

"So it wasn't just a lucky shot?"

I nodded. "No, it wasn't. I hit what I was aiming for. Besides, it would have been hard to miss at that distance."

"Thank you," James said. "Your father would be proud of you. He taught you well."

I looked away, fighting to get the next words out. "There's more. Have you ever wondered why I never talk about my family?"

"I hadn't really thought about it. There's a reason?"

"Yes." There was no pretty way to put this, so I just stated it bluntly. "My father killed himself when I was seventeen, with one of his handguns. My mother didn't take it too well, and more or less drank herself to death, although it took her five years to destroy her liver. She wouldn't let me get rid of the gun collection, even though she hated it. I didn't tell her, but I made sure the guns were disabled, so she wouldn't be able to do what my father had done. As soon as she was gone, I sold the lot of them. I never wanted to see them again. I never wanted to touch a gun again."

Wisely James made no move toward me. I

was afraid I would fall apart if he touched me. "Nell, I'm so sorry. I'm sorry it had to happen to you. I'm sorry that this thing brought it all back."

"It's not your fault. Part of me was glad I knew what to do — to save you."

James nodded once, acknowledging what I'd said. "Is it a problem for you that I carry a gun?"

"To be honest, I never really gave it much thought. I mean, I know you do, but . . ." I couldn't seem to find words that made sense. I knew James was not my father, and in his hands a gun was not an evil thing. Or maybe I cared enough about him that it didn't matter. ". . . I can handle it," I finished. "It's part of who you are and what you do. Maybe what happened was some kind of cosmic balancing act, good compensating for evil."

But somehow that didn't seem to be the whole story . . . until at last the pieces fell into place and I saw what had been holding me back — not just with James but with so many other things in my life. "Oh God," I whispered, more to myself than to him.

Now he made a move to get up, to reach out to me, but I stopped him with a gesture. "No, wait, please . . . I have to work this out." I took a swallow of wine, then another, mostly as a stalling tactic — and to keep me from hyperventilating. How could I have been so stupid for so long?

And James watched and waited, his concern etched on his face. He knew, he had always known, that I had to be ready.

Another deep breath helped. "I know what the problem is, but I never saw it before. I guess I never had a reason to look too hard before now." *Before you.* "I loved my father, and I worked hard to get close to him. He was a complicated man, I can see that now. And then he killed himself, with no warning, and I was shocked, and hurt. He left my mother, and he left me, with no explanation. Maybe there was a reason, or maybe he was just depressed, but to me he was simply . . . gone. And then because of that my mother withdrew from me, too, although it took longer. But somewhere inside, I felt like they'd left because I wasn't good enough for either of them. That I didn't matter enough to stick around for. I know, it's not rational, but I think that's why I've never really committed to anyone since. Because it would hurt too much when they left me."

I took another sip of wine, and I noticed that my glass was empty. I reached out to retrieve the bottle and refilled it. "You know

378

I was married once before?"

"Yes."

"And it ended. Not badly, but there just wasn't a lot holding us together. He was a good guy, and after we split up, he married someone else and had a couple of kids. He's happy. But the worst part was, I really didn't miss him. We'd been married for three years, and when he was gone, I felt . . . relieved, I guess. I didn't have to worry anymore about making him happy or wonder why things weren't working and if it was my fault. It seemed like the right thing to do at the time, but we never should have gotten married at all. I couldn't let him in. I couldn't let myself care about him too much. And there hasn't been anyone since, not anyone that mattered. Until you."

"And that's why you've been pushing me away?" James asked quietly. "Because you do care? Too much?"

"But I didn't want to push you away! I didn't mean to. It's just that this whole thing between us has me scared."

"And my getting injured didn't help."

"Weirdly enough, it did. Not because I got to play heroine and save you, but because it forced me to recognize how much I cared about you and that I didn't want to lose you. But as soon as you started talking about moving in together, I started backing away."

"I noticed," James said wryly. Then he turned serious again. "Nell, I could say something trite here like 'You're never going to lose me,' but you're an intelligent woman and you know I can't promise that. My job can be dangerous, as you know all too well. When I joined the Bureau, I had only myself to consider, and it didn't make a difference to me. Now it does. I don't want to inflict that on you. I can quit, find something else to do."

"No!" I stood up abruptly, unable to sit still like a calm, rational person, which at the moment I wasn't. "I don't want that. I mean, I don't want that for *you*. It's an important job, you like it, and you're good at it. I don't want to be responsible for telling you to change your life, not because I have baggage. I don't have the right to do that, and I don't want to."

Now he stood up, too. "What about what *I* want? What if you're more important to me than any job?"

"How can I be?" I whispered. He was standing close, so close . . .

"You are."

We stopped talking for a while. A long while.

Later, we lay in the dark, propped up by a dozen or so pillows — this was a *nice* little hotel — finishing up the last of the wine, now room temperature. "Thank you," I said.

"For what? This?"

"Yes, this, but mainly for not giving up on me. First Marty, and now you — you keep telling me how to fix my life, and I can't even resent it because I know you're both right, in your own ways. I'm getting a little old to be scared of messing things up. It's time I figured out how to commit." I pulled myself up and rolled onto my side to look at James, or at as much of him as I could see in the light that trickled in from the courtyard below. "Don't quit your job. What you do matters. I know that. I understand that because I've had a little taste of it myself."

"And given me palpitations when you do," he grumbled.

"Look, there are idiots who go skydiving or swimming with sharks, looking for danger. You risk your life because you're helping someone else. And that's all I'm trying to do. If I have knowledge that matters, I'm going to act on it. And pass it on to you."

"Does it have to be in that order?"

"We'll see. And I'm sorry I've been dragging my feet about finding a place — I just needed time to process the idea. You gave me time. So let's do this thing."

"What are you doing tomorrow? Or I guess I mean later today."

"The only thing on my schedule is meeting with Mitchell Wakeman to present Lissa's report, at two."

"Will that include what you guess about Eddie Garrett?"

"It doesn't have to. We can simply call the bodies two unknown Revolutionary War soldiers from opposing sides, lying side by side through the centuries."

"Good spin. What about George Bowen's death?"

"That might be trickier, but it doesn't have to go into the Society's report. If anyone asks, I'll just refer them to the police, or you."

We drifted into sleep, entangled, and woke up the same way. "What time is it?" I asked, not that I was in a hurry. After all, I was only a few blocks from work.

James rolled over. "Looks like . . . seven something. There's a buffet breakfast downstairs — part of the package."

"Sounds good. Can I have the first shower?"

"Go for it."

I rolled out of bed and realized I hadn't

even checked what Marty had included in the overnight bag she had so thoughtfully provided — I'd never gotten around to opening it. I assumed she'd raided what I kept at James's place and knew what was appropriate for a day at work. She had included one new item, a slithery silk nightgown — that we hadn't had a chance to try out.

We did the normal morning things, and Marty's choices were fine. I hated to leave our little universe — James's brilliant idea to get us out of our respective nests and into a place where we were on equal footing had paid off.

Downstairs, breakfast was served in a large, brightly lit room lined with bookshelves, its tall windows facing the street. A diverse array of hot and cold foods was laid out in silver-plated dishes, and we served ourselves and found a table a comfortable distance from the few other people in the room.

"Maybe we could just move in here," I joked. "The food is good, someone else does all the cleaning, and we could both walk to work."

"It might be a bit beyond our combined budget," James said.

"Oh, pooh — you're no fun. Maybe you

could moonlight as their in-house security and get a discount."

"I'll take it under advisement." I didn't hear a phone ring, but James must have set his on vibrate, because he reached into his jacket pocket and pulled out his cell phone. He looked at it, then stood up, and said, "I need to take this," and walked into the adjoining room. He was back in under two minutes, his expression somber.

"What?" I asked.

"Eddie Garrett was found dead in his home this morning when police went to question him. He committed suicide with an old shotgun. He left a note, confessing to George Bowen's murder."

I couldn't speak for a long moment, buffeted once again by memories of my father. But then I realized they didn't hurt as much as they had — before I'd told James the story. "Poor Eddie," I whispered, fighting tears once again.

James reached across the table and took my hand. "Don't blame yourself, Nell. It would have come out one way or another."

"That doesn't make it hurt less. I feel responsible."

"I know. There's something else."

I wiped my eyes and faced him. "What?"

"You were right — he was the one who'd

been holding the gun that killed his brother. He never really got over it, and dealing with the exposure of those two early Garrett brothers was too much for him. He said all that in the note. It's not your fault, Nell."

"I know, or at least the rational part of me does. But it still hurts. Funny how history comes back to haunt us, isn't it?"

CHAPTER 30

Even the sad news about Eddie Garrett couldn't dampen my spirits altogether. After talking things through with James, I felt like a huge burden had been lifted from my shoulders — one I hadn't even recognized I was carrying. For years I'd done a good job of *not* thinking about a lot of things, like what had happened with my family and my marriage, and I hadn't realized how much it was dragging me down. And it had taken a catastrophic event to make me understand it. And James.

I still wasn't entirely sure I deserved James. He was smart and good at a job he liked and nice to his extended family and honest and brave and true and all that good stuff — and he loved me. Of that I had no doubt, for how else could anyone have put up with my vacillating?

We finished up our breakfast quickly and packed up what little we had, and then strolled out onto the street, side by side. The sun was shining, there was a cool breeze, and all that was missing were a few bluebirds and butterflies and maybe a rainbow. At the corner I turned toward the Society, and James followed. "Wait, don't you work in the other direction?" I teased.

"I'm escorting you home — figuratively, at least."

"Oh. Thank you." We took our time covering the few blocks to the Society building, enjoying the moment. When we arrived, I said, "Will there be more fallout from . . . Eddie's death?"

"For me, possibly. I can keep you out of it."

"I'm already in it — I just want to figure out what to say to Wakeman. I bet he thought the whole deal would be easy when Ezra agreed to the sale, and now all this happens. Oh, and I should talk to Janet, too — I don't know if she'll have heard the news. Will I see you tonight?"

"I hope so. I'll call you during the day if there are any new developments."

"Let me know where we're going to be, okay?" If I recalled, my car was still parked across the street, with a whopping bill, no doubt. But, oh, last night had been worth it!

I let myself into the building and went upstairs to find that Eric had beaten me to the office yet again. "Hey, Eric. Can we use the conference room for our meeting with Wakeman? He may decide to bring his staff." Or he might not bring anyone at all, if he was discouraged by the events that kept springing up like mushrooms around his beloved project.

"Already booked," he said.

"I should have guessed. Have you by any chance seen Lissa yet?"

"She's in your office. You want coffee?"

"Sure."

When I walked into my office, Lissa was sitting on the settee, scribbling edits on printed pages. "Did you ever go home last night?" I asked.

She looked up, dazed. "What time is it? No. I figured I'd go over this with you, then run home for a quick shower and change before our meeting at two. It is still at two, right?"

"Yes, but I have some new details and you may have to make a few changes." Eric appeared with a mug of steaming coffee, and I waited until he'd returned to his desk before resuming, glad of the delay. "You know about my meeting with Janet Butler and Eddie Garrett yesterday. This morning James got a call that Eddie Garrett killed himself sometime during the night. He left a note confessing to the murder of George Bowen." It still hurt me to say that. Although I know it wasn't rational, I felt responsible for pushing Eddie to such a drastic solution. The fact that the whole story was likely to have come out eventually was little comfort.

"Oh my God," Lissa said, trying to process the new information. "Oh, wow. Do we assume Wakeman will know about this?"

"Probably somebody on one or more police forces will tell him, right?"

"Yeah, sure. He's got friends everywhere, doesn't he? So what do we put in the report?"

Based on my half hour of absorbing the news and its ramifications, I said, "I think we go with the straight history part of it — who owned the land over the centuries. I think you can put together a separate appendix about the dead soldiers and Eddie Garrett's connection to them, for Wakeman's eyes only, and let him decide what he wants to do with it. I don't think it's our place to tell the world, no matter how juicy a story it might be. Wakeman asked for a simple report on the history of the farm, and that's what we'll give him. If he wants more, let him ask."

Lissa thought hard for a moment, her fatigue clear on her face. "I think I agree. And it makes my job easier, because the core stuff is done. You want to see another draft?"

"No, I think what you've already done is great. Make those last few changes, print me out a copy, give one to Eric to make copies for the meeting, and go home and take a nap. Well, once you add that other bit, just for Wakeman's copy."

"Thanks, Nell. You want me at the meeting, right?"

"Of course I do. You did all the work."

"Then I'll see you later."

After she had left, I checked the time. It was still early, but maybe Janet would already be in her office. I'd rather she heard the news from me than from a cop or not at all.

She picked up after the first ring. "Nell?"

From the tone of her voice I could tell she knew. "You heard?"

"I did. A friend who works for the township called me. What an awful thing. I feel so guilty. And so bad for Eddie."

"I know what you mean. Maybe no one could have accused him of killing George Bowen, but I guess he couldn't handle having everyone know about his role in his brother's death, which was bound to come out once the dead soldiers had been found. There was no putting the genie back in the bottle."

"Poor Eddie," Janet echoed my comment. "What are you going to tell the Wakeman people?"

"I told Lissa just now that we should stick with the simple history. I'll let him know the rest of the story, but privately. If he wants to use the information, it's up to him."

"Fair enough. Thanks for calling, Nell. Despite everything, I enjoyed working with you."

"Me, too. And I was serious about that idea for an exhibit. Let's talk about it later, when the dust settles. Keep in touch." As I hung up I wondered if Wakeman would go as far as to shut down the project, but somehow I doubted it. From what I'd learned, he'd had his heart set on this for a long time.

I muddled through the next few hours. I made a few phone calls, including one I'd been putting off for a while. But my mind was somewhere else, or rather several some-wheres, bouncing from yesterday's conversa-tion with Eddie Garrett and the way his face changed when he realized I knew the story, to several memorable moments last night with James. For all that he was a government agent, he was an extraordinarily kind and patient man. I was staring into space, no doubt with a small smile on my face, when Eric, followed by Lissa, came in to announce that Mitchell Wakeman was waiting downstairs.

I brought my wandering attention back to the present. "Thank you, Eric. Will you go down and get him, and escort him up to the conference room?"

"Sure thing. Everything's set up in there."

When Eric had left, I asked Lissa, "Are you ready?"

"I hope so. No matter how it goes, Nell, thanks for this opportunity. I think we academic types tend to forget that history is still very much with us, and we've seen that this week."

"I know what you mean. Well, let's do this thing."

We were waiting in the conference room when Mitchell Wakeman stalked in — alone. I wasn't sure whether this was a good or bad sign.

"You heard about Garrett?" he demanded.

"I did."

"You know why he did it?"

"I do. Why don't we sit down and talk

about it? Will Scott or anyone else from your team be joining us?"

"Nope. I wanted to get the facts first. I'll pass along whatever I think they need to know."

He dropped into a chair. I handed him one of the copies of the reports. "We decided to break this up into two parts. The first is the history of the farm and its place in the community. The second is about those two soldiers — for your eyes only, if you choose, and there's more I can add that we didn't write down."

"Let me read 'em first." He took them both, then started leafing through the first report. I glanced briefly at Lissa, and then we sat in silence while Wakeman read. Thank goodness he was a fast reader, and it didn't take long. When he was finished, he put the papers down, sat back in his chair, and rubbed his hands over his face. "You said there's more?"

"Yes. We know the dead soldiers were brothers, and we suspect that they were members of the Garrett family, fighting for opposite sides, and that the family passed down the story. And that's why Eddie killed George Bowen, and then himself. He was involved in the shooting death of his brother when they were both children, and he couldn't face it all coming out again."

"You got proof?"

"We can compare Eddie's DNA with the others, if it's necessary."

"Who else knows?"

"Apart from Lissa and me? James Morrison, the FBI agent you called in, and Janet Butler in West Chester. No one else."

"Will it come out?"

"Do you want it to?" I parried. "Odds are high it will reach the press eventually, since there's already been coverage about the bodies' discovery. If you want to put your own spin on it, now's the time. Do you plan to move forward with the project?"

"Hell, yes. I've got too much invested in this to walk away now. And I don't mean just money. Let me think."

He thought. Lissa and I waited. I wasn't even sure what outcome to hope for.

Finally he sat up again and slapped both hands on the table. "First, I've got to thank you for finding all this out and then for keeping it quiet. I think you're right — it's too good a story for the press to ignore, and there's probably somebody nosy enough to keep digging, so I'll turn it over to my people and let them work out how we can use it. But I owe you — both of you here — and you'll get what's coming to you. And I guess I owe that lady in West Chester, too. Look, I'm going to put together another press conference, and I want you on the podium."

"I won't sugarcoat it."

"I didn't ask you to. You can't mess with history, and I wouldn't want to."

"I'm glad to hear that."

Wakeman stood up abruptly. "I gotta get this thing rolling. Thanks for everything. We'll be in touch." He strode out of the room, and I rushed to catch up so I could take him downstairs.

In the poky elevator, I asked him. "Why is this project so important to you?"

Wakeman sighed. "I've built a lot of things around here. I'm proud of them, and I've made a lot of money. This one, though — it's not about the money, it's about what's the best way to live in the world today. I wanted to make a model for the future. And then the past popped up in the middle of it. Maybe there's a lesson in that. But the idea is still good. It'll work."

"I hope it does." I let him out of the elevator and watched him head toward the front door, and then the elevator doors closed and I pressed the button for the third floor again.

Upstairs, Lissa was still hovering anxiously

outside my office. "Everything okay?" she asked.

"You know, I think it is. When I first met the man, I hoped he was basically a decent guy, and I haven't seen anything to change my mind. Don't worry. If he doesn't come up with a check soon, I'll make it right with you and then I can hound him so you won't have to. But it occurs to me that the Society could probably use you for other assignments like this, as a contractor. You know, the genealogy of building sites or houses or the like? On a project-by-project basis. If Wakeman puts in a good word for you, more people might be interested."

"That sounds great, Nell! And I could fit it in around my graduate course work. Thanks a lot!"

"Hey, we all win — you did a great job on this, with too little time and a few unexpected distractions. Now take the rest of the day off and have some fun."

"I'll do that." She left my office with a smile on her face, but I noticed that instead of heading toward the elevator she went down the hall toward Ben's cubicle. Interesting.

Eric came in and handed me a few message slips. "Agent Morrison called while you were in your meeting. He said I didn't need to interrupt you, but he'll stop by at five and pick you up."

"Did he say anything else?"

"Nope. Just to meet him outside — he'll be driving."

CHAPTER 31

I was on the sidewalk outside the Society waiting for James when he pulled up. He opened the door for me. "Get in."

"You do remember I have a car parked across the street?" I said, climbing in anyway.

"We'll deal with that later. Buckle up."

"Where are we going?" I said as I complied.

"You'll see."

The man was full of surprises these days. I wondered if Marty had had a hand in this one, too, or if she'd just given him instructions on how to woo reluctant me. I wasn't going to complain. Besides, James looked like he was enjoying himself.

I was mildly curious when he took the Schuylkill Expressway heading west, which meant we were actually going north. I made a point of studying his profile as we passed the Fairmount Water Works on the other side of the river. That was the site where James had been injured, and it was going to be a while before I could look on that view without feeling a pang. The traffic was surprisingly light, given that it was a sunny Friday, one of the last of the summer, although generally most of the traffic escaping the city was heading east for the shore.

After a few miles, he asked, "How was your meeting with Wakeman?"

"Surprising. He came alone — no entourage. I think he was expecting bad news and wanted time to digest it before he shared it."

"So he wasn't surprised by what you told him?"

"Not entirely. He read through our report, and he took it well, though — kind of sad, and quiet. I guess I expected more bluster. He thanked us, and he said we'd get something for our efforts, although he didn't say what, and I didn't ask. By the way, I think I'm going to try to keep Lissa on at the Society as a researcher for hire. She did a good job, and her specialty is local history, so maybe we can create a new niche for her — building historian or something like that. Do you think Ben will be happy about that?"

"Ask him. Or Lissa. I told you, I don't mess with other people's romantic lives."

"Ha! So you're saying they might have one."

"No, I'm not. But if they do, I wouldn't mess with it."

"Obviously you're much too busy managing your own romantic life, right?"

We talked happy nonsense for a few more miles as we wended our way around the western edge of the city. Then he veered off on Wissahickon Avenue, still traveling west, away from the city. I knew the area, but not well. James seemed to know exactly where he was going. The farther we went, the greener the streets became, and the larger the houses, with more space between. Chestnut Hill, I guessed, a beautiful — and pricey — neighborhood.

A few more turns, and then he pulled into a driveway that led up a hill. There was a house sitting on a rise in the middle of a surprisingly large expanse of lawn. He stopped in front of a set of steps and parked.

"Are we meeting someone here?" I asked.

"We're meeting a house. Come on."

He climbed out of the car and came around to my side and politely opened my door. I closed it behind me and looked up at the house. Late Victorian, I guessed, fieldstone, its trim painted a rich, dark red. Three stories with a mansard roof and a porch running across the front, with what looked like original gingerbread woodwork. I looked at James, who was watching me with a peculiar expression that seemed to combine excitement and apprehension.

"Are we going in?"

"Yes." He let me precede him up the steps, and then pulled a key from his pocket and unlocked the door. He held the door open for me to enter.

I stepped inside and stopped in my tracks. *Oh my.* My first impression was that the interior was largely untouched: no idiotic remuddling or well-intentioned "improvements." The second was that it had been lovingly maintained. All the woodwork was gleaming with varnish but looked as though it had never been painted. The ornate door and window moldings had to be nearly a foot wide.

I stepped tentatively forward. Living room — no, parlor — on the right, running the full depth of the house, with a glorious bay window at the back and an original fireplace with an elaborate overmantel and tiled surround that had me salivating. I hated to tear myself away from it, but I knew there was more to see. I crossed the hall to a narrow dining room, and behind that was a fully remodeled modern kitchen with a huge refrigerator and tiers of cabinets. Back stairs led upward, and beyond the kitchen I could see a wall of windows suggesting a sunroom.

I turned to James, who had followed me like an eager puppy. "Okay, what are we doing here?"

"Do you like it?"

"I think it's spectacular."

"Five bedrooms, three baths, over half an acre of land, and parking for three cars," he recited. "Oh, and it's three blocks from the train line."

"James, what are you saying? You're seriously considering this place? For us?"

"Yes for us, but only if you like it."

I couldn't imagine living in such a splendid place, but I knew I wanted to. "Can we possibly afford it?"

James named a figure that made me gulp. "What's that come out to in real-world terms? Like how much we would pay a month?" I wasn't good at calculating mortgage payments in my head. The answer he gave meant it would be tight, but between us it was doable . . . particularly if we could pay a good chunk up front. Like the kind of money the psychiatrists were offering for my carriage house.

"Okay," I said.

He stared at me. "You mean, yes, you like

it? Yes, let's do it?"

Poor man, he was almost quivering with eagerness. "There's something I've been meaning to tell you." I fished around in my bag and pulled out the offer letter — I'd brought it with me that morning. I pulled the letter out of its envelope and handed it to James.

He scanned it quickly, then looked at me. "They're serious?"

"They are. I told them yes this morning."

"We're buying this house?" he said, just to be sure.

"Yes. We are."

He let out a long sigh. "Good, because I made an offer for it this morning."

"Smart man."

I caught a glimpse of the happy, boyish James — the one the Bureau had never met — when he grabbed me up then and swung me around, right in the kitchen.

"Now that I've already agreed, you might as well show me the rest of the house now."

"That's right, I can't believe you said yes before you even looked upstairs."

"You had me at the fireplace," I said cheerfully. "Let's go on up. And can we take the back stairs? I've always loved back stairs — they're like one step above a secret passage."

After we looked around from the attic to the basement and back again, we circled the spacious yet private yard. I said, "I thought you said you weren't going to mow lawns. There's a lot of lawn out here."

"With what we'll be paying monthly, we can afford to hire someone. You're sure?"

"Yes, I'm sure. Oh, wait — did Marty have anything to do with finding this place?"

"She did not. She hasn't seen it. I found this one all by myself, thanks to all that online research."

"You are brilliant. When are we going to tell her?"

"I'm guessing in about an hour — we made plans to meet for dinner. She's bringing Ethan along."

"Have you met him?"

"Nope, not yet. You?"

"No. She's been very secretive about him. I'm glad she's got someone, though. She wasn't just feeling competitive, was she, now that she's got us settled?"

"Hey, Marty does what Marty wants to do."

Since we had time to spare, I had to go back and study the fireplace again. It looked even better the second time around. Then I drifted back to the ornate window overlooking the lawn. James came up behind me and folded his arms around me.

"Happy?" he said into my hair.

"Very. You are an extraordinary man, and I love you. When can we move in?"

"I think the paperwork may take a month. We can stay at your place until then. Or we might have to stay at a hotel . . . I think I know a nice one."

We beat Marty and the mysterious Ethan Miller to the restaurant and ordered a bottle of champagne, because I was certainly ready to celebrate. And we could surprise Marty, which was a rare occurrence.

But in the end, Marty surprised us first. She grinned at us as she made introductions. "Ethan, this is my cousin Jimmy, and my friend and colleague and sometimes partner in crime Nell Pratt."

We shook all around. Then Ethan said, "Marty didn't tell you, did she? My mother was a Korean war bride, and my father was a GI Mayflower descendant — the best of two worlds, I always thought."

I decided I liked Ethan. Before we could all sit down again, I had to tell Marty. "We bought a house!"

"Without consulting me?" Marty said in mock dismay. "Where is it?"

And we opened the champagne and described our new home in glowing terms, I realized that I was as happy as I could ever remember being.

And we were going to need a lot more furniture to fill all those rooms.

The employees of Thorndike Press hope you have enjoyed this Large Print book. All our Thorndike, Wheeler, and Kennebec Large Print titles are designed for easy reading, and all our books are made to last. Other Thorndike Press Large Print books are available at your library, through selected bookstores, or directly from us.

For information about titles, please call:
(800) 223-1244

or visit our Web site at:
http://gale.cengage.com/thorndike

To share your comments, please write:
Publisher
Thorndike Press
10 Water St., Suite 310
Waterville, ME 04901